Mitakola Waste Omy Go...

Mitakuye Oyasin
(We all are related)

Wicahpi Win
(Star Woman)

Bonnie Jo Hunt

Lawrence J. Hunt
June 8 2003

THE CRY OF THE COYOTE

FIVE MEN FACE THE GALLOWS. THREE ARE BELIEVED INNOCENT; WILL THEY HANG, TOO?

---

by

Bonnie Jo Hunt

and

Lawrence J. Hunt

"They spoke very loudly when they said their laws were made for everybody, but we soon learned that although they expected us to keep them, they thought nothing of breaking them themselves. . . ."
Plenty Coups, Crow

A Lone Wolf Clan Book, Vol. VIII

THE CRY OF THE COYOTE

Copyright 2003 by Bonnie Jo Hunt and Lawrence J. Hunt

First Printing, 2003

Library of Congress Catalog Number: 2003100073
International Standard Book Number: 1-928800-07-6 (Vol.VIII)

Cover designed by Ricardo Chavez-Mendez and Michelle Marin-Chavez -- website www.orofineart.com
Buffalo from painting by Lyman A. Rice displayed in Buffalo County Courthouse, Kearney, Nebraska

Published by:

Mad Bear Press
6636 Mossman Place, NE
Albuquerque, New Mexico

Words of Appreciation

The Lone Wolf Clan historical series is the work of many talented people. As usual we are indebted to our fine editorial staff without whose assistance we would be lost. The comments, corrections and suggestions of Barbara Lee Hunt, Juyn Krumm and Susan Shampine are invaluable.

The Cry of The Coyote is the eighth and final volume of Lone Wolf Clan Books. When we began this series we wondered if readers would be interested in early western history written from an American Indian point of view and told in the style of traditional storyteller. It seems there are many. Right from the first volume, The Lone Wolf Clan, the acceptance has been phenomenal. Lucile Bogue, talented author of twelve books including Salt Lake and Blood on the Wind, wrote of Land Without a Country, "Oh what a magnificent book. I have never read a better one in my whole lifetime!"

The success of the Lone Wolf Clan historical series comes from thousands of enthusiastic readers like Lucile. We love you all and have worked hard not to let you down.

Among the special people who contributed extraordinary help in the promotion of the Lone Wolf Clan series are Barbara Bastle, Harriet Braden, Jim and Phyllis Gilbertson, Betty and Vern Hunt, Lydia French Johnson, Dee McLaughlin and Joan Lovelace. Our appreciation for their generous, unsparing efforts is immeasurable. Pilamayaye (thank you) so much.

Mitakuye Oyasin (We all are related)

Bonnie Jo Hunt and Lawrence J. Hunt

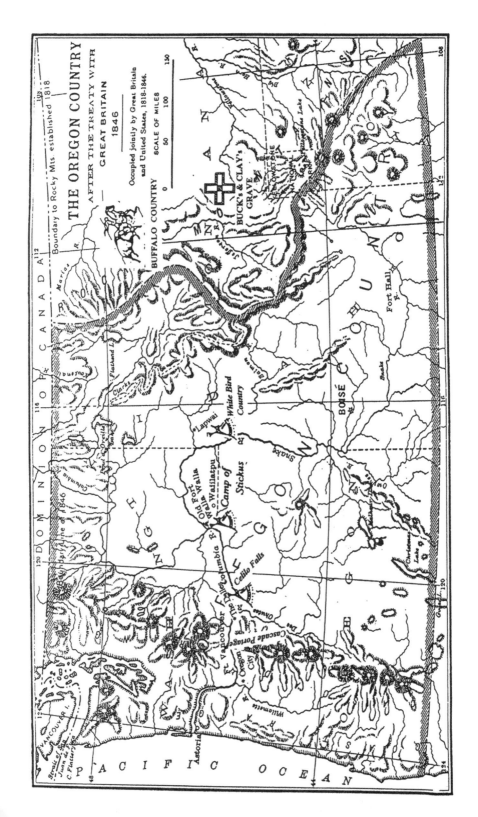

THE OREGON COUNTRY
AFTER THE TREATY WITH
GREAT BRITAIN
1846

Occupied jointly by Great Britain
and United States, 1818-1846.

SCALE OF MILES
0   50   100   150

Boundary to Rocky Mts established 1818

BUFFALO COUNTRY

HISTORICAL BACKDROP

"Lacking only the slow torture of hacking and flaying and burning, it (the Whitman Massacre) stands among the most atrocious of Indian atrocities," wrote William Barrows, 19th century historian.

To understand this murderous assault on a Christian mission, Mr. Barrows went on to say, certain facts must be taken into account, especially the two policies of the British and Americans in regard to Indian lands. Using the great trading organization, Hudson's Bay Company, as its enforcer, the British maintained a policy of keeping its vast North American empire in its wilderness state -- a game preserve to produce furs. They restricted the production of "civilized" grains and grasses, the plow and hoe and water-wheel. All who came to settle the country, to develop it, and "civilize" the Indians, Hudson's Bay kept back. All schools for Indian people were opposed, as were all Christian missions, except those of the Anglican and Roman Catholic faiths.

The purpose of the British was to keep their North American holdings (an area one third larger than all of Europe) for their brigades of trappers and network of trading posts. This pleased the Indian, especially when intermarriage and an accommodating life met him half way.

On the other hand, the Americans wished to build the United States on Indian lands. The factory dam must take the place of the beaver dam; wheat fields, the place of buffalo ranges; stationary brick and mortar buildings the place of moveable tipi lodges. This displeased Indian peoples, as they lost their lands, their game and the pleasures of a wild free life. No two policies could be more in contradiction: one fostering all the tastes and habits of the natives; the other demanding a total change in the modes and grade of life.

At the time of the Whitman Mission tragedy the Indian people were convinced the Americans wanted their lands, while the British did not. Moreover, they believed the Americans wished to change the entire life of the Indian -- religious and civil -- while the British wished only for fur, an aspiration in which a "civilized" Indian would be a hinderance. These two contradictory policies created a friction that had to burst into flame -- which it did, at Whitman's Mission in the homeland of the Cayuse.

THE CRY OF THE COYOTE

I

*"The United States further engage to build for the head chiefs
of the Walla-Walla, Cayuse, and Umatilla bands each
dwelling-house, and to plough and fence ten acres of land
for each, and to pay to each five hundred dollars per
annum in cash for the term of twenty years. . . ."*

Article V Treaty With Walla Walla, Cayuse, and others, 1855

The clouds hung heavily -- dark and threatening -- above
the lands of the Cayuse. The sound of thunder resounded against
purple bluffs. A distant shower sent a blanket of silver arrows
slanting down to disappear into the gray carpet of sagebrush. The
downpour of raindrops formed pools. The pools joined, making
rivulets that raced down hillsides, swelling into streams quickly
becoming torrents. Soon the thunder and rain ceased, the clouds
disappeared and the sun shone brilliantly again.

On a hillock a lone horseman watched the storm grow in
strength, then subside and finally pass from sight. It was like life,
he thought, all of Mother Earth's creatures started small, grew in
size and strength, finally weakened and passed into nothingness.
And like the storm, life had its threatening moments but ended in
restful silence. Thoughtfully, the horseman reined his mount away.
It did no good to worry and fuss. The Great Mystery's plan was
set. Whether it be storms or creatures, while on Mother Earth
The Great Creator guided them all along the same path.

In spite of this sanguine belief, worry consumed the horseman. His name was Stickus, leader of the Upper Umatilla band
of Cayuse. His people's welfare weighed heavily on his mind.

Stickus was only one of many troubled Indian leaders.
For eight winters tribulation after tribulation afflicted Columbia
River plateau dwellers. But the tribe called Cayuse suffered the
most. These once proud people whose name for themselves meant
"Superior People," were in disarray. War and pestilence had re-

duced their numbers so drastically they no longer could call themselves a nation.

"What had launched this tragic turn in their lives, and how long would they be dogged by misfortune?" These questions were on every Cayuse tribesman's mind. Did their troubles start with the arrival of the missionaries . . . were they to blame? Yes, their coming had created discord but, actually, for six winters after their arrival life had continued much the same. Many of the people came to rely on the mission medicine man, Marcus Whitman, and his pleasing looking woman, Narcissa. Yet, after much thought, and in spite of being a friend and follower of Missionary Whitman, Stickus concluded that the missionary was responsible for the endless troubles suffered by his people.

It had been during his fifth winter in the Cayuse homeland that Missionary Whitman had departed so abruptly. One cold morning in the Season of Falling Leaves, he left his Cayuse flock without explanation. That was the day the troubles began. In Waiilatpu, the location of Whitman's mission, the people watched in astonishment as the missionary doctor mounted his special horse named "Cayuse" and, with one companion, two pack animals and a dog named "Trapper," took the trail east. Stickus later learned starvation had forced the travelers to eat one mule and the dog, "Trapper."

Whitman's sudden departure left people aghast. What urgency had made him abandon the mission, his woman and his Cayuse flock who he had labored so hard to "civilize?" No sane person attempted to cross the "Big Open" in the Season of Falling Snow. To confound the Cayuse people even more, shortly after her husband's departure, the missionary doctor's woman, Narcissa, and Whitman's two adopted children also had left. Now the Cayuse truly felt abandoned and affronted. The missionaries were guests. It was inexcusable for guests to depart without one word of thank you or farewell.

To add to the people's consternation, without warning, a pompous man named Elijah White had arrived in the Cayuse homeland. Calling the elders together, he announced he was the Indian Agent appointed by the white father in Washington. As Indian Agent he was responsible for the affairs of all Indian people in Oregon Territory. He brought a code of laws that had to be observed. Punishments for not obeying the laws relied mainly on hangings and whippings, methods totally repugnant to the Cayuse. The people were horrified. They fled into the hills, refusing to meet with Indian Agent Elijah White.

The Indian Agent was not to be denied. He traveled to the adjoining tribal lands and, with the help of Missionary Henry Spalding, imposed the laws on the Indian people called Nez Perce. Using the Nez Perce as an example, Elijah White returned to wrangle the Cayuse into adopting the onerous code of laws, too.

This was a dark day for the Cayuse people, but a darker day soon was to follow. In the Season of Turning Leaves Missionary Doctor Whitman returned. Behind him, like a trail of ants on the scent of a honey tree, came a string of immigrant lodges on wheels and herds of cloven-hoofed animals called cattle.

These hairy faced people, in their land canoes, brought with them more than their possessions and cattle. They brought a deadly weapon called measles. There was no defense against this merciless, silent killer. Nothing, not even the shedding of blood, diverted it from its deadly mission. From the moment of its arrival the Cayuse Nation was doomed.

These "Superior People," who relied on the Great Mysterious to guide them along life's pathway, began to wonder if this almighty deity had deserted them. Ill luck seemed to dog them in everything they did. Even the full moon that rose the evening after the storm, had given the horseman who watched over the herd a feeling of apprehension. The mighty orb, bright and shiny as polished silver in the rain washed air, sent brilliant rays down to turn the valley into a shimmering lake of sage. The unusual brilliance kept the nocturnal raccoon, badger, kangaroo rat and other nighttime foragers in their shelters. Jackrabbits and hare normally out to feed in grassy areas, remained in their lairs. Horses

whinnied and snorted, shying at their own shadows. The horseman watched his uneasy charges with misgivings. The herd was
the only wealth his band of Cayuse had left, and he, alone, was
responsible for protecting it from harm.

Gradually, like a slowly forming ocean wave, the horses
began to move. The animals were so closely packed together,
one horse appeared linked to another. Suddenly, stallion after
stallion reared up, uttering unearthly cries. With heads tossing,
manes flying, tails held high and thunderous pounding of hooves,
the stallions led the wave of animals down the valley, crashing
through the ghostly sage like ocean breakers pounding a rocky
shore.

"Hi-yah!" the night herder shouted, urging his mount into
a gallop. Once the horses hit the flat lands they would scatter to
the winds. The horseman's sturdy mount, dodging through the
sage and buckbrush, raced toward the lead stallions. The animal
crashed through a thick patch of brush then suddenly faced a
thicker and higher patch. Again he leapt, but too late. The big
body careened sideways and fell. The horse struggled to get up
but dropped back to lie still. The rider, unhurt, shouted for help.
Those who were light sleepers heard the call. Hurriedly, men
mounted prized horses kept close to their lodges.

"Hey! Hey!" they shouted, racing up to the downed herder.
The horses that had been running relentlessly for the far end of
the valley were racing back. Behind them the sage was turning
dark. The bright shimmering surface of the sage lake was gradually disappearing.

"What is it?" an arriving horsemen shouted frantically.

A youth pointed skyward. "Sister Moon is turning black!"

The sight was so awesome in the camp behind the hill the
women began the piercing mourning cry. "Aiiee! Aiiee!" Children ran to hide. Dogs howled and barked. On a nearby hilltop a
band of coyotes pointed their muzzles skyward, adding to the din
with their haunting cries.

Panic would have set in if Stickus had not appeared. He

rode back and forth shouting, "Have no fear. This has happened before. Somehow Mother Earth is passing between Father Sun and Sister Moon. Only The Great Mystery knows why and how it is done."

Except for whimpering children, the crowd grew quiet, but eyes remained fastened on the awful creeping darkness that was eating away the great silvery orb. An excited youth pointed. "There are live things trying to escape."

The people gazed, awestricken. Even the medicine man stared, open-mouthed. The herder who was trying to get his mount on its feet, stopped as if shot. The awesome sight made his skin crawl. Just as the youth said, ahead of the creeping darkness indistinct figures darted as if fleeing for their lives.

"Its a flight of geese," a man declared. "Can't you hear them honk?"

The herder heard nothing but the herd thundering up the valley. Then, just as suddenly as the curtain of gray had blanketed the lake of sage, the bright shimmering light of the moon's rays began to return. Slowly, but surely, Sister Moon in all her shining glory became whole again. Women and children dried their eyes and hooted at each other in their relief. The thunder of galloping hoofbeats faded away. The restless horses had stopped to graze.

The fear was over but the herder kept his eyes on Sister Moon. No one could tell him differently; he had seen moving things. They were not geese flying north; they were people in great trouble. Like spiders dangling from a web, they had been hanging in space. Thoughts buzzed in his brain like hornets in a nest trying to make sense of what he had seen.

"Oh-hah!" The realization struck the herder like a thunderclap. He pulled the saddle and bridle from his prone mount and ran to catch a healthy horse.

\#

To the east, in the homeland of the Nimpau, people were less distressed than their Cayuse neighbors. The trail through

Oregon Territory did not cross their lands. The fearful onslaught of hairy faces and their lodges on wheels had left them virtually untouched. Yet, they were not without their troubles. The missionary couple who tended their spiritual and educational needs had left. The sawmill and gristmill were quiet. The classrooms and pulpits were abandoned. Those who resented the missionaries' rules and demands were delighted. It was like the old days when they were free to do what they wished.

Lone Wolf, the former leader of the Lapwai band of Nimpau, especially was happy over the absence of the missionaries. Spalding's edict outlawing hunting and trading trips, particularly had nettled him. On that very evening of the moon's eclipse, memories of old hunts and trading journeys had left him restless. Lone Wolf reached for his alder stick. Even that effort made him wince.

He groaned. "A few more winters and I will be no more." He pushed aside the elk skin robe that hung over the opening of the long lodge. He lifted his lined face to the fresh night breeze. How wonderful it felt after the thick inside air where 20 families had prepared and eaten the late meal.

Momentarily, Lone Wolf stood listening to the chorus of frogs who seemed not to fear two-leggeds. It always was good to hear the little creatures of Mother Earth happily sing and speak. They brought him back to his boyhood when his father had passed on precious words of wisdom.

"During spring and summer every creature is rich," his father had said, "even lowly earth worm. Food and water are plentiful. The land we live on and the air we breathe are free. All Mother Earth's bounty is at one's feet. We arc free to do as we wish. We can go anywhere, even to the shores of The Great Water where boats with wings may be seen."

Lone Wolf limped down the path, the light of the moon so bright he could see where the trail ended at the edge of the Kooskooskie. Overhead a flight of honkers flew over the creek, to disappear beyond the high far bank of the river.

"Flying north! Flying north!" the flailing wings whispered. For honkers to fly at night was so unusual, Lone Wolf looked up to follow their path. But the sky had darkened. The birds were no more than blurred shadows flitting overhead.

He groaned. Like his mate, Quiet Woman, had The Great Mysterious taken away his sight? The thought made him shudder. What good would a blind man be on the next buffalo hunt?

Lone Wolf leaned on his stick. "That ill-fated trip 20 winters ago still haunted him. Second Son, Vision Seeker, had warned him not to go, disaster would strike. First Son, Many Horses, had lost his scalp and later his life. The buffalo had been slow in coming. The entire hunting party was on the edge of starvation.

The trouble had begun during the time of the circled moon when three hairy faced strangers appeared out of the snow. Once again Vision Seeker had warned of trouble ahead -- these men were bad medicine. Again Second Son had been right. The hairy faces had many items for trade. They encouraged Lone Wolf and his people to travel with them to a place called rendezvous where there were many more trade items, so many he had gasped in awe.

Yet, rendezvous was where fate had dealt them its harshest blow. Near the encampment Blackfeet warriors had attacked a group of trappers. In the melee, First Son, Many Horses, was shot, scalped and left for dead. There, too, Daughter Raven Wing, had become obsessed with the many trade items, especially an elk hide dress owned by the hairy face, Little Ned. To satisfy Raven Wing he had invited the hairy faced trader to become a member of the family. Lone Wolf sadly shook his head. Those few days at the rendezvous forever had altered the lives of the Lone Wolf Clan.

Lone Wolf audibly groaned. He was in his 80th winter. He had witnessed many changes, some good, some bad. Should the Great Mysterious call on him to live another lifetime, what transformations would take place? What would life be like?

The thought of another 80 winters filled him with dismay.

The freedom his father had spoken of had faded away like melting snow. Their villages had been invaded by missionaries who insisted they live by the newcomer's religion and rules, settlers came wanting their lands, and now a great column of Blue Coats had arrived with guns as large as tree trunks to rule the region.

Gradually Sister Moon brightened. The gray curtain that had dimmed his vision disappeared. He could see the glow of a frog's eyes on the far bank of the creek. The Great Mysterious was not taking away his sight, but had sent him a sign. Just like the hunt of long ago, a spirit had called to him. "It is time to seek the buffalo." So powerful was the message, he could not resist.

Lone Wolf threw the alder stick away. Suddenly he felt ten winters younger. The blood that flowed through his veins took on new vigor. The Great Mysterious intended for him to go on one last buffalo hunt. He must get started. First, scouts should go ahead. It was said buffalo were becoming scarce. White hunters slaughtered them by the thousands just for their hides and tongues. The thought made him cringe. Could he face the plains covered with skeletons of the great beasts?

With his mind tracing the route to the buffalo grounds, Lone Wolf limped back to the long lodge to fall exhausted on the buffalo robe covered sleeping pallet. Quiet Woman, sensing something had agitated her man, put out a hand to comfort him.

Lone Wolf gestured her away. "I have work to do. While the mission people are gone I must make one last buffalo hunt."

Quiet Woman started to scold, then held her tongue. She must take care. That long ago buffalo hunt had hung over her mate's head ever since. While he still could breathe and walk he had to prove he could carry a hunt off with success. But perhaps there was another reason for his wanting to make this last hunt.

Many Horses, their firstborn's name, was never mentioned. That did not mean he was forgotten. First sons never die in a father's heart. Lone Wolf had to travel to buffalo country and say good-bye to the boy he had laid to rest in that lonely, stark grave hidden in the grasses of the windswept hunting grounds.

II

A few more moons, a few more winters, and not one of the mighty hosts that once filled this broad land . . . will remain to weep over the tombs of the people once as powerful and as hopeful as your own.

Seattle, Duwamish

Vision Seeker, Lone Wolf's second son who had predicted the dire events that took place on the long ago buffalo hunt, made it a practice to rise before sunup. Standing on a hilltop and bathed in the first morning rays, he silently thanked Father Sun for bringing forth a new day.

This spring morning he prayed with extra fervor. Somehow his father had enlisted a few elderly hunters into making one last trek to buffalo country. He had attempted to change his father's mind, reminding him of the hazards they previously had encountered along the trail, but Lone Wolf was adamant.

"What does it matter?" his father retorted. "Sooner or later we all must make the journey to the Great Beyond. Time or place is for The Great Mysterious to decide."

Knowing well how obstinate his father could be when bent on something close to his heart, Vision Seeker said no more. Once Lone Wolf made a decision nothing anyone could say would sway him from carrying it through. In his youth Lone Wolf often awakened his family during the night to start on a hunting or trading trip. How did his mother, Quiet Woman, endure such treatment?

Vision Seeker's ruminations were diverted by the sound of hoofbeats. Someone in a hurry was riding hard along the bank of the Kooskooskie. Louder and louder the pounding hoofs approached, the noise echoing back from the opposite riverside bluffs. Suddenly the hoofbeats faded until nothing could be heard. Then they resumed, softly and more slowly.

The horseman is a stranger, Vision Seeker thought. He had reined his mount into the swale, the soft earth cushioning the sound. Unwittingly, the rider had endangered both his horse and himself. In early spring water seeped into low areas, turning them into bogs. An animal could lose its footing and fall, breaking a bone or suffering a strain. Sometimes they were stuck in the goo, frantically snorting and struggling until they either pulled free or sank beneath the surface to smother a slow, painful death.

The thought made Vision Seeker shudder. At least this rider's mount had not become a victim. The pounding of hoof-beats resumed. The horse again was on firm ground. Over the ridge and into Lapwai village the horseman galloped, scattering barking dogs and squealing children. A village guard hailed him.

"What brings you to Lapwai village?" the guard asked.

"It is important I see the person called Vision Seeker, your tribesman who sees into the future." The words drifted clearly and distinctly up the hillside. Glumly, Vision Seeker watched the stranger rein his mount away and up the slope. He could tell by his dress and riding gear the horseman was Cayuse, a member of the neighboring tribe to the west.

Vision Seeker had no wish to meet this man. Although the Cayuse spoke a different dialect of the Shapaptian language than the Nimpau, they understood each other very well. Many Cayuse and Nimpau were related by marriage. The two peoples often met in council and joint festivities. Yet, a barrier of cool-ness recently had risen between the two tribes. From the ranks of the Cayuse came the evildoers who had set the plateau aflame.

The dark face bobbed over a ridge and into view. "Cut Lip!" In his surprise the name easily came to Vision Seeker's tongue. He knew of this young Cayuse man but had had little to do with him. What possibly could bring him to seek counsel? From the intense expression on the dark face, it had to be of con-siderable importance.

Vision Seeker held up a hand in greeting. "Give your animal and yourself a rest. We will smoke and talk."

Cut Lip's forehead remained creased with a frown. All
the way to Lapwai he had been forming the proper words to say.
Before he forgot them he wanted to blurt them forth at once. But
he swung down. He loosened the cinch that held the blanket
saddle in place, led his foam lathered pony to a patch of grass and
squatted cross-legged to politely watch his host prepare the pipe.

Vision Seeker took his time. Out of the corner of his eye
he examined his Cayuse visitor. He could tell the youth was distraught with the news he brought. It was only politeness that kept
him from speaking forthwith. Good, Vision Seeker thought. Many
young people these days had abandoned the ways of their forefathers. In the old days young men were taught never to blurt out
bad news. It was to be delivered thoughtfully and softly but not
before the speaker carefully had thought it through.

"Now, my friend, what brings you all the way from your
homeland to this Lapwai hillside? If the matter is as grave as
your actions would lead one to believe, it should be placed before a council of elders."

Cut Lip nervously fingered his long braided hair. "I had a
vision . . . a message from The Great Mysterious. Five men soon
will be hanged by the hairy faced ones; among them is my brother."
The youth's lips trembled so, he could not continue.

Vision Seeker glanced away until his visitor could com-
pose himself. "Where and how did this vision come to you?"

The young Cayuse told of the darkening of the moon. He
described the awesome changing color of the sage that caused
the herd to run wild. In hushed tones, he recounted the spider
like objects dangled in space. "They were not spiders, they were
people hanging from ropes. One of them was my brother!"

Vision Seeker thoughtfully mulled over what the youth
said. It was obvious he had suffered through a harrowing experience. Of course the eclipse of the moon had taken everyone by
surprise. Many of his own people looked upon it as a warning of
evil days ahead. Yet, it had had the opposite effect upon his father. It had made him young again -- young enough to send him

off on an impossible buffalo hunt.

Vision Seeker studied the Cayuse lad. Except for his agitation, he appeared to be a sensible being. One barely noticed the deformity of his lip. He had an intelligent face, even handsome. Yet, the disfigurement surely must have been a trial to bear. As a child playmates eyed him curiously. During young manhood he was left out of hunts and games. Undoubtedly, the boy had led a lonely life . . . probably still did. He was Cut Lip, a person on whom The Creator had put his mark . . . a mark that identified him as an imperfect being. In the old days his mother might even have left him by the trail, she would have been so ashamed.

Vision Seeker's heart went out to the youth. He must treat him with care. "Why should your brother be in danger? Has something happened in the Cayuse homeland?"

It was Cut Lip's turn to take stock of the Nimpau man. Didn't he know of the danger that threatened the Cayuse people? In the camps of the Cayuse they said this man read the future as easily as carvings on a sandstone cliff. He spoke with The Great Mysterious as though they had known each other from birth. It was rumored that during these talks The Great Mysterious revealed the future . . . the things that would befall all peoples.

Cut Lip thoughtfully sucked on the pebble he had place in his mouth to keep away thirst on the long journey. Perhaps this man, looked upon with such reverence, was not as Godlike as everyone believed, but a mere human like himself.

"Five Cayuse men are held prisoner on the banks of the Great River at a place the hairy faces call The Dalles."

"That is so," Vision Seeker agreed. "These people are from Waiilatpu, followers of Tiloukaikt. It is believed they are the ones who killed the missionary people. Your family should not worry. Is your family not of the band of Stickus?"

Cut Lip raised his forefingers to the inside corner of his eyes, the sign for weeping. He continued in Shapaptian. "On the day of the killings Brother Kia-ma-sump-kin was visiting relatives in Tiloukaikt's village."

Vision Seeker grimaced inwardly but remained silent.
"My brother is a man of soft heart," Cut Lip entreated.
"He could not do the bad things that took place that day."
"Why are you so certain he's held prisoner?"
"After the sign in Sister Moon, I rode to the place on the
Great River where the Cayuse men are held prisoner. Young Chief
has his men guarding them: Tiloukaikt, Tomahas, Ish-ish-kais-
kais, Clokamas and my brother. I spoke with them. They say
they are to be taken to a place called Oregon City and hanged."
Vision Seeker stared into the distance. The Cayuse indeed were unfortunate. Their members died by the dozens from
the disease, measles. In desperation they attacked what they believed was the source of the disease. They killed Doctor Whitman,
his wife and others. They were following the ages old Cayuse
tradition that medicine men whose patients died had to forfeit
their own lives. But, according to Indian Agent Elijah White's
code of laws, this was murder. The penalty was hanging.
Vision Seeker glanced at Cut Lip who patiently waited.
Like the crimes of the Cayuse, there was more to this young man
than met the eye. He was exhausted and emotionally spent. Riding
to The Dalles and all the way back to Lapwai was a hard four-day
journey. But why did he come to him? Did he believe he, Vision
Seeker, in some miraculous way could set the prisoners free?
Of course, like many plateau people, Cut Lip believed he
possessed supernatural powers. "Take your problems to Vision
Seeker. He has the answer." Hardly anyone thought of him as a
mere human like themselves. Just because on occasions his senses
told him of events the average man could not foretell, people
thought he knew everything the future held. What did he know
that would comfort this young man? His mind was blank. He
only could offer words from Agent Elijah White's code of laws.
"If your brother is innocent he will go free. According to
the laws only the guilty will be punished."
"White man laws!" Cut Lip blurted. "Our people say white
man laws are like a dog with many masters and many tails. One

master speaks, a tail wags. Another master speaks, another tail wags. Governor Chief Lane now is big man. The dog waves his tail for him. When Chief Lane leaves, a new chief comes . . ."

"Enough of this tail talk," Vision Seeker said impatiently. "You did not come to tell dog stories. I know Governor Lane will soon leave, and I know he wants to have this trial over before he goes. Now, tell me exactly why did you come to me?"

"On the banks of the Great River the Cayuse are holding council. Stickus is taking his people. Five Crows is taking his band. Peu-peu-mox-mox and the Walla Wallas will come. The gathering will decide the prisoners' fate. There is need for hurry. Governor Chief Lane soon will take the prisoners to Oregon City. Some say prisoners should not go with the governor chief. Others say they must go. Stickus fears if they do not go terrible things will happen. Stickus seeks your help. You know white man ways. You speak their words. You know their talking paper. . . ."

Vision Seeker glanced from the anxious face to the lodge where his blind mother was approaching the end of her time and his 80 year-old father believed he was young again. He could not leave Lapwai. Yet, how could he refuse his friend Stickus? The existence of the entire Cayuse tribe was at stake. If they did not hand over the prisoners as promised, Governor Lane surely would order the Mounted Riflemen into action, plunging the plateau into war. Terror would reign, not only among the Cayuse but also among the Walla Walla, Umatilla, Palouse . . . even the Nimpau.

"When will Governor Lane come for the prisoners?"

Cut Lip held up three fingers. "Three, maybe four sleeps."

Vision Seeker frowned. Events in the Cayuse affair had progressed too far for anyone to turn them back. He started to tell Cut Lip so, but the youth's hopeful expression made him hold his tongue. The lad was right. He had to go. Perhaps he even could do some good.

"Come," he said to Cut Lip, "let's get you a fresh horse."

III

The two great "civilizers" were whiskey and gunpowder, and from the hour we accepted these we had in reality sold our birthright and unconsciously consented to our ruin.

Ohiyesa, Dakota Sioux

Reveille came as always at 5 A.M., a hefty hammer pounding against an iron triangle. The jarring sound ricocheted against the river banks and echoed back to rattle poorly hung doors and precious window glass in the sleeping town of Oregon City. The dissonant clangor made exhausted housewives groan, small children whimper and men of the house swear and threaten the hammer wielder bodily harm or banishment to a region of everlasting fire. The troop, the Regiment of Mounted Riflemen, that had settled in to guard the citizenry from harm and thus provide an environment of peaceful comfort, had instead become a nuisance almost too annoying to bear.

The clanging triangle was not impartial. Indians hunkered beneath tattered, moldy woven mats on the wooded escarpment, the gristmill operator, the sawyer at the sawmill, the blacksmith, ladies of the street, priests at the Catholic church, even Dr. John McCloughlin, founder of Oregon City, asleep in his fine Main Street mansion, endured the same rude awakening.

Besides this ungodly racket at dawn, the soldiers made daylight hours a trial. Instead of remaining on the grounds set aside for them, they flooded the muddy streets, jostling shoppers, taunting workers, uttering cat calls and lewd suggestions to womenfolk and teaching young boys to curse, chew, spit and smoke.

It was the hours after dusk when people were eating supper and holding evening prayer service, that the rough nature of these protectors of society caused the greatest distress. Congregating in establishments serving strong drink, they launched into bouts of roughhousing patrons and fighting among themselves.

Townsmen getting involved, could well find themselves returning home with blackened eyes, bloodied noses and sometimes naked as plucked turkeys. The situation became so intolerable Colonel Loring, the commandant, ordered public houses to close their doors.

Merchants, church people, especially tavern owners, appealed to local officials to bar the troops from the city. But authorities like US Marshal Joe Meek, turned a deaf ear on the complainers. He enjoyed his spirits as much as anyone, and stood by the Mounted Riflemen. He had traveled across the country during the winter of '48 to lobby government officials for their presence. To demand they leave now would make him look a fool.

Among those aroused this early May morning was a robust fellow with a shock of hair that swept up from a high forehead like a haycock. After a fitful night of tossing and turning, the man had finally managed to capture a couple of hours of sleep. An old soldier and frontiersman accustomed to sleeping lightly, prepared for any eventuality, he swung off his cot and reached for his boots. Otherwise, already fully dressed, he stood and made ready to move out. He stomped across the squeaky floor planking toward what he took for the opening of a field tent, then abruptly stopped. The light that filtered in came through window glass. He rubbed his eyes and stared down. He was on the second story of a frame building

"Ah, yes!" he muttered, exasperated with himself. He was acting like a first year recruit. He was no longer a field soldier. He was Joseph Lane, the territorial governor. He made his way back to the cot, slipped off his boots and started to tuck his feet into the warm covers, then jerked himself upright. What was the matter with him? He couldn't lollygag around like some ordinary foot soldier. He had important things to do and so little time in which to do them.

Joe Lane was not the regular run-of-the-mill settler of Oregon's Willamette Valley. He had fought one war, and if those Cayuses, Walla Wallas, Palouses and Umatillas up-river gave trouble, he was prepared to fight another. But there was no need of that. Right from the beginning he had let the Oregon citizenry know he meant business.

One of his first acts as governor was to march up river and straighten out the Indian mess. He met with Indian leaders, smoked with them, received and gave gifts. The leaders said his heart was good. From now on he was their chief, "Chief Joe" he would be called. The governor accepted the honor but warned they could not become friends until the killers of 13 victims at Whitman's Mission in November of 1847 were brought to trial. Unless five of the murderers surrendered he would send an army into their homelands and hunt the culprits down. The arrival of a Regiment of Mounted Riflemen from the east made it clear "Chief Joe" was capable of backing up his demands.

In May, 1850, the five murderers Lane demanded had surrendered. They were held at the Columbia River port called The Dalles. The next move was up to Governor Lane -- to bring the accused prisoners to Oregon City for trial. The white populace was impatient for justice to prevail. They expected no less than a hanging. If Joe Lane did not satisfy them as speedily as possible they very well could take matters in their own hands and do the job themselves.

"Sam," Lane shouted for his orderly. "Take a message to Colonel Loring. . . . No, never mind, I had better speak to him in person," Lane said as the sleepy fellow appeared. During the Mexican campaign friction had developed between Loring and himself. The colonel was a West Pointer and he, Joe Lane, with no formal military schooling, had scrambled up the chain of command to the rank of general. Then, here in Oregon, the gulf between them had widened. He had taken Colonel Loring to task for the lax way he handled his command.

First it was the Mounted Riflemen's obnoxious behavior that kept the locals in high dungeon. Later it was the alarming rate of desertion that gave him cause to upbraid the colonel. One hundred twenty men audaciously formed up outside the Mounted

Riflemen's compound quarters and marched south toward the California gold fields, claiming to settlers that they encountered they were on a legitimate military mission. The deserters were so daring and well organized they even requisitioned supplies against government vouchers along the way.

"Waugh!" Lane growled. What had happened to the bloody army? Military discipline had degenerated so badly enlisted men actually thumbed their noses at officers. When the deserters marched away Loring had hopped around like a frog in a dry lake, hollering for help. He begged him, Governor Lane, for civilian volunteers to pursue the runaways. He should have told the colonel to take a flying jump, instead, he went along with the request. It was a good thing that he did. The Joe Lane group of volunteers rounded up 70 deserters. Loring's party only managed to bring back seven.

The whole business stank of disaster. The ranks left to guard Oregon City had been nil. If unrestful Indian tribes had got wind of the chaos that reigned among the forces of law and order, they could well have stormed and sacked Oregon City. Panic would have reigned throughout the valley. All of his peace efforts would have gone for naught.

Upon his return from the deserter fiasco he vowed never again to leave the settlements so vulnerable. Now, he had to march off to The Dalles and collect these Cayuses. Could he depend on Loring to keep the valley from harm in his absence? He pulled a boot on with such force he nearly crushed his little toe.

#

Colonel Loring, commander of the Regiment of Mounted Riflemen, also awakened that morning with a start. He had lost an arm in the Mexican campaign and, when tired or out of sorts, the stub of the missing limb gave him fits. The previous night had been one of those times. Until the wee hours of morning severed nerve ends burned and twitched. He rolled out of the blankets and reached for the laudanum, but the painkiller did little good. Instead of driving away the pain, it made him groggy and grouchy. When Governor Lane rapped on the door the sound struck his ears like the rat-tat of the post drum. Thinking it was the first sergeant, Loring uttered a growl.

"Dunderhead! Don't stand out there pounding like a ninny. Come in and do it quietly. Ah!" he gulped when the governor's head appeared. With his one good hand he fumbled futilely at the undone uniform buttons.

"Never mind, there's no need for that," Lane said. "I'm here about the criminals held at The Dalles. A detachment must be made ready straightway to escort them to Oregon City. The sooner we get after this lousy business the better."

"Yes, sir," Loring answered, apprehensively eyeing the governor. He should have been on top of that . . . sat down last night with the first sergeant and made up a detail roster and had a platoon on the way up river by first light. It was the blasted arm he left at Chapultepec that was to blame. This damp Willamette Valley weather played havoc with his stump. Instead of sticking to business, he had dismissed the sergeant and taken an extra long pull on the bottle of painkiller in hopes he could sleep.

"I'll get right on it," Loring promised.

Before he could get up, Lane waved him back. "No, I think it best I manage this. There is no point in a large detachment going up river. It'll only make the tribes nervous. Ten or 12 handpicked men can do the job."

"Hmm!" Loring grunted. The governor was afraid to let him handle the assignment, and for good reason. He probably would lose half the troop along the way to desertion. Why didn't these men have an ounce of loyalty? On the entire march from St. Louis enlisted men walked off whenever it took their fancy. He had blamed Major Cross, regimental quartermaster, for the high rate of desertion. He was so certain of it when they hit The Dalles he had sent Cross packing. He had wronged him. After the major left, the situation went from bad to worse.

"Damn it all," Loring muttered to himself. "This is my job." He glanced at the governor. "If you don't mind, I would like to deal with this. The reason the Mounted Riflemen made the march west was to round up and bring in these criminals. It is my rightful duty to see that these orders are carried out."

Joe Lane hesitated. He understood how the one-armed colonel must feel, and he didn't want to create any more friction than already existed, but he had to keep the big picture in mind. The townspeople were upset with Loring and his riflemen, thought them blundering oafs. Would they trust Loring to bring in the criminals? He doubted it.

There also was his own situation to consider. His term of office was coming to an end. As a final act it would be a feather in his cap to see that justice was done, leave the territory at peace. Political bigwigs back east would take note. Already his people in Indiana had their eye on him. He could run for state representative, perhaps senator. Look at that homely Abe Lincoln of Illinois, the state next door. In spite of his awkward ways and homeliness, Abe had run for office and won.

The silence in the room grew unbearable. Not only was this mission personally important to each man's career but neither man had the desire to take issue with the other. Memories of past dissensions and disillusionments kept coming to mind. Colonel Loring's lack of discipline stuck in Joe Lane's craw. He probably didn't have the loyalty of a single platoon.

Colonel Loring saw before him a man who had clawed his way up the ranks from private to brigadier general. Through politics and rash action he had made his ruthless way to the top. Now he was about to pull the same scurvy trick on him by seizing the opportunity that should be his.

A sharp rap on the door broke the brooding silence. "Urgent message, sir," the orderly announced. "A sizeable fast moving body of Indians have been seen descending on The Dalles. Messenger reports they appear to be hostile." Loring and Lane stared at each other, a myriad of disastrous possibilities racing through their minds.

IV

Many of the whites always seemed to say by their manner when they saw an Indian, "I am much better than you," and the Indians did not like this.

Big Eagle, Santee Sioux

News of Indians on the move in the up-country sent shock waves through Oregon City and surrounding countryside. Weapons were brought out, cleaned and loaded. Mothers ordered their children inside. Men gathered on street corners and in public places to contemplate the implications, all of them bad.

"Thet damned government, it's to blame. We'd be better off lettin' half-witted imbeciles take charge of keepin' the Injuns in hand," a surly Oregon City householder complained.

"Well, what kinda people yuh think we got? Ole Joe Meek, an' those boozin' Mounted Riflemen ain't got nothin' 'neath ther hats 'cept hair," his companion bitingly observed. "I say, speakin' of the devil . . ."

US Marshal Joe Meek, dressed in buckskins and armed to the teeth, came riding down the street. "Keep yer shirts on," Meek advised. "Nuthin's goin' to happen 'cept a hangin' of five Cayuses thet I'm personally conductin'."

Grumbling, the crowds dispersed, but the Indian threat was not forgotten. For months townspeople and homesteaders had been on edge. Instances of violence kept their fears honed. The previous year a band of Snoqualmies had attacked the Hudson's Bay fort at Nisqually. The plan of the attacking force was to steal sufficient lead, powder and weapons to drive every white person from the lower Puget Sound.

To the south settlers had run-ins with the Umpqua and Rogue who seemed to get bolder with every passing day. Emotions ran so high that when the young son of an Umpqua leader was overheard making what was considered a lewd remark to a settler's daughter, the youth was promptly lynched and his body burned.

Emigrants who had followed the Applegate Trail across Nevada's Black Rock Desert and into the Willamette Valley from the south, were haunted by tragedies that happened along the way. They could not forget nor forgive the Pits, Modocs, Klamaths and Rogues who, in their own lands, had made the travelers' lives miserable every dusty step of the trail.

Many homesteaders were disenchanted and disgusted with life in general. They had left comfortable homes in the east. The trek across country was envisioned as the adventure of a lifetime; a chance to get away from dull, drab lives and to financially better themselves. For some it was an opportunity to run away from responsibilities they wished to avoid.

After enduring untold hardships, establishing new homes and living under primitive conditions through several years, people realized they had not especially improved their lot in life. They were sick of experiencing exciting adventures and had far more pressing responsibilities than they ever had endured before.

Also, among the neurotically inclined, there was a growing belief the red man whose homelands they had confiscated, was taking his revenge by haunting them. Like silent ghosts these previous inhabitants of the acreages homesteaders now called their own, could be seen flitting through the shadowed glens and meadows of the dark virgin forests.

Householders never knew when a native might appear on their doorstep. Usually they demanded a handout. With guttural, unintelligible words and emphatic hand signals, they made their wants known. Their dark, expressionless faces beneath shocks of hair held in place by little blocks of cedar wood or strings of fur, were sufficiently startling to send timid housewives screaming and children to have nightmares.

When problems affecting communities occurred, it was common procedure for Willamette Valley homesteaders to come together to seek solutions. The meetings generally were orderly and civil. Yet when, what was referred to as "The Indian Question" arose, orderliness and civility went out the window. This was the case at a town hall meeting in the community of Rickreall, a market center a few miles west of Reverend Jason Lee's Methodist mission.

A bushy bearded settler with a few drinks under his belt started things off. "This valley ain't goin' ta 'mount ta a hill a' beans 'til we quit hidin' in our barns an' houses afeered ta take a deep breath. The answer ta this Injun business's simple: we march up-country an' blast every blasted one of 'em inta eternity."

"That's nonsense an' yuh know it," the bearded man's large wife scolded.

The chairman of the meeting rapped for quiet. The volume of the din rose louder.

"Mrs. Huggins's right. The military should punish the Injuns. Ain't thet what they's paid to do?" a voice declared.

From the back of the hall came sarcastic words of support. "Yeah! Thet's the thing ta do; call on those valiant sojers, if yuh kin find 'em. Half of 'em're over the hill minin' gold nuggets in Californi. The other half's asleep in the barracks or oglin' womin on the streets of Oregon City."

"Yer tellin' it straight, brother, might as well call on a den of foxes to guard a chicken roost."

"All right!" the chairman shouted. "Let's take up the topic we came to discuss."

The first item on the agenda finally was addressed, the rising loss of livestock to coyotes, wolves and mountain cats.

"How can we control these livestock killers?" the chairman asked. "At the present rate there'll not be a calf, colt or lamb left in the valley. If anybody has an idea, let's hear it."

A scrawny man with flaming red beard and hair, wearing a ragged canvas coat, leapt to his feet. "How do we know it's four-footed predators thet're doin' all this livestock stealin' an' killin'? In my 'pinion we're lookin' in the wrong direction."

The man's penetrating voice made those sitting near clasp

hands to their ears. "What 'bout two-legged predators? I'm speakin' 'bout the red savages."

"Hear! Hear!" someone applauded. "Those Injuns hev me ol' womin as jumpy as a flea an' crabby as a snappin' turtle."

"We been settin' traps an' guardin' our herds an' flocks but ain't come up with hair er hide of coyote, wolf er cat," the man with flaming hair continued. "It's as plain as the nose on yer face where yer heifers, lambs an' pigs're goin' -- right inta the cookin' pots of those pesky Injuns. Fer once Brother Huggins's talkin' sense -- blast everyone of 'em ta kingdom come."

"Ah! Sit down an' shut up," came a voice from the crowd. "From the traps I seen yuh set, yuh couldn't catch your backsides with both hands."

A skinny, sharp-faced woman leapt to her feet. "Who said thet? Yuh foolish man, me husband's jest tryin' ta open yer eyes fer yer own good. Havin' dealin's with Injuns afore, he knows what he's talkin' 'bout. Yuh should be thankful someun got the gumption ta stop lettin' these murderin' savages steal us blind. Soon's they finish off our animals they'll be after us'ns next."

The chairman, who had launched the topic of controlling the damage created by coyotes, wolves and mountain cats and had remained standing through the outburst, held up his hands for quiet.

"I know these meetings are supposed to be democratic, a place where everyone can say what they wish, but it seems to me this is getting out of hand. Instead of making sound arguments, this has turned into an unruly shouting match.

"Personally, I think we should let the matter of Indian re-lations rest. From what I understand the Whitman Mission kill-ers have been apprehended and are in custody at The Dalles and will soon be escorted to Oregon City to stand trial. I don't be-lieve this rumor that Indians are on the warpath. Likely as not, they're just as nervous as we are. Now is not the time to do anything that's apt to rile them up."

Both the man with flaming red hair and his sharp-faced

THE CRY OF THE COYOTE   27

wife were on their feet. "Yuh're absolutely wrong, my good man.
Now is perxactly the right time ta swing inta action," the husband
bluntly interjected. "We should hustle up river straightway an'
grab those slimy murderin' savages an' string 'em ta the nearest
tree branch. They showed no mercy ta the missionary folk. Why
should we treat 'em differently? Besides, thet would git the
'tention of all the blasted critters, damned if it wouldn't."

"Yeah! Yeah!" the wife cheered her husband on. "These
heathens hev no right ta trial. As the Good Book says, 'a eye fer
a eye an' tooth fer a tooth.' Nobody kin spell justice out better'n
God did when He said thet."

"Amen!" a burly man shouted. "Thet's the spirit. Let's
git after 'em."

"Wait a minute," a steely voice cut through the din. A
tall, slender, buckskin clad youth thrust his way through the crowd.
Redhead took a step backward. His wife uttered a squawk like a
disturbed setting hen. The youth paid them no attention, his startling blue eyes coolly surveyed the gathering.

"You people should be ashamed of yourselves," he chided
in a clipped New England accent. "Talk like this is foolish and
dangerous and those of you with a brain in your head know it.
Taking the law in your own hands is anarchy. You will be just as
guilty as the Indians who killed the missionaries."

The face of the man with flaming beard and hair turned
livid. He jabbed a wrathful finger at the speaker. "I know this
man. He's a Injun lover. He gotta Injun half brother. An' his
paunchy sidekick with the bald head lives amongst Injuns, has
Injun wife an' kids.

"I know 'cause me an' me missus traveled cross country
with 'em. Don't yuh believe a word these galoots say. They
looks white but they's Injun through an' through."

The buckskin clad youth gave his castigator a look of pity.
"I'm sorry for you folks, letting this empty-headed fellow lead
you astray. He is properly named. His name is Short. He's short
on brains and short in regard for his fellow man. He can't get it

through his head that Indian people are human beings just like you and me.

"So, you have had Indian trouble. Who hasn't had troubles of one kind or another in this life? How have you dealt with them? I would guarantee there is hardly one of you that resorted to killing and hanging, so why should you start now? Put yourselves in the place of the Indian people. If someone settled on your land and began to shoot the animals you had counted on for food, what would you do, stand idly by? Of course you wouldn't. You would resent it just like they do. . . ."

The group that favored blasting every Indian dead began to hoot and holler so loudly the buckskin clad youth could not be heard. He, his paunchy companion and several more, including the chairman who gave up trying to keep order, sidled out through the back door.

"I guess this is a free country and everyone has a right to express his or her opinion but . . ." The chairman shook his head. "If these rabble-rousers have their way we may be caught up in a situation that'll make the Whitman Mission tragedy look like a tea party."

V

We made up our minds to be friendly . . . But we found this
difficult, because the white men too often promised one thing
and then when they acted at all, did another.

Plenty-Coups, Crow

Vision Seeker was sore of heart. He had no idea how long the mission with Cut Lip would take. He had said a hurried good-bye to his parents. His blind mother, Quiet Woman, had pressed her hands against his face as though she were molding his features into her memory like a piece of clay. He would feel the loving pressure of her hands, long after the chatter of Lapwai children and bark of village dogs had faded away.

Lone Wolf, busily organizing his gang of elderly buffalo hunters, hardly had noticed his son's departure. "Bring back much meat and skins," Vision Seeker finally had said, attempting to attract his father's attention.

"Yes-yes," Lone Wolf muttered without looking up.

Vision Seeker had turned away to hide his dismay. What suddenly had given these old men the idea they needed one last hunt? Yet, who was he to discourage them? They were having so much enjoyment it made him envious. But it would not last. A few nights on the Lolo Trail would see to that.

Down the Kooskooskie Cut Lip and Vision Seeker went. The silvery, whispering waters of the swift river gurgled its time-less tune, one to which Vision Seeker had put words to as a child:

"I'm the Kooskooskie on the way to the Great Water.
Someday I will return to make brooks and lakes,
morning dew, spring rain and winter snowflakes."

Vision Seeker shook himself free of his reverie. He was on a serious mission yet daydreaming like a six-year old. What must Cut Lip think? Probably he had expected to meet a youthful warrior eager to do battle rather than a man of middle years who hated to leave his home village.

The two riders rode in silence. Except for a knife at his belt, Vision Seeker went unarmed. Early in life he had come to the conclusion a man who walked and talked with The Great Mysterious had no need for weapons. There was good in every living thing. Mother Earth would not have it any other way. Once a person wholeheartedly believed this he had nothing to fear.

Cut Lip, who rode in the lead, had no such faith. He carried his long barreled rifle loaded, ready for instant use. His eyes shifted uneasily back and forth. Not only was he passing through land he did not know well, but was on a mission that filled him with dread. If things went wrong his people were in for another season of turmoil. How his Nimpau companion could ride along as calmly as if they were on a trip to gather wild honey, was beyond his imagination.

Suddenly, almost from beneath the horses' hooves, a flock of northern geese flew out of a patch of bulrushes and whirred overhead. Instinctively, Cut Lip threw up the rifle barrel and pulled the trigger. To his amazement the lead bird uttered a squawk and fell to earth. While Cut Lip hurriedly reloaded, Vision Seeker rode to where the goose fell, dismounted and picked up the bundle of feathers. He held the bird aloft and said a silent prayer to the departed spirit of the northern goose.

"I am at fault. I shot without thinking," Cut Lip apologized, cringing from the scolding he fully expected to receive. Instead, he was shocked to hear praise.

"You did good. The Great Mysterious must have guided your hand. I have never seen finer shooting. The bird died without pain and will provide us with food for the night."

The following morning the two men arose at dawn. Before mounting up, standing together, they murmured a prayer, thanking Father Sun for the new day. They forded the River Snake and cut across the rolling land that one day would be great fields of grain. They forded the Tucannon, Touchet, Walla Walla rivers, finally to arrive at the camp of the Cayuse leader, Stickus, on the upper Umatilla. Two guards greeted the riders and escorted them into the tipi village where Stickus and a group of elders stood with arms folded, waiting to welcome their honored Nimpau guest.

The formalities were few. The traditional smoke was cut short. There was little talk. Time was precious. If they were to arrive at The Dalles in time to be of help, they must leave at once. Normally, it was a two-day ride but it had to be done in one. Herders brought fresh mounts for Vision Seeker and Cut Lip and a drove of extra horses.

It was a small number of riders but, with the extra drove of horses sending up a long trail of dust, it appeared a formidable force. There was little wonder scouts catching sight of the fast moving body of horses and horsemen took it for a band of hostiles and reported it as such to Colonel Loring and Governor Lane.

Unaware of the threatening impression they created, the riders pushed steadily westward until they came to the escarpment overlooking The Dalles. The riders pulled up. Ahead, against a backdrop of green, stood a cluster of stately white tipis. In a field of luxuriant grass grazed a herd of horses. Beyond gleamed the white ripples of the Great River's rapids called The Dalles. In the curve of the river, a line of canoes and other small craft lined the south river bank. In the hazy distance loomed the white mountain peak the hairy faces had named Hood.

The sight of the majestic mountain always gave Vision Seeker a feeling of awe. An ancient legend claimed when life first appeared on Mother Earth a tribe of giants occupied the great mountain's slopes. The men were as tall as evergreen trees, even taller was their chief. His giant followers could walk upright beneath his extended arms. But inside the mountain dwelled evil spirits. Spewing fire and red hot rocks, the evil spirits destroyed the giant's homeland and killed their chief. Starved and weakened, the giants' offspring gradually became stunted and were doomed to remain so until another giant chief appeared to conquer the evil spirits. When that happened the people again would become giants.

Vision Seeker jerked his thoughts back to the business at hand. Riders on spirited shaggy ponies were galloping pell-mell toward them. They pulled up a short distance away. The leader of the group rode forward, his hands clasped before him in the sign of peace.

"You come to make council?" he queried. His wary eyes glanced suspiciously over the armed group. Their dusty appearance, lathered mounts and spare extra horses, told him these people had ridden hard and far. Was the unarmed man on the Appaloosa a prisoner brought in to surrender to Chief Governor Joe? He hoped not. The camp already was in turmoil over the five men held prisoner.

Stickus held up his hand palm forward. "Yes, we come to join the council," he said somewhat sharply, annoyed by the wary reception. "Riding with us is our Nimpau guest."

Vision Seeker held up his hand in the traditional greeting. "I am Vision Seeker," he said pleasantly. "Your markings are of the tribe, Walla Walla."

The horseman's surly demeanor promptly turned friendly. "Welcome to our camp, Nimpau man. We know you are the shaman who sees into the shadows of tomorrow. Our leader, Peupeu-mox-mox, awaits to greet you."

The Walla Walla tribesman escorted them around the cluster of tipis to an open space where a sizeable group of men were seated in a circle. On the far side of the circle a heated discussion was taking place. As the newcomers appeared to be welcomed and seated, the angry exchange ceased but tension hung heavily over the council gathering. One of the men involved was Five Crows. The Cayuse leader whose band lived along the middle Umatilla River, was vehemently opposed to surrendering the five prisoners to Territorial Governor Joseph Lane.

Vision Seeker was not surprised by the man's stand. Two years previously Five Crows had led the fight against Colonel Gilliam's invading army of volunteers who had been sent to cap-

THE CRY OF THE COYOTE   33

ture the Whitman Mission murderers. During the campaign's first battle Five Crows had been badly wounded and his war party humbled. Perhaps his wounds and shattered ego still tortured him.

Vision Seeker glanced around the crowd. Peu-peu-mox-mox silently greeted him with a slight motion of lips and chin. Also present was Kah-lat-toose of the Palouse. Both men had good reason to be unhappy with the territorial government.

While on a trading trip Peu-peu-mox-mox's son had been killed by a white man. The youth, who was his father's pride and joy, had been educated at Jason Lee's Methodist mission school and given the name Elijah Hedding. Although his death was an outright case of cold-blooded murder, Elijah's killer never was charged. The fact that little or no attempt was made to bring the man to justice had been a bitter pill for the Walla Walla leader to swallow. He had no confidence in the white man's so-called system of justice.

Kah-lat-toose of the Palouse also had little reason to place trust in the laws of the white man. The Palouse had played no part in the Whitman Mission tragedy, yet the same army of volunteers that wounded Five Crows blatantly invaded a peaceful Palouse village and absconded with the people's horses. A battle ensued in which a number of Palouse were slain.

"Cayuse - Palouse . . . what's the difference?" Colonel Gilliam had remarked when members in his command objected to invading the peaceful village. "They're Indians. For my money all of them are guilty of the Whitman Mission killings."

A place was made for Vision Seeker in the first circle of elders. He sat down with a feeling of unease. What right did he have to be here? These council members had the power to shape Northwest history for decades to come. He glanced across the circle of faces to see the dark, impassive eyes of Peu-peu-mox-mox upon him. Was this man's destiny already determined? Had he joined with Five Crows and Kah-lat-toose in opposing the release of the five accused murderers to Territorial Governor Lane?

Did he have a premonition that one day he would fall before the white man's guns?

The Cayuse leader, Young Chief, who conducted the meeting, called a recess and reached for his pipe. It was only polite to give the newcomers time to collect themselves before taking part. He took a pinch of tobacco, sage and sweet grass from a beaded pouch; rubbing the mixture together, he began to fill the red stone bowl. He attached the pipe stem to the bowl and reached for a burning ember to light the pipe bowl's ingredients. The pipe went around the circle of men and back to where it started. A second pipe made the rounds and then a third.

Young Chief purposefully delayed putting the pipe away. How could he control the firebrands from dominating the meeting? So far Five Crows hardly allowed anyone else to speak. He claimed it a cowardly act to surrender their fellow tribesmen. Five Crows was for war -- seeking peace with the white man was impossible. Never would he accept an agreement with Territorial Governor Joe Lane.

After the third smoke Young Chief carefully and slowly placed the pipe into its fringed carrying case. He took time to smooth the fringes. Finally, he turned toward the men who silently waited, his face as dark and expressionless as the overcast sky above.

Although he had started the meeting with a prayer, again he raised his eyes to seek help from above. "Great Mysterious, guide us," he beseeched. "The lives of five men are in your hands." But the problem was far greater than that. The very existence of his people could well depend upon what decision they made today. He cleared his throat to speak but no words would come. He avoided looking at Five Crows. He had no wish ever again to hear his tiresome, spiteful tirades.

Young Chief had placed himself in a difficult position. He was not a follower of Missionary Marcus Whitman but a Catholic. He had given his home to be used as a base for incoming priests. Two years prior to the death of Missionary Whitman,

Young Chief had gone to the missionary doctor with a list of complaints. He had spoken first of the death of his nephew who had died while attending the Red River Mission school.

"You people are careless with the lives of our youth," he had accused. "No more Cayuse children will I send to your schools." Missionary Whitman was not concerned as almost all of his mission school students were white.

"The people you bring from beyond the River of Many Canoes are taking our land," Young Chief had continued. Missionary Whitman replied this was not true.

Young Chief ended with a third accusation. "These people that come in their land canoes bring with them infection and disease. You go to the sick and say you will make them well, instead they die. You, and the people you bring not only take our lands but also our lives." This charge had struck home. After the meeting with Young Chief, Whitman wrote to a fellow missionary, "I am so nervous that I cannot govern my hand."

Young Chief thoughts were bitter. His complaints had made no difference. Increasing numbers of intruders in their land canoes had poured into the Cayuse homeland. Offspring of the newcomers crowded the mission school classrooms until there was no room at all for Indian children. The disease death toll among the Cayuse had continued to rise, faster than ever.

"Ah!" He should be siding with Five Crows instead of opposing him, Young Chief thought angrily. Instead, he had made the pact to surrender the prisoners to Governor Joseph Lane, believing to do so was best for the tribe. Now that the decision had been made, he had to go through with it. Unlike the white man, when a Cayuse made a promise, he kept it.

Young Chief glanced at the circle of men who waited for the meeting to continue. They should all join together and speak with one voice, but how could that be accomplished? Perhaps the Nimpau wise man had the answer.

"Our good friend, Vision Seeker, has journeyed all the way from Lapwai to give us the benefit of his wisdom," he began, turning to the tall Nimpau. "Our brother knows the language of the white man and the mysteries of their talking paper. . . ."

Five Crows threw up his hands. "Why call on the Nimpau? I can tell you what the pale skins say and write. Lies! Lies! Promises and promises they never keep. I know these things. I learned all these things at Spalding's Mission School."

Young Chief, made a sharp negative motion with his hand. "There is no need for our brother to speak of what we already know. He has made it clear that he is against surrendering our tribesmen to Governor Joseph Lane. We would like to keep our brothers from harm, but laws have been broken. Wrongdoers must be punished."

"What about pale skin wrongdoers?" Five Crows shouted. "Why do they not stand before us and answer for their crimes?" He turned on Vision Seeker. "What answer does our wise Nimpau friend have for that?"

Vision Seeker searched his mind for an appropriate response, but what could he say? Five Crows was right. The white man had committed many grievous crimes against Indian people that went unpunished.

"Oh-hah!" Five Crows jeered, "our Nimpau wise man has no answer." With a final glare at Vision Seeker, Five Crows motioned his followers to depart. The Cayuse council members who remained stared at the ground, too embarrassed to speak or look at each other. One of their own had insulted an honored guest, one to whom they had called upon for help.

Instead of feeling insulted, Vision Seeker's heart went out to his Cayuse friends. They had lost control of their people at a time when they all should be working together.

VI

If the blind lead the blind, both shall fall into the ditch.

Matthew, XV:14

"I'll need a strong second-in-command," Governor Lane said, pulling on his ear lobe, a habit he had formed as a youth. He glanced over the roster of available officers and enlisted men. "Lieutenant Addison? His record is fairly good and he's already at Fort Vancouver. Perhaps you can send him a message, something like: 'hire six good boatmen with river craft ready to move.'" Receiving no response, Lane seized a pad and scribbled a note. He called for his orderly. "See that this gets off straightway?"

Colonel Loring looked on grimly. They were in the headquarters orderly room with a peaked-faced corporal taking notes. Right from the first he had disliked the place. It smelled of dampness and rats. The original posting was for the regiment to occupy quarters at Fort Vancouver but upon their arrival they found the fort facilities in shambles. Leaving a small cadre at Fort Vancouver, he had ordered the men south to take up accommodations in Oregon City. When they arrived he found them even worse than those in Fort Vancouver.

The poor housing plus the hostile environment of the citizenry made the troopers resentful. They had marched 2,000 miles across the country in answer to the locals' call for protection from fractious Indians only to be treated like dirt. Little wonder the men in his command had deserted in droves.

"What about these fellows?" Lane asked, handing over the roster with ticks against the names of the men he had selected. "We need a good noncom, someone dependable and able to get along with men. Here's a Corporal Coombs -- a 20 year veteran. What happened to him? He retired with the grade of sergeant and six months later reenlisted as corporal?"

Colonel Loring massaged the stub of his missing arm.

"Yeah, while crossing the plains Corporal Coombs made some dubious decisions . . . ran into an ambush on Barlow Road . . . got himself shot up. Shortly afterward he asked to be discharged. I don't know whether he had a belly full of the army or an emigrant woman caught his fancy. Anyway, he got married and homesteaded in Tualatin Plains.

"I had my doubts, but being shorthanded, especially of experienced noncoms, I decided to take a chance on him. So far he's worked out fine. If his womenfolk keep their distance . . ."

"Ah, yes." Lane pulled on his ear lobe. "Family trouble is the bane of a soldier's existence. Womenfolk, whatever respect they show a man to his face, sure as shooting secretly they'll view him as an ass and regard him with pity. Maybe what this good man needs is to get away for a spell and let the air clear."

Colonel Loring nodded and kept his lips sealed. Let the governor find out for himself about Corporal Coombs. He had been a good man but then got mixed up with that Beamer bunch. They had caused more trouble on the cross-country trip than all the rest of the regiment put together.

"Here's this fellow Beamer," Lane commented as though reading Loring's mind. He's getting long in the tooth but he must know his way around these parts. I see he received a commendation for bravery."

"Agh!" Loring could no longer remain quiet. "Putting Coombs and Beamer together is like planting a lightening rod in a barrel of gunpowder."

"Whatever you say. What about O'Hara?"

One by one they went through the roster. The peaked-faced corporal made notes and Colonel Loring gave opinions on the men. He still did not know who would lead the party, Lane or himself. The indecision wore on his nerves. He kept rubbing his stump, shifting uneasily in the chair.

Lane sensed Loring did not approve of the men selected or, was it because he didn't like the way he was taking charge? Let him sulk. It was the governor's responsibility to get the prisoners to Oregon City. He handed the marked roster to the colonel. "If you kindly will notify these men to collect their field equipment and draw supplies for a four day march, the party, led by myself, will leave at first light in the morning. You won't have to worry about a thing except keeping the locally stationed troops on the alert." Lane abruptly turned and strode out.

"Bagh!" Colonel Loring uttered to the closed door, forlornly massaging his stump. Lane made it quite evident he did not have sufficient confidence in Loring to command the escort that would bring the prisoners in from The Dalles. If that was the case, what made the governor believe him capable of guarding Oregon City while he was gone? Lane was taking the best men he had. Those left behind were about as worthless as a half bucket of horse droppings. What was to keep the reported war party from circling around and plundering Oregon City?

The colonel did not have time to brood. He had to get Lane's party ready to leave in the morning. Whatever happened the crucial thing was to get the five Cayuse safely to Oregon City. If the assignment failed -- if somehow the prisoners escaped -- he and the entire Regiment of Mounted Riflemen would be the ones in the soup.

"Smith, on the double," he shouted to the headquarters clerk. "Find Corporal Coombs, and tell him to report at once."

Corporal Coombs, busy with a garbage detail, was not in the best frame of mind. Since rejoining the army every dirty duty seemed to fall to him. He responded to the Colonel's summons with profanity. "What bloody chore has that dimwit thought of now," he growled at the messenger who delivered the summons. He stomped into Loring's office and saluted. Without glancing up, the colonel acknowledged the salute with a wave of his remaining hand and motioned Coombs to a chair. Coombs sat down, stiff and upright. He didn't at all like the colonel's taut expression.

Of course Colonel Loring had no reason to like him. He had left the service far from being in the colonel's good graces, just at a time when Loring needed him most. Lucille, his wife to be, had not given him much choice. The wounds he received during the battle on the Barlow Road had left her distraught. She made it quite clear if Sergeant Coombs wanted her hand he had to leave the service and settle down at once. She did not want him out of her sight.

"Now that you've had time to accustom yourself to army routine again, it's time you begin earning your pay," Colonel Loring said bluntly. He studied the veteran trooper who had accepted the reduced rank of corporal without a grumble. Why had he returned after such a short period away? From what he had been told his young wife was a beauty, the best looking woman in the entire upper valley.

"Yes, sir," Coombs grudgingly responded. "I'm ready, willing and able."

"Good, because we have an important duty to perform. As you know, the criminals we came to apprehend are being held in The Dalles awaiting transfer to Oregon City. Governor Lane has asked for a detachment of trustworthy men to see that these prisoners arrive safely back here to stand trial. A responsible noncom is needed to take charge of the enlisted men. It's a challenging assignment. Can I count on you to manage it? It has to be done by the book. There cannot be the slightest mishap."

"Yes, sir," Coombs answered. As he thought, another dirty task. "I'm only a corporal. You need someone with more rank. You know what these men are like."

"Hmm!" the colonel grunted. "Quite so. From this moment on you are Acting Sergeant Coombs. If you manage this assignment well, the rank is permanent. Round up the men on this list and prepare them to leave first thing in the morning. Governor Lane, himself, will lead the escort."

Coombs groaned. Tomorrow was market day. Lucille and her family planned to be in town and he had promised to show them around. Already he was in the dog house. His in-laws were furious with him for reenlisting. What was he to do?

THE CRY OF THE COYOTE   41

He wanted those sergeant stripes back. If he refused to carry out
Colonel Loring's order, he could kiss them good-bye forever.

Unaware of his new sergeant's predicament, Colonel
Loring continued giving orders. "Draw your supplies from the
quartermaster building. If I'm not mistaken, Beamer, who just
arrived from sick bay, is in charge. He may still be weak, apt to
make mistakes. As you know he's not too reliable at his best."

"Yes, sir," Coombs agreed, but in good conscience had to
put in a word for the men. "Beamer and his Two Feather cousin
did mighty good work, too. In the battle on the mountain they
saved the wagon train. Beamer took so much lead its a wonder
he's alive. . . ."

"Yeah, yeah," the colonel interrupted, "the fellow has the
constitution of a mule. Wasn't he supposed to have taken sick
with cholera and died on the way out?"

"Ah, he was just play acting then. He . . ." Acting Sergeant Coombs hesitated. What was the matter with him, spilling
the beans to the commanding officer like a raw recruit? The
colonel liked Teamster Beamer even less than he, himself. Acting Sergeant Coombs abruptly stood and saluted.

"Sir! The quicker I get to work, the quicker I'll have things
in hand."

Colonel Loring rubbed his stump, wondering what the acting sergeant had left unsaid and if he had made a mistake by
giving him the prisoner escort detail. Well, who else in his miserable command had the experience of Coombs? No one. Most
of them were untrustworthy as a balky team of mules.

The colonel went to the window to watch Coombs plodding through the mud toward the quartermaster shed. Beamer
was waiting, his belly as large as an oversized watermelon. He
gave Coombs a mocking salute and mouthed a ribald greeting.

"Hello there, Corporal Coombs." Beamer's small eyes
glinted mischievously. "Whatcha been upta? Heerd yuh'd left
the army an' got yerself hitched. Sure wish yuh an' yer missus
well. Yuh gotta woman any fella'd give his eye teeth ta hev. An'

what 'bout those corporal stripes? Didja git busted?"
Coombs eyed the teamster uneasily. Beamer had saved
his life in the mountain shoot-out, but that didn't entitle him to be
privy to the unhappy details of his life since then. Only his wife
and himself knew the terrible truth. Who would have thought
robust, virile appearing Sergeant Coombs was unable to consum-
mate his wedding. Only after returning to the army did he regain
his manhood. No wonder the marriage had a rocky beginning.
No woman wanted a husband minus his manhood.
    Out of the quartermaster quarters stepped a gangly figure
with a mop of hair that stood straight up. "Hiya, Sarge."
    Loring swore. "Grasshopper Stillings, back from sick bay
too! Trouble-trouble-trouble," he moaned. "It comes in threes."
    "Ain't yuh goin' ta tell watcha been upta?" Beamer asked.
    "It's a long story," Coombs said, avoiding Beamer's pig-
like eyes.
    "We ain't goin' nowhere, is we Stillin's?" The big man
leaned against the wagon wheel and took a chaw. He liked nothing better than listening to someone's troubles. During the past
year he'd had enough of his own. His gimpy leg and irksome
hunk of lead in his shoulder was proof enough of that.
    Coombs stiffened. This was no way to start earning his
sergeant stripes -- gossiping with privates like they were kins-
folk. Abruptly he became his old demanding sergeant self.
    "Nothing has changed," he snapped. "The colonel has
just returned my rank as sergeant. My marriage is nobody's business. Right now we have an important job to do, bringing those
five Cayuses from The Dalles to Oregon City. Get cracking and
fill my supply order. If I'm not mistaken Colonel Loring is watching us right now. He believes all three of us are irresponsible,
lazy, good-for-nothings. Let's show him differently."
    Colonel Loring, who indeed watched, was amazed how
sprightly the big teamster and his gangly companion, Stillings,
began to scurry about. Perhaps reinstating Coombs to the rank of
sergeant had been the right decision after all.

VII

*We made these little gray houses of logs . . . and they are
square. It is a bad way to live, for there is no power in a
square. . . . Everything an Indian does is in a circle and
that is because the power of the world always works
in circles and everything tries to be round.*

Black Elk, Oglala Sioux

Tildy Jennings Laird glanced out the kitchen window. At
the end of the lane stood a solitary horseman. She shaded her
eyes. Horse and rider were silhouetted against the setting sun,
motionless, still as if carved in stone. There was something about
the fixed way the man stared at her log cabin home that sent a
chill racing up her spine. His face was in a shadow but she could
tell by the intent posture, he was studying it as if counting every
shake, chink and log.

Tildy set down the dish she had been drying and reached
for another. Her heart pounded so fast and fiercely she felt faint.
This man looked as menacing and mysterious as the dark forest
that cloaked the hills on the far side of the river. And, like the
evergreens, the stranger was slender, tall and dark. A thin black
line like a lightening shattered treetop rose above the back of his
head.

Tildy dropped the plate she held and uttered a stifled
scream. The horseman was Indian. The line above his head was
a long, black and white feather. Joshua Short, the vociferous
redhead who warned the town hall meeting crowd, had been right.
These Indians were lurking in the shadows just waiting for the
right opportunity to strike.

"Macon!" she shrieked, then remembered her husband was
outside taking care of the chores. Except for her three year-old
child, she was alone. She forced herself to look again. The horseman was gone. Had it been an illusion? There was not a trace of

horse or rider. They had vanished as mysteriously as they had arrived.

Tildy sat down and tried to still her pounding heart. She had to get her nerves under control. She had lived in this dark land with its dusky people for nearly four years and should be taking incidents like this in stride. Yet, she could not forget the loss of her first husband who had been shot dead by the Cayuse during Gilliam's '48 campaign to capture the Whitman Mission murderers.

Unsteadily, Tildy pushed herself upright and began to set the table. Soon the men would be in for supper. She should be ashamed of herself, letting a lone Indian upset her. After all, her own father had taken an Indian woman for a wife and begat a dark-faced son. Even so, she could not imagine Father living and loving an Indian woman, no matter how beautiful she was.

"What possessed Father to do this?" she had asked herself time and time again. It would have broken poor Granny Jennings' heart. In a way it was a blessing the prim old lady had passed on. She never would have accepted the Indian wife and grandson into the family circle. It was Granny's belief each race had a place of its own in the Lord's scheme -- not to be tarnished by mixing the blood of one race with another -- when this rule was broken the all powerful God would bring forth plagues to scourge the land as he did in the time of the Pharaohs.

#

The tall, slender horseman, sensed he would not be welcome, certainly not at this late hour. Like the fog and drizzle overhead, fear hung over the valley like a shroud. Settlers he met on the road gave him wide berth, watching over their shoulders as if they feared that if given the chance he would turn about and do them harm. Once he had asked a man and wife driving team and wagon for directions. Instead of answering, the homesteader whipped the team into a gallop, taking off as fast as he could.

The Indian man wheeled his mount around and made a beeline for the edge of the forest. Beneath a cluster of tall firs he pulled the saddle from his horse, rubbed his four-legged companion down and staked him in a grassy open space. Only after making certain the campsite was well hidden from prying eyes, did he unfold a single blanket and sit on it with his back against a tree trunk. From here he had an unobstructed view of the log cabin. He methodically studied it, chewing on a piece of dried meat.

His thoughts were as unappetizing as the food on which he dined. The council meeting of plateau Indian leaders had ended in confusion. Five Crows and his men, so violently opposed to handing over the prisoners to Governor Lane, had left before the meeting was over.

Kah-lat-toose, the Palouse, had ridden up river to council with tribal elders. Young Chief and a few elders chose to await Governor Lane's arrival as did Cut Lip, the Cayuse youth who sought the release of his brother. At the last moment Peu-peu-mox-mox, the Walla Walla leader, who had remained uncommitted, approached him.

"Nimpau brother, what think you? Does the White Governor Chief speak with straight tongue?" he had asked.

"I believe he does," Vision Seeker replied.

Peu-peu-mox-mox nodded. "Good. You go, see, return and tell what the white man says and does. If the white man speaks with a straight tongue and does right, we will store our war paint pots. If the white man lies . . ." The Walla Walla left the sentence uncompleted.

Before Vision Seeker had had time to digest the conversation, wan faced Cut Lip came to renew his plea for help in freeing his brother, Kia-ma-sump-kin. Then Stickus approached to report that two more of the five prisoners insisted they were innocent. Ish-ish-kais-kais and Clokamas said they had been present at the mission that tragic day but had taken no part in the bloodshed. Would he seek their release?

Vision Seeker did not have the heart to say there was little hope. Right from the start he knew they were asking the impossible. Men called lawyers spent years studying books and working in places called courthouses and still were ignorant of many aspects of the judicial system. That was among the many bits of information Buck Stone the Harvard educated mountain man had imparted to him long ago during winter nights spent trapping the Bitterroot. How he wished for the council of his educated friend now. Even after all these years he could hear Buck's clipped voice explaining words taken from the thick black covered books he carried in a waterproof sack.

Buck Stone likened the system of justice to a spider web. Threads of the web caught and strangled the weak and unfortunate, but the rich and powerful slashed through them and escaped. He said that knowledge of laws was important but more valuable was having influential friends. A few words in the right places could turn a man free or keep him imprisoned. It was this slim chance that brought Vision Seeker here. In the log cabin lived the only person he knew that could help him find these men with the power to save the lives of the innocent Cayuse prisoners.

As darkness fell, Vision Seeker watched candle flares light up the cabin windows. From the tall building called "barn" a lone figure came toward the house, swinging a lantern. The cabin door opened, outlining a man as tall and slender as himself. Then, from somewhere, a second man appeared, short and round. A flicker of disappointment made Vision Seeker frown. Neither man was the one he had hoped to see. He waited for the door to open again but it remained closed.

When the cabin windows ceased to glow, Vision Seeker pulled the blanket around himself, laid down and closed his eyes. He would sleep until the darkest hours of the night, then awaken and go scouting -- look into the barn and outbuildings. Perhaps he would find what he wanted there.

A dog growled. Vision Seeker answered with a friendly word. He understood the language and feelings of animals, even those that ran wild knew from his manner he was their friend. The dog came forward, wagging its tail. Vision Seeker ruffled the hair behind the canine's ears. The dog licked his hand.

"My good fellow creature, guide me to your four-legged companions," Vision Seeker asked. As if it understood, the dog trotted toward the barn where a horse snuffled and another stomped a hoof, their heads turning to watch the newcomer approach. It took a moment for Vision Seeker to accustom his eyes to the inner darkness. The horses accepted the presence of the tall stranger as complacently as had the dog. Soft lips nibbled at the fringes on Vision Seeker's buckskin shirt. A muzzle thrust itself in the crook of his arm. He singled out the face of a blaze, the blotched side of a pinto, two other animals were dark shadows, then, against the far wall, was the pony he expected to see, a light colored rump covered with dark splotches as if made by mud slung against a whitewashed wall.

Vision Seeker sidled along the rough barn wall to circle behind the horses. He patted one rump after another until he came to the Appaloosa. Just as he put a hand on the animal, a sharp click, like breaking of a dry stick came from the shadows.

The deadly sound of a rifle cocking made no impression on the tall, slender intruder. He would have been disappointed if something like this had not occurred. He ran his hand down the Appaloosa's side and uttered the pony's name, "Magpie."

From the shadows came a gasping sound. "Vision Seeker! What are you doing here? I could have shot you."

"My dear nephew, you would never have done that. You would have been afraid of injuring your four-legged companion."

The shadowy figure lowered the weapon and wrapped his arms around the intruder. For a moment the two men clung to each other, too overwhelmed to speak. Silently, uncle and nephew left the barn to walk to where Vision Seeker had made camp, the dog trailing along behind. They built a small fire that could not be seen from the log house. They sat and quietly talked, pausing for moments on end to listen to the chorus of distant coyotes, savoring their companionship and taking delight in the beauty of the night.

Vision Seeker did not speak of his fears that his mother

and his nephew's grandmother, Quiet Woman, might soon make the journey to the Great Beyond, or that Lone Wolf had reverted to childhood and likely would kill himself on the dangerous trek to buffalo country. In moments like this, one did not speak of fear and heartbreak. Nor did Vision Seeker give the slightest hint why he had come and Michael Two Feathers did not ask. He knew his uncle did not converse until he felt the moment was right.

When the first rays of Father Sun peeped over the eastern hills, the two men stood in silent prayer, thanking The Creator for the new day and for bringing them together. Only then did Michael Two Feathers invite his uncle to enter the log cabin lodge. He did so with apprehension, fearful of what Vision Seeker would think of the comfortable way he lived.

Tildy, who saw them coming, sucked in her breath. The slender horseman had not been an illusion. Here he was walking up the lane with her half brother. Was he a member of her dead father's Indian family? Was what she had feared most taking place? It was said without invitation Indian people moved in on relatives like salmon coming home to spawn. For her half brother's sake she could not turn the stranger away, but where would she put him? The cabin and the lean-to in back were chock full. If the newcomer brought family . . . ! Tildy uttered an audible groan. What would the neighbors say and do when they discovered an Indian family in their midst?

"What's the matter, Sis?" her brother, Joe, asked. He pushed back a chair from the kitchen table and came to stand alongside his sister. "Why, I do believe it is Michael's uncle, Vision Seeker. You'll like him. He is said to be the wisest native in the entire Northwest. What in the world brings him here?"

There was the scraping of another chair being pushed back. A bushy bearded man with head as bald as a new laid egg, peered out. "I do declare, yer right. Isn't he a sight fer sore eyes? I members when the lad was jest a sprout. Takes me back ta the winter we spent together on the Bitterroot. If only our ol' pardners,

Buck Stone an' Little Ned, could see him now, wouldn't they turn over in their graves?" He flung open the door and rushed out, seizing the tall stranger by the hand with Joe following close behind.

Tildy watched as the men met, all talking at once. She glanced at her husband, grandfather and stepson, who remained sitting at the kitchen table. Her three year-old son of her own blood and flesh took that moment to tumble down the stairs from the loft. He started to cry, then glanced out the door that stood open and fell silent. Wide-eyed, he studied the tall man and the big horse that reared its head up behind him. He clapped his hands.

"What a nice man. He brings pony," he chortled. He toddled through the door, waving his chubby arms. "Ride, ride, me ride that pony."

Tildy ran to pull the boy back. She was so near the tall stranger she could see gray flecks in his eyes. "Boys are so impetuous. They see something they want and go after it without thought of the consequences," she explained, flustered by the position the child had put her in, then became more flustered when the man called Vision Seeker hardly glanced at her, keeping his eyes on her son. Of course, she had blundered. He didn't understand English. With her eyes she appealed to brother, Joe, to come to the rescue. He, too, remained silent.

"Yes," the tall Indian finally replied, the impeccably spoken word had the Boston ring Tildy loved to hear. "Small children are the same wherever they may be found. They have no fear, their tongues are straight. They see the world with open minds and open hearts. To them things are not good or bad, they are just there to enjoy. Oft times I wonder if that is not the way the gods want us to live, accepting everything Mother Earth offers as having a place in The Creator's scheme of life."

Tildy was so surprised by the thoughtful, meaningful speech, she was struck dumb. Unable to speak, she waved a hand inviting the stranger into her log cabin home.

Vision Seeker hesitated. He nearly was as flustered as his hostess. He had come to find his nephew, Michael Two Feathers. He then had planned for both of them to travel straightway to Oregon City where the five Cayuse soon were to be imprisoned. Michael was the one person who could help find that someone needed to cut the threads of the legal cobwebs. His nephew had spent years in missionary classrooms, for a while lived in the land of the Bostons and had marched with the Blue Coats. He was on speaking terms with US Marshal Joe Meek. Most important of all, he had led the party that saved the column of Mounted Riflemen that had taken the Barlow Road across the Cascade Mountains. That act alone should make the citizenry of Oregon Territory beholden to him.

Now that he had found his nephew it was important they get busy and do what had to be done. But here he was, trapped, caught up with this family of pale faces. It was not polite to refuse their hospitality, certainly not when they were related to him by marriage. Also, he could not very well leave without having a smoke with his long ago trapping partner and one of the very first white men he had known, Deacon Walton.

Vision Seeker handed the halter rope of his horse to Michael and, stooping a little to enter the cabin door, followed the woman with hair the color of ripe corn. Once inside, he met two more men and a boy, the mate, grandfather and stepson of the lady of the house. Vision Seeker lowered his eyes but they came forward with hands outstretched, introducing themselves: husband, Macon Laird; grandfather, John Jennings; and adopted son, David Malin Laird.

To keep them straight in his memory, he carefully noted each face and the sounds that came from each set of lips. From his speech the husband, Macon Laird, was obviously from a different land. He spoke in the precise manner of newly arrived redcoats who came to work in the trading posts of Hudson's Bay. Grandfather Jennings spoke with a Boston tongue, much like his son, Little Ned, who sired nephew, Michael Two Feathers. The boy, David -- his speech was that of a mission school boy.

Vision Seeker combed his memory. There was something familiar about the youth. Suddenly it dawned on him, he had seen the lad playing in the Whitman Mission compound. Yes, David Malin was the eight year-old who was left behind when the survivors of the Whitman Mission tragedy sailed away in the rescue bateaux.

McBean, the Hudson's Bay factor at Fort Walla Walla, would not let the child go, claiming the lad was a British subject and had to stay among his own kind. David had been heartbroken. His adopted family and mission school classmates had left him for good. He stood on the river bank weeping until the Englishman, Macon Laird, promised to take care of him as though he were a son. Vision Seeker responded to the adopted boy's father's greeting with an extra warm handshake.

For a while confusion reigned in the small kitchen. Macon Laird attempted to make a place at the table for the guest. Deacon, who had known Vision Seeker and his family for more than twenty years, wanted to reminisce. David Malin found his voice and began to ask innumerable questions. The baby, Little John, stood sucking his thumb and staring wide-eyed at the tall, dark stranger, getting in everyone's way. Tildy busied herself at the stove frying eggs and bacon, fearful the meal she prepared would not meet with the approval of the visitor. Michael and his half brother, Joe, leaned against the wall, watching the tall Indian trying to cope with all the attention.

Vision Seeker found himself sitting at the table looking at the plate of food Tildy had placed before him. He reached for a piece of crisp bacon and quickly drew his hand back. This was not a trapper's lean-to in the woods. Among people like this, one did not eat with fingers. Then he remembered mission school children were taught to pray before partaking of food.

Folding his hands, as he had seen Michael do, Vision Seeker silently thanked The Creator for the good things Mother Earth provided and then asked for guidance in dealing with the situation he faced. How did he eat this food without giving offense? Which one of these shiny utensils laid beside the plate did he use first?

When Vision Seeker finished praying, Grandfather Jennings, who seemed to sense the meaning of the silent prayer, uttered a resounding, "amen," and said a short prayer himself.

"Thank you, Lord, for this bounty and for the companionship of all these good people who are present to partake of it."

Youthful David Malin then answered Vision Seeker's prayer by showing the proper utensil with which to eat. The hungry boy seized a fork and began shoveling bacon and eggs into his mouth, all the while chattering like a magpie. He had to ride that big horse. When they finished eating could they go outside and go riding? Little John pulled the thumb from his mouth and announced he had asked first. David would have to wait his turn.

"Ah! Shucks," David muttered. "You're just a baby. You'll probably fall off and break a leg."

"Me won't," Little John retorted. "Me ride as good as you."

"We'll not have any quarreling at the table," Tildy admonished.

"And Little John you are not going anywhere until you eat your breakfast," his father, Macon Laird, said sharply.

Vision Seeker suddenly felt very comfortable. The babble and confusion reminded him of the days when he was a youngster. The long lodge, half buried in the earth and covered with reeds, limbs and grasses, housed as many as 20 families. At meal time 20 fires might flare up at once. Dozens of women dropped what they were doing to prepare food. Untold numbers of hungry, clamoring children gathered around to watch. Men hovered in the background, visiting and occasionally reprimanding a child.

Meal times were much the same, Vision Seeker thought, whether in the nest of an eagle or in a white man's log cabin.

VIII

When our young men grow angry at some real or imaginary wrong, and disfigure their faces with black paint, their hearts, also, are disfigured and turn black. . . .

Seattle, Duwamish

At dawn Acting Sergeant Algeron Coombs had his men standing at parade rest in front of the headquarters building. Should former General Joe Lane wish to inspect them, they were ready down to the last polished brass button. It had taken all of Sergeant Coombs' rank and locking a dissenter in the guard house to do the job. "No lazy lout is going to stand in the way of getting my stripes back," Sergeant Coombs vowed.

"Atten'chun!" The sergeant's strident voice echoed back from the far side of the river. "Now listen to me, you clumsy, dog-faced yokels, one false move and I'll personally have your hides. Better yet, I'll turn you over to the bloodthirsty plateau Indians and let them have a turn at you. In the mood they're in, likely as not they'll be more than happy to take your scalps.

"Just because the Cayuse fugitives are in irons doesn't mean we're home free. Indians have more tricks up their sleeve than county fair magicians. If you want to come back from this trip with a whole skin, keep your eyes and ears open . . . stay alert every step of the way to The Dalles and back to Oregon City."

"But we'uns is goin' by water the orders said," a weak voice at the end of the front rank spoke up.

Coombs was on the speaker like a cat after a mouse. "Shut up! Who gave you permission to speak? We probably are going by canoe, another reason you fellows had better stay alert and be light on your feet. One slip of your clumsy clodhoppers and there's a hole in the skin of those things. You'll be swimming for your lives and believe me, I'll not pull you out 'cause I can't swim."

All the way to Fort Vancouver, Sergeant Coombs had badgered the enlisted men until even Governor Lane's nerves were rubbed raw. However, rather than say anything, the governor held his tongue. He knew that to keep the men on their toes they had to have a firm hand, an experience these chaps seemed never to have had. Yet, he couldn't help but think the sergeant was carrying on the strict discipline act largely for his benefit.

At Fort Vancouver Lieutenant Addison met the detachment with a half dozen Klickitat boatmen. Several troopers would not go near them. When Sergeant Coombs remonstrated, two men tossed their rifles aside. "I jined up ta be with me own kind, not savages thet murder missionaries," a pimply faced youth declared.

For once Sergeant Coombs did not wield an iron fist. He turned to a post noncom. "Are there some Indian prisoners in the guard house?" he asked.

"Yep," the noncom replied. "Several sleepin' it off . . . a little too much firewater."

"Good. Throw these two men in with them, and keep them there until we get back."

"Might get kinda crowded. There's a big native shindig tonight -- powwow, Injuns call it. For certain some of 'em'll be swillin' a bit of rot gut."

"Great, the more the merrier. It'll give these two a chance to get acquainted with the natives."

The reluctant troopers were appalled. "Yuh cain't do this to us," Pimple Face shrieked, "keepin' us locked up with a bunch of drunken Injuns. Criminy, those people're inhumane, we could lose all we hev an' git scalped ta boot."

"You'll just have to take your chances, won't you?" Coombs replied. He glanced at the governor, but Lane made a point of looking the other way. Losing two men would weaken their strength but perhaps it was for the best. Discipline had to be maintained. In fact, the manner in which Sergeant Coombs handled the situation pleased him. There was a noncom in the Mexican War who was equally as uncompromising. When things went wrong his company had been one of the few that had faced situations squarely, turning potential disasters into victories.

The wisdom Sergeant Coombs had shown in maintaining tight discipline clearly was revealed at Cascade Portage. A band of Indians, in numbers far greater than those of the detachment of troopers, appeared on the escarpment. Painted and armed, they silently watched as boats and baggage were transported to the upper side of the falls. Unable to keep their eyes off the apparent hostiles, the men stumbled and fell against each other like frightened schoolboys.

"All right dog faces, straighten up," Sergeant Coombs ordered. "These Redskins are just looking us over. When we return with the prisoners, that's when they'll show their colors."

The presence of the war party also gave Governor Lane a queasy feeling. Had his agreement with the Cayuse fallen through? He attempted to identify the tribe, but in war paint one warrior looked much the same as another. Perhaps this was the party of hostiles sighted traveling toward The Dalles, possibly Cayuse renegades.

Of course there were other groups who were bitter about the way the perpetrators of the Whitman Mission tragedy had been hunted and finally forced to give themselves up. Peu-peu-mox-mox of the Walla Walla was an example. More than once he had questioned the white man's system of justice, and with good reason. Six years ago his son had been killed by an American and the killer had yet to be brought to justice.

"Aagh!" the governor muttered. If one of his sons were killed and the killer went scot free, would he feel any differently than the Walla Walla chieftain? Why shouldn't as much effort be put behind solving and punishing that crime as the present Whitman Mission murder case?

The territorial legislature would be furious if he attempted to revive the Hedding's case. He seriously doubted that even at the time the Hedding crime was committed that lawmen had given it much thought. But now that a trial of great publicity was on the docket everyone wanted to get involved. Lane uttered a deep sigh. All this talk about justice being free and equal to all was pure poppycock.

The Governor forced the disagreeable thought from his mind. He had enough on his plate without worrying about past misdeeds. Right now his task was to bring the Whitman Mission murderers to trial.

#

Five Crows and members of his war party who watched Governor Lane's detachment pass over the portage made mental notes of the number of men and their arms. He rubbed his hands together in satisfaction. His party outnumbered the Blue Coats two to one. Unless the Governor Chief brought reinforcements on the return trip his men would pick them off as easily as frogs snapping up flies.

Five Crows and his cohorts had confidence in their plan to overwhelm the prisoners' escort, but had given little thought as to what they should do afterward. They would have to find a hideout, but with so many hairy faces in the territory it was difficult to know where they would be safe. He had counted on Peu-peu-mox-mox and his warriors joining him. Their two parties would create a formidable force, but the Walla Walla leader the whites called Yellow Serpent, refused. It was such a bitter blow Five Crows had lost his temper and made matters worse.

"You speak of white man's justice! Bagh! Did the hairy face who killed your son hang by the neck until dead? No! Not a hair of his head went to pay for that crime. Why should Indian people hang when they kill white man and when white man kills Indian white man goes free?"

"Do not judge the white man hastily, my friend," Peu-peu-mox-mox had replied. "Governor Chief Joe speaks good words. If innocent Cayuse prisoners go free, then his heart is good -- his tongue straight. There will be peace."

The Walla Walla leader's response was so ridiculous Five Crows swung his mount around and galloped away.

IX

You might as well expect the rivers to run backward as that any man who was born free should be contented when penned up and denied liberty to go where he pleases. . . .

Chief Joseph, Nez Perce

At the bend of the river a sharp wind made the river craft pitch and yaw. Governor Lane wiped a gust of mist from his brow. The Dalles landing was crowded with Indians and horses. For a moment he wished he had come with a larger force of men. Were those people waiting on shore hostiles or friendlies? The mist and wind blinded him. He could not tell. Behind him a trooper cocked his rifle. Another thrust his head over the side and was sick.

"All right, dog faces, shape up." It was the voice of Sergeant Coombs. "There's no need to puke or arm your rifles. These people respect courage and hate cowardice. All along you have been thinking you're better than they are, so act like it."

A churning sensation suddenly left Governor Lane sick to his stomach. Cold perspiration popped out on his forehead. Was he boat sick? No, it was the memory of the battle with Santa Anna. The sergeant who had stemmed the rout had said almost the same words as Sergeant Coombs.

The governor gritted his teeth. Would he ever live down the ignominy of that day? Although outnumbered, he had had the Mexicans on the run, then gave the order to halt and then to retreat. That was all Santa Anna's forces needed. They took heart. Instead of fleeing, they turned back and mounted a charge that sent his forces reeling. Fortunately, he had rallied the men. Thanks to that unknown sergeant, defeat turned into victory.

"Steady men." It was the voice of Sergeant Coombs again. "We're within rifle range now. If these Indians are hostile they would be putting up a show, daring us to come in."

Governor Lane, whose stomach continued to churn, forcibly took a grip on himself. Sergeant Coombs was right. The prisoner escort had to put on a brave face, most of all, the man in charge. To show weakness now could undo all the good he had accomplished. He squared his shoulders, disembarked and waded up the rocky beach to hold up a hand in greeting to Young Chief and the other Cayuse leaders who stood waiting on shore. The size of the gathering continued to amaze him. They could easily overwhelm his small escort but there was no war paint. The leaders' expressions were grim but not hostile.

"Why the big turnout?" he asked the interpreter.

"People come to say farewell to the five tribesmen."

"Hmm!" the governor grunted. "What a strange society. They treat these murderers more like heroes than criminals."

An officer stationed at The Dalles hurried forward, abashed at his tardiness. He had been at his post but when the governor's party approached an Indian youth broke through the ranks of greeters to shout, "I must see the Governor Chief."

The disturbance did not upset the governor's composure. "The natives take our laws literally," the greeting officer explained. "The law says those accused of a crime are innocent until proven guilty. In their minds the prisoners have yet to be proven guilty. Therefore, their belief is that these men are innocent."

The governor shook his head. "How naive can they be?" Yet, it was he who had taught them that this was the basis under which they would be judged. They were innocent until proven guilty. Perhaps it was he, not they, who was naive.

#

Meanwhile, back in Oregon City US Marshal Joe Meek stood on his balcony viewing his domain. The sight of four horsemen approaching made his eyes narrow. Who was this mixed gang, two Indians and two white men? Except for the older, taller Indian, they were well armed. The packs tied to the saddle straps meant they were riding afar or planning to stay a while. If the latter was the case he'd put a stop to it right now. He had no intention of letting outsiders make a mess of things. There was that bunch from Rickreall led by loudmouthed redhead named Short. He had sent them packing with their tails between their legs.

"If you people know what's good for you, you'll go back to your Rickreall homes an' mind your own business," he warned. "I'm the one who's goin' to hang those five Cayuses, an' I ain't goin' to have no busybodies like you hornin' in."

Yes siree, that's what he'd told them and sent them scurrying. Whether Governor Joe Lane and Colonel W. W. Loring realized it or not, he, Colonel Joe Meek, US Marshal personally appointed by President James Knox Polk, was legally responsible for seeing that territorial criminals were properly punished.

To make himself equal in rank to the commander of the Mounted Riflemen, Joe Meek had adopted the title of colonel. This did not set well with Mexican War veteran and hero of the battles of Contreras and Chapultepec, Brevet Colonel William Wing Loring. The garrulous, roughhouse, former mountain man, Joe Meek, disgusted professional soldier, Loring. Every time the two met, Joe Meek's overbearing attitude and overinflated ego left Loring fighting mad.

Even now as he watched Joe Meek go about his duties, the disgust Loring felt rose in his throat like bitter bile. Every chance the irascible former mountain man got he threw his weight around. Just this morning he stomped through the outer office, brushing by the headquarters orderly and pounded on the door.

"What's this I hear, puttin' thet blasted striped ape Coombs in charge of the prisoner detail? I want you to know when those Cayuses get to Oregon City I'm takin' over. The only reason your men are on the job's 'cause I ain't got no one to spare an' the Legislature's too poor to pay."

Colonel Loring did not reply. A small worm of wisdom, kept wriggling away in his brain waving a flag of warning. Whatever he said only would make matters worse. This obnoxious man stalking the floor before him had high friends in Washington. He had it on good authority Meek was a shirttail relative of

President Polk, hobnobbed with the likes of General Winfield Scott and had traveled across the country with Governor Joe Lane. In spite of all this, the colonel had no inclination of backing down to a man who was near illiterate. It was said when Joe Meek went to dine at one of Washington's better restaurants he had held the menu upside down. When the waiter turned it around, Meek waved it away. "Never mind, I know jest what I'm hankerin' for . . . a hunk of antelope meat."

Colonel Loring scowled. He was not about to allow this ill-mannered, blustering, braggart interfere with his plans for prison and courthouse security. He folded his good arm over his chest and placidly waited until US Marshal Meek had vented his wrath.

Meek stomped out of Loring's office more infuriated than when he had stormed in. "That one-armed, uncooperative, haughty Blue Coat pig," he exploded. "If it's the last thing I do I'll bring that uniformed swellhead to his knees."

Joe Meek was still in that frame of mind when the four horsemen cantered into Oregon City. He rode toward them, holding up a commanding hand. "Who goes there?" he demanded. "If you're plannin' to hang aroun' for the trial, I'll collect your weapons, here an' now."

"Why, yuh ol' buzzard, what's the matter with yuh? Yuh know a man cain't go 'round these parts unarmed," blurted a voice that could be heard all over town.

"Ain't yuh heerd, there's bad uns plannin' a lynchin' party an' a gang of Injuns waitin' ta snatch yer prisoners. If'n I had yer job, I think I'd be worryin' 'bout things like thet rather than fussin' 'bout collectin' honest citizens' weapons. Who knows when yuh might be needin' a leetle help in keepin' the peace."

"Who the hell are you?" US Marshal Meek, jabbed his heels into the ribs of his horse, making the startled animal leap. "Whoa there!" he shouted, sawing on the reins.

"Consarn it, Joe, yuh don't hev ta put on a dog an' pony show fer usn's. We know the kinda tricks yuh kin do," the voice admonished. "Anyways, we's jest ridin' through wantin' ta say howdy ta ol' friends like yerself. Maybeso, chew the rag 'bout ol' times, like when yuh was near shot an' scalped on the Yellerstone. I'll betcha those Blackfeet're still hankerin' fer yer hair."

"Wh-who are you?" Meek stuttered. This was a voice out of the past. Only old fur trappers knew about his narrow escape from the Blackfeet. He calmed his mount and studied the face of each horseman. For certain the speaker was a trapper who knew him in the old days. The tall Indian had the look of Nez Perce. He should know, he'd had two Nez Perce wives. The first of the two had given him his cherished daughter, Helen Mar. The memory of mother and daughter brought a stab of pain. The wife had run away and sweet Helen Mar was dead, buried in the Whitman Mission compound along with the massacre victims.

Thoughts of the dark-eyed girl haunted him. At the time he'd left Helen Mar in the care of Narcissa Whitman he had been footloose. It seemed the only sensible thing to do. He had not given the consequences a thought. He knew those Cayuses were stirring up trouble, yet he had left Helen Mar to die a captive of these bloody, murdering heathens. He hated himself nearly as much as he did those five Cayuse murderers.

The only thing he could do to make up for his negligence of Helen Mar was to see every one of those Cayuses dangling from a hangman's noose. Stiff-necked Loring, bound up in army regulations, would never understand how he, the rough tough former mountain man, Joe Meek, had loved the pert, dark-eyed girl better than anyone on earth.

In his heart he agreed with blabbermouth Short and his band of vigilantes. Holding these killers for trial was nonsense, all done so a few egotistical stuffed shirt lawyers, judges and politicians could show off and make names for themselves. Those five bloody Cayuses were going to hang. They were unfeeling savages who had looked on and done nothing while his poor sick Helen Mar suffered and died from neglect before their eyes.

Meek thrust the painful thoughts aside and continued his study of the four horsemen. What business did the tall Nez Perce have here? He was not a run-of-the-mill Indian. The self-confident way he sat his horse, the austere expression on his face and the quiet but watchfulness of the dark eyes, made it clear he was a man who feared nothing. He was here for a reason, not passing through to say howdy as the old mountain rat claimed. If he came to help his Cayuse brothers, Meek didn't want him around.

The buckskin youth who rode by his side had Indian blood too. Ah! He recognized him. He was the mission boy Helen Mar called Two Feathers. The two white men -- he didn't know the young man, or did he? The old bushy bearded goat -- yes, he had seen that face before.

"Keerist! It's Deacon Walton," the name popped into Meek's mind. "I ain't seen yuh since the last rendezvous, must be goin' on ten years."

"No need ta blaspheme," Deacon retorted. "If'n I heerd kerectly, yuh ol' muskrat, in '38 yuh was preachin' up a storm amongst the Flatheads, or t'was it some other tribe? Anyways, yuh was thinkin' on hitchin' a third woman. . . ."

"Ahem!" Meek interrupted. He urged his mount forward. He had to get this old mountain rat aside before he really spilled the beans. He was the US Marshal. It was important he maintain a good name. Likely as not this old goat would start gabbing about Mountain Lamb, who had been given to him by his fur trader friend, Milt Sublette. Then there was his second wife who ran away while he was dead drunk.

Juicy tidbits like that would keep the tongues of Oregon City's womenfolk flapping for weeks. With election coming up the gossip of these old gals very well could sink him at the polling booths. Also, he had to think of his present wife and family. He didn't want to lose them because of some loose-tongued rendezvous buffoon.

X

Providence sees to it that no man gets happiness out of crime.
Vittorio Alfieri - Orestes

Unaware that son-in-law and husband, Sergeant Algeron Coombs, had departed for The Dalles, the Morgan family packed the light wagon with a few essentials, mainly food and bedding, and set out to meet him in Oregon City. They were late. The changeable spring weather made it difficult for the womenfolk to decide what to wear.

"Come on!" Morgan finally shouted. He had been against the trip from the start. If the son-in-law wanted to make an ass of himself by rejoining the army there was no reason why it should make the rest of the family miserable. For weeks wife and daughter moped around the house as melancholy as whipped hound dogs. Only the thought of getting Algeron back into the family fold brought them to life. They had had days to prepare for the journey yet, here they were sorting through a frugal supply of baubles and gewgaws like schoolgirls on a first walkout.

"Quit lollygagging around. Everyday clothes will do," Morgan shouted again. "After all, we ain't hobnobbin' with the gentry."

Still worrying over a few items, the ladies hurried out and piled into the wagon. Before they could get settled Morgan snapped the reins sending the wagon off with a jerk, making wife and daughter grab for something to keep them from falling beneath the wheels. Even though he'd kept the team scampering at a fast trot, dusk was beginning to fall when they pulled into Oregon City. The grounds where they had agreed to meet Algeron were crowded, forcing them to camp on a rocky hillside. Morgan was beside himself.

"I told you to stop lollygagging," he growled. "We promised we'd be here in time to sup, and look, it's nearly dark. Algeron is as punctual as a seven-day clock. He's probably been here and given us up. Maybe we can still save the day. You girls whip something together. I'll walk over and leave a message for Algeron with the folks that have camped where we told him we'd meet."

Hardly had Morgan disappeared from sight when a voice out of the past asked after the ladies' well-being. Lucille Morgan sucked in her breath. Her mother gave an audible gasp. In the shadows two mounted horsemen were outlined against the fast fading sky. One wore a broad brimmed hat, the other was hatless but two feathers stood upright from his long, braided hair. The rider with the hat politely removed it and made a slight bow.

"We didn't mean to startle you ladies," he said, "but you appear alone and unescorted. . . ."

"We . . . ah're just getting settled," Mrs. Morgan stammered, "but thank you for your concern."

"Yes, thank you," Lucille said without turning around. "We're in no danger. Our men folk'll be here soon."

"Very well," the rider with the hat said. "Have a pleasant stay in Oregon City." The two horsemen reined their mounts away. Only then did Lucille turn to wistfully watch them disappear. How ironic, instead of her husband, the man just encountered had been the first to capture her heart. "Why couldn't Algeron have been here to stand by me?" she cried. "What can anyone think but that after six months of marriage I've been abandoned."

Mrs. Morgan put a comforting hand on her daughter's shoulder. "I guess we should have expected something like this. But we can't hide like hermits the rest of our lives. You're just going to have to get a grip on yourself. As some ancient sage once said, 'Time . . .'"

"If you tell me once more that time heals everything, I'll scream. I never have felt this badly -- never in my whole life."

#

The lynch mob led by Joshua Short, had not dispersed as US Marshal Joe Meek had ordered. Instead, the group of heavily armed men rode south out of Oregon City, then turned northeast to follow the foothills of the Cascade Mountains. They struck the Columbia River almost across from Cascade Portage. There, Short called a halt.

"I don't like the way that current is swirling about," he said, studying the rushing waters. "Me thinks it wise to hike downstream an' take Switzer's Ferry, not all at once, mind you. We don't want to draw attention. Another set-to with that puffed up Meek would ruin everything."

The next morning, when Short called his troop together on the north side of the river, he counted heads and uttered an obscenity. "Someun's missin! Anyone still poopin' in the brush?"

There was a stunned silence until a man with a mouthful of crooked teeth scratched his nose and swore. "I think it's thet fella thet rode alongside me yestiday. He bounced 'round like a hen on a hot griddle. I ask 'im if'n his saddle was all right. He give me a look as if I'd asked ta borry his missus fer the night."

"Well, we don't need him nohow," Short said. "We'd better start lookin' to how we're gonna git this job done. If my guess is right, the party escortin' the prisoners'll be comin' down river in one of those flat-bottomed Mackinaws. At the landin' there'll be plenty of confusion. The first thing we got to do is disarm the troopers an' then grab the prisoners. If everybody does his job we can have those murderin' creatures hangin' from tree limbs afore you can say Jack Spratt."

"Thet sounds simple enuff," a dirty, big-bellied man said. "What're we goin' ta do after we hang these critters? Thet red hair of yers shines up like a bonfire on a dark night. Those sojers'll recognize yuh quicker'n yuh kin spell Jack Spratt. Every law abidin' citizen in the territory'll be after us like a pack of hounds on a fox hunt."

"I don't think it necessary," Short said, "but to be on the safe side we kin do like road bandits, pull sacks over our heads. Besides, we'll strike so fast those sojers won't know what's hit 'em. Jest stick to the plan. We'll be in an' out afore they kin collect their wits, if they have any. Anyways, once the murderin' savages have bit the dust, no one's goin' to object seriously. Some, like Marshal Meek'll be out of sorts for a while, but it'll blow over. Everybody'll be thankful we saw our duty and done it. We'll be looked on as heroes."

#

Unbeknownst to Short and his gang of ruffians, on the far side of the next ridge of hills from where they camped, Five Crows' men were daubing war paint on their horses and themselves. A scout caught sight of the would-be lynchers' camp and returned to report their presence. Five Crows called his men together.

"There is a camp of hairy faces an arrow flight away. They are armed, prepared for war. Do they come to make battle with us, or do they plan to ambush Governor Chief Joe and seize our Cayuse brothers?"

"Why should they take prisoners?" someone asked. "Already they are in the hands of the white man."

Five Crows thoughtfully rubbed his chin. Yes, for a group of hairy faces to seize prisoners from their own Blue Coat warriors did not make sense.

"Let us attack the hairy faces before they know we're here," the scout who brought in the report suggested.

"No, some might escape and tell of our presence," Five Crows said. "We wait. We watch. We will do nothing until we learn why these hairy faced ones are here."

Five Crows spoke boldly but a feeling of uneasiness made him scowl. He had not foreseen the presence of a band of armed hairy faces. Had the hairy faced ones learned of his plan to attack the portage? Would they sneak up on his camp during the night? For certain the camp guards should be doubled. Perhaps he should do as the scout suggested, lead his men over the ridge, descend on the enemy and slay them to the last man.

"Don't be foolish," he cautioned himself. He was too near success to let a band of hairy faces upset his plans now.

XI

Nothing lives long, except the earth and the mountains . . .
George Bent, Cheyenne

Governor Joe Lane expected to have a short parley with
Cayuse leaders, and then whisk the five prisoners away. Instead,
he found himself involved in council meeting after council meeting, each preceded by ceremonial smokes and lengthy speeches.
The Cayuse leaders hated to part with their tribesmen. The longer
they delayed Governor Chief Joe and his Blue Coat escort, the
longer it would be before the accused would face trial.

There also was the faint hope that their shamans could
conjure up a miracle . . . in some way be able to demonstrate to
the hairy faces that the five Cayuse prisoners had good reason to
act the way they did. Their lands had been invaded by missionaries who said they came to show them the pathway to everlasting
life. Behind the missionaries came a wave of invaders called
homesteaders. In their canvas covered wagons they brought unseen killers more devastating than locust plagues. One terrible
white man's sickness after another swept through the Cayuse
homeland. Instead of everlasting life, the missionaries and those
who followed brought everlasting death.

They had called for help but when the missionary doctor
came the spirit of death continued to take its toll. They went
back to their old medicine men and sweat lodge ways, but they,
too, were no match for these sicknesses that sneaked unseen into
lodges and took the lives of young and old. The people became
desperate. They had to do something to save themselves, their
loved ones and their tribe. They struck back at those who brought
this terrible scourge into their midst. Was it not Mother Earth's
law to protect your own kind from harm, especially those closest
to you: sons, brothers, daughters, mothers and wives?

Time and time again Young Chief and other leaders related the way grief had turned to panic and finally vengeance. "What does the white man do when terrible things like this happen?" Young Chief asked the governor. "Do they turn away and do nothing, saying it's God's will? When these five men stand before the people who judge them, will the reason why they did these deeds be told?"

Joe Lane kept repeating that the laws of the land must be respected. Epidemics were not crimes but acts of nature that no one could predict or control. Even so, the jury the accused faced would take everything that had a bearing on the crimes into account. Those found guilty would be punished. The innocent would be set free. "When this is over the Cayuse and the white man will be friends," he said. "Life on the plateau will return to what it was before the Whitman Mission tragedy occurred."

The governor said these words with a straight face but an erratic heartbeat warned him he spoke with a crooked tongue. Too much had happened for either side to forget or forgive. Even if all five prisoners were executed, the white citizenry would not be satisfied. If all five prisoners were freed, the Cayuse still would be tormented. Nothing ever would be the same again.

After two days at The Dalles, Governor Lane considered the counseling and farewell ceremonies were sufficient. He had done his best to smooth things over. He met with Young Chief and the elders one last time. The five prisoners, who had been held in a large tipi lodge, were led out and down to the makeshift dock. First came Tiloukaikt, followed by Tomahas, Clokamas, Ish-ish-kais-kais and Kia-ma-sump-kin.

As the accused men filed toward the craft that would carry them down river, a great burst of emotion poured forth from the gathering. Children ran alongside the prisoners tearfully trying to touch their departing loved ones for the last time. The prisoners' bereft womenfolk tore at their clothes and hair. Some dropped to their knees beseeching the gods to interfere. For the most part the men stood to one side, painfully looking on.

The soldier escort, unprepared for the emotional outburst,

was unhinged. Sergeant Coombs, who was sick with worry about his wife and in-laws awaiting him in Oregon City, purposefully strode up and down, trying to keep the situation from getting out of hand. One false move by a mounted rifleman, like a discharged gun, could very well trigger mayhem.

"Remember the drill, men," Sergeant Coombs snapped. "Right, left. Right, left. Get in step. One-two-three-four," he chanted. "Act like soldiers and no one will know you don't know your right foot from your left."

The prisoners boarded the flat-bottomed craft river men called Mackinaw. The hired crew took their places along the rail. Governor Lane stepped aboard and raised a hand in a fare-well salute. The Cayuse leaders responded. A scattering of boys gave the ungainly craft a shove, wading waist deep, making certain it cleared the rocks that cluttered the shore.

"By George," Lieutenant Addison exclaimed. "I'm glad we're safely away from that."

Joe Lane shook his head. "Don't count your chickens just yet. We have the portage yet to cross."

The current pulled the boat into the rushing waters that formed the main channel. Directly ahead the mighty river narrowed to curve through a canyon. On either side high dark cliffs rose skyward. For a moment the unwieldy craft bobbed and bounced on the waves like a cork. Passengers seized any handhold within reach. With a jerk, the man at the rudder swung the bow on course. The paddlers dipped their oars to hold it steady, then, except for a few swipes, passively allowed the current to carry them along.

The pilot stood upright in the bow. He wore a band of buckskin around his head, his long black hair dangling halfway down his back. The dentalia decorations on the head band gleamed in the sun's morning rays. It was said this man knew the location of every rock, trough, curve and rapid through this stretch of river. He read the force and direction of the winds by the way the trees swayed and white caps popped up on the crest of rushing waters. His eyes were busy, but he said nothing. The boat paddlers watched his buckskin clad back for signals. With mere movements of head or shoulders, the pilot directed the boatmen to veer right or veer left. The rowers responded immediately, maneuvering the craft to take full advantage of the surging current. Sometimes the flat-bottomed Mackinaw careened ahead at the speed of a galloping horse. On these occasions the men's grip, including those of Governor Joe Lane, on the side rails tightened until their knuckles turned white.

The manacled prisoners, who if pitched overboard would surely drown, did not seem to mind the wild ride. Stoically they rose and fell with the swells as if riding unruly horses. When gusts of spray burst over the rails they did not blink. Death coming from the river would be preferable to rope nooses strangling them like neck-wrung quail.

Within a mile of the upper landing of the portage, the water picked up speed to flow through the narrow gateway of the Cascades. A line of breakers bounced against boulders, some standing as high as three-story buildings. Just above the landing an enormous granite rock thrust its algae covered bulk above the white-capped water like a giant thumb. With a shout and a flurry of activity, the boat skimmed by it to grind its bow into the embankment where a line quickly was secured to shore.

The troopers, remembering the war painted warriors that were sighted at the portage on the way up river, apprehensively staggered ashore. At this point men and supplies had to pass over a five mile stretch to where the waters were navigable again. As soon as the boat was pulled up the embankment the entire party would be as exposed as sitting ducks. Fully aware of this, Governor Lane called his men together.

"Expect trouble at the portage, probably an attack from the hillside slope. We'll use the boat for protection. By pushing and pulling it on its side, the thick bottom planking will take the brunt of arrows and lead. But keep on your toes. Those Cayuses are certain to descend on us like a pack of hungry wolves."

XII

*The Ancient One built this cascade as a sort of dam for the
Indians and often he would cause a strong east wind to
blow the waters back as Indians could take their open baskets
and dip fish from the pools left at the foot of the cascade.*
Klamath Legend

Long before the coming of the white man the plot of
ground that became known as Oregon City was a favorite place
of Indian people. Primarily it was the falls on the Willamette
River that drew them to this picturesque location. The base of
the falls was a good place to spear and net fish. The hills on
either side of the river were abundant with game, berries and root
crops. The high river banks provided protection from enemy attack and storms that blew in from the great water called ocean.

When the white men arrived they coveted the location for
different reasons. They saw the frothing cataract, that plunged
40 feet, as the source of power to turn the wheels of gristmills,
sawmills, weaving mills and other production facilities that were
turning the so-called civilized world from dependence on agri-
culture and cottage industry to mass production. In this new world
there was no place for the humble tasks of spearing and netting
fish, gathering roots and berries and hunting game in the hills.

Dr. John McLoughlin, the ruler of Hudson's Bay's Northwest fur trading empire, took the first step in bringing the location that he would name Oregon City into this new era. In 1829
McLoughlin built a mill race and some cabins at the falls. But
the natives, apparently envisioning this as the start of something
that would destroy their way of life, burned the cabins to the
ground.

As with everything else the Indian people did in the attempt to hold onto their land and way of life, their efforts were in
vain. In 1841 a Willamette Falls' powered gristmill was in op-

eration, followed by a sawmill in 1842. By 1844 seventy-five buildings of one kind and another were counted along the east river bank below the Falls of the Willamette.

Now, in 1850, Oregon City had more than doubled in size. The citizenry took pride in *The Spectator*, the first newspaper west of the Missouri River, the first Roman Catholic Church in Oregon Territory and the first Federal Court and Land office on the Pacific Coast. It was little wonder then that semiliterate US Marshal Joe Meek, in charge of law and order in Oregon City, was proud of his position and determined that no one would knock him off his perch, certainly not a ragged, baldheaded mountain man who had known him when he was a down and out beaver trapper.

Meek sourly worried over what action to take. He had induced the four horsemen to make camp a mile or so north of the center of town. At present they were out of nuisance range but should trouble arise it wouldn't take long for them to be right in the midst of it. He didn't know about the other three, but that man, Deacon, could create more havoc than a treed mountain cat.

Meek leaned over the rail that encircled the second story porch where he maintained guard over the city and spat into the muddy street. For the 20th time, he glanced toward the road that led to Fort Vancouver. According to his reckoning the Cayuse prisoners and their escort should have arrived long before now.

Was that someone coming? He rubbed his bleary eyes for a better look and then had to grab for the rail to keep from falling into the street below. Strangely, the height made him somewhat dizzy. He must be getting old. That was the excuse he gave himself, but in fact he had attempted to drink that mountain rat, Deacon Walton, under the table the previous night and miserably had failed. His stomach throbbed like a well-worked butter churn and his mouth tasted as sour as spoiled milk.

Meek scowled. That de-frocked preacher, Deacon, had taken him in like a greenhorn fresh on the frontier. The old buzzard claimed in his old age he had given up the jug -- it wasn't right to guzzle booze in front of his Cheyenne kids.

"Yuh know how 'tis when Injuns git a few sniffs of fire-water," Deacon said in all confidence, "they gits a bit looney. Besides, me father-in-law, Bear Claw, would not take it lightly if'n I stagger inta camp with a snoot full. So I been tetotalin' fer a long spell. Jest one leetle sip'd be refreshin' though, an' I must say, when I goes back ta Sweetwater country an' tell the folks I had drinks with US Marshal Joe Meek, their eyes'll grow big as cart wheels."

The smooth talking varmint, it was those words of flattery that did Joe Meek in. He had walked Deacon Walton to the backside of a tavern that had been closed down by orders of Colonel Loring. With a special key he opened the door and invited the baldheaded rascal inside. They went through one jug and started on the second when a bat flew down from the rafters and scared them half to death. Deacon swore it was a creature Satan had sent to warn them of the fires of hell.

But that didn't finish the drinkin' bout. "Ta steady the nerves we'd best hev 'nother swig," Deacon suggested. They polished off the second jug and stumbled out and made for home. He couldn't get the front door open, and they had to crawl through a window.

"Agh!" Meek groaned. What a shameful night. He never should have invited the old de-frocked preacher to his house. The very first thing, the bumbling fellow stumbled over a chair, dropped on the floor and passed out. He, himself, made it up stairs to bed but didn't remember a thing until his wife pulled the covers away to find him fully clothed. His muddy boots had given him away, leaving a track up the stairs and across her freshly polished floor and into the sheets.

"Dammit!" Meek swore, it was all the fault of that bushy-bearded mountain goat. He should have run him out of town on sight. Now that the old goat had a taste of his stashed-away fire-water, he would hang around until it was gone. "Aagh!" His past had caught up with him. How could he ever live it down? When would his wife allow him back in her bed? He was so distressed he failed to recognize the rider who passed by, loping in from the north. Only when the horse pulled up in front of Colonel Loring's headquarters building did he realize that the horseman was a member of the blathering redhead's Rickreall lynching gang he had ordered to disperse. From the lather on the horse and the way the rider raced up the steps two at a time, it dawned on US Marshal Meek that trouble had arrived.

"Blast it! Did that damned redheaded idiot and his bunch go against my orders?" he angrily muttered. Down the steps and over to the regimental headquarters Meek ran as fast as his unsteady, wobbly legs would move.

Colonel Loring's orderly hardly had announced the presence of the rider before Marshal Meek pounded into the colonel's office. "I'll take charge of this man," Meek blurted. "He comes under my jurisdiction."

"What do you mean, he's under your jurisdiction? He's reporting to a United States Army installation. And what's the matter with you, charging in here like a mad bull bison? This is my private office, not an open city market place where any drunk and fleabitten hound can enter whenever he or it pleases. If you think you're pulling the wool over my eyes, think again. I know where you have that rotgut stashed. I have a good mind to send a detachment straight over and bust every jug in the place."

Meek flushed. How did Loring get wind of the liquor, anyhow? Did that gossipy mountain rat spread the word? He'd fix him good, but right now he had more important things to do.

"I beg your pardon, Colonel, but I ordered this man an' his bunch to go home an' mind their own business. I'll be dammed if I'll have him disobeyin' the orders of US Marshal Joe Meek."

"Look, Meek," Loring remonstrated. "You're getting entirely too big for your breeches. You may be related to President Polk and a camping sidekick of Governor Lane, but that doesn't give you the right to bust in here and browbeat my office guests. From the smell of your breath you should be home soaking your head in a bucket of soap suds."

Meek started to open his mouth and quickly closed it. What was the matter with him? There was a time to speak and a time to be quiet. The colonel was right. Now was not the time nor place to be throwing his weight around.

"Colonel, I'm truly sorry," he said contritely, "but I beg your permission to question this man. Why is he disobeyin' my orders? His gang was out to do mischief -- waylay the prisoner escort and lynch the five Cayuses."

Colonel Loring blinked. "Is it true what the marshal says?" he demanded of the horseman who impatiently waited to speak.

"Yes, it's true. Short and his vigilantes are waiting right now to attack the prisoner escort. And there's a war party of Injuns waitin' to do the same. I'm tellin' you, all hell's goin' to break loose unless somebody does something mighty soon."

"My gawd!" Meek uttered. "Get somebody to bangin' on that iron triangle yuh wake the troops up with. Turn out every dog face in camp. . . ."

"Let's not go off half-cocked," Loring cautioned. "Before we act we need to explore the facts. Besides, if we send our troops on a wild goose chase, who's to guard the city? Be just like those tricky Cayuses to make a feint toward Cascade Portage. While we're trying to protect the prisoner convoy, they could well ride in here and sack the town."

"Yeah! Yeah!" Meek growled and then turned on the youth who reported the news. "I told yuh fellas to go home an' leave this business to me. Now yuh come whinin' fer help." Meek stomped back and forth. "Well, thet's water over the dam. Now, how didja happen onto the bloody Indians?"

Loring glared at Meek. "Why didn't you report this lynching plot at the beginning? If you had, we could've locked up the ring leaders and nipped this in the bud. Now, what're we to do? I haven't enough men to deal with this and guard the city, too."

"You mean you don't have nobody yuh kin trust to git the job done," Meek growled. "What about those supply guys out theya? They don't seem to be doin' nothin', probably chompin' at the bit to get in a little action."

"You mean Beamer and Stillings? They would be more trouble than they're worth. All across the plains they were in one mischief after another."

Meek peeked out the window. "I must say, they don't look like they have much get-up-and-go. Why do you keep them around? That skinny fella couldn't lift a saddle on a horse if he tried, an' that guy with the big gut'd probably eat all the rations before we made it to the first campsite."

Meek paced the floor. "Maybeso, I can round up a few able-bodied men in town. Looks like everybody and his dog is comin' in for the trial. By golly! There is a party that came in yestiday. One of 'em, an ol' mountain man, kin shoot the eye out of a squirrel. Also, there's a couple of young men thet marched across the country with your regiment, an Indian lad an' his half brother, the sons of a mountain man I knew back in the old days.

"Then there's a fella thet looks to be a full blood Nez Perce. He ain't carryin' a weapon but I'll bet my socks when the chips're down he kin hold his own against three of those blowhard vigilantes. Yes sireee, there'll be only five of us -- six countin' this fellow." Meek jerked a thumb at the ex-vigilante. "I'll have a fightin' force thet'll have those would-be lynchers runnin' for home like turpentined cats."

XIII

No man's knowledge . . . can go beyond his experience.
John Locke, *"An Essay Concerning Human Understanding"*

The place where Marshal Meek had urged the four horsemen to camp was a pleasant, sunny glen north of town. White flowered dogwoods and multicolored rhododendron bushes made it a beauty spot only Mother Earth could devise. Vision Seeker, usually so attuned to the wonders of Mother Earth, hardly glanced at the colorful surroundings. He presented his usual serene expression for all to see, but his inner being was in turmoil.

Any day his mother could make the journey to the Great Beyond. His father, Lone Wolf, probably already had run into trouble on the trail to buffalo country. On the long ago trip up the Kooskooskie a landslide occurred in which a boulder knocked two geldings off their feet and into the gorge hundreds of feet below. Then, near the summit a wind storm struck so severely it uprooted cottonwoods and sent lodge coverings sailing away never to be seen again.

Of course that disastrous journey was made in the Time of Turning Leaves, a season noted for its storms. But even in the spring there were a myriad of dangerous things that could happen: lightening bolts striking with such force they lopped off the tops of mature evergreens or smashed huge branches into kindling, and there was the constant threat of killer landslides. Even small difficulties could turn nasty. Lone Wolf was traveling with a group of elderly companions. It was questionable how capable they would be in dealing with emergencies.

Worry over his parents was bad enough but the business at hand was impossible. Vision Seeker's presence at the white man's village, Oregon City, was a farce. He had come to try and help his Cayuse brothers . . . save the innocent from the hangman's noose, but in this anthill of white faces Indian people were as helpless as fish out of water.

He had explained his mission and the need to find the key to cutting strands of the legal web to nephew, Two Feathers, and his white brother, Joe. They had been of little help. Yes, they knew US Marshal Meek, but this man had lost a daughter while captive of the Cayuse. He was adamant. Innocent or not he was for hanging all five prisoners.

The Blue Coat officers also would be of little help. The Mounted Riflemen were in such ill repute with the citizenry it was a wonder they had escaped the hanging ropes themselves, and Governor Lane was in a hurry to get his affairs in order before he quit office. He wouldn't touch anything that might lengthen the trial.

"You are up against a system that is made up of many men, some of whom don't even like each other," Michael's half brother, Joe, explained. "When this system is set into action it must run its course. Yes, sometimes a person along the route can raise objections and slow things down or speed them up, or if great cause is shown, stop them all together. We could hope for something like that to happen but it is a very faint hope."

Joe hesitated. How could he make this clear when there were so many cogs in the process: prosecutors, defenders, judge, witnesses and jurors, all with individual personalities and motives? Joe grimaced. He didn't understand it himself, so how could he help Vision Seeker understand?

Vision Seeker, who had been trying to follow Joe's explanation, held up a hand. "You mean when you start this thing called legal system it's like taking a journey down river? Boatmen can encounter sandbars or rapids which can slow them down or speed them up? At the journey's end they are at the ocean where everything opens up? The obstacles have all been overcome and there is no going back?"

"I guess you could say the Oregon Territorial legal system is something like that," Joe agreed, but inwardly quaked. Vision Seeker had translated his explanation into the world he knew, but in actual fact the legal process was far more complicated than navigating a river. No matter how wise, Vision Seeker's experiences and the environment he lived in had conditioned him into a way of thinking far different than that of the men who would be conducting the trial. Joe's heart reached out to this man who by marriage was related to him. He tried so hard to do what was right but had no idea of the challenge he faced. As he watched the trial unfold Vision Seeker was certain to receive many rude awakenings.

There was another reason Joe wished he was any place but Oregon City. An old wound he thought had healed suddenly opened up to torture him. Although he tried as hard as he could to submerge memories of the intimate moments Lucille and he had shared on the trail, they returned to haunt his every waking hour.

"What do you suppose was eating on them?" Joe asked his half blood brother. "You'd think we were complete strangers. They wouldn't even look at us . . . treated us worse than mangy camp dogs."

Michael Two Feathers did not reply. His brother knew as well as he did why the two women acted as they did. Right from their first meeting Lucille Morgan had decided Joe was the man she wanted to marry. In more ways than one she had demonstrated her love, but fate intervened. When Joe's presence was needed most, he was laying wounded in an enemy camp. Sergeant Coombs, who was present, pressed his case and won her hand. Now Lucille and her mother, who had urged her daughter to accept the sergeant's proposal, were too embarrassed to look the rejected lover in the eye.

Michael sympathized with his brother. He, too, had a love locked away in his heart, a maiden he had loved and lost in a much more tragic manner than the Joe Jennings/Lucille Morgan affair. He never once had mentioned her name. Their love was too precious to reveal to even Vision Seeker or his brother. Besides, she had gone completely out of his life, perhaps had gone to the Great Beyond.

Deacon, the only cheerful member of the party, glanced at his companions and shook his head. "What's the matter with yuh fellas? From yer looks yuh'd of thought the Cayuses was already hangin' from a noose an' they ain't even hit town. Why, anythin' kin happen. Ol' Joe Meek could git blind drunk an' fall inta a well. More likely his ol' woman'll belay him with a rollin' pin, knockin' out what little brains he has."

The mountain man's attempt to bring cheer to the camp was met with stolid silence. So it was with some relief when US Marshall Joe Meek jogged up and made his needs known.

"Yep, we know all 'bout thet gang of vigilantes," Deacon said. "We was thinkin' those rascals was goin' ta hev ta be put down somehow. Thet guy Short's mighty stuck on hisself . . . struts 'round like a turkey gobbler in a pen of hens . . . got more gall than a buzzard after a hunk of dead meat. The hotheads he's got backin' him ain't much better, act meaner'n rabid skunks, an' they sure got a hate agin' the Cayuses. If they git hold of those prisoners they'll lynch 'em fer certain."

The mountain man's partners, the two half brothers and the Nez Perce said little, but did not hesitate when Meek asked for their help in diverting the vigilantes.

"Yer right, Joe," Deacon said agreeably "We kin not afford any more bloodshed. Things're bad enuff as 'tis."

Up the north trail out of the city they went, crossing the Columbia at Switzer's Ferry to the Columbia River's north bank. Guards at Fort Vancouver hailed them but Meek showed his badge and they continued east toward Cascade Portage.

"No need to let them in on our business or they'll be wantin' to come along, probably want to take charge," he said. "This affair should be handled quietly. People're plenty spooked without addin' to it."

Michael and his brother Joe, who knew the country well, scouted ahead. They passed through an area thick with trees and then through a large meadow-like clearing. On the far edge of the clearing Michael pointed to an area cropped clean of grass. Broken branches and a ring of rocks laid out to contain a camp-fire and clusters of horse dung, made it clear a body of horsemen had made a stopover here.

"White camp," Michael said without getting off his horse, "stayed a day, maybe two."

"How many would you say?" Meek asked.

"Fifteen - 20 men and a like number of animals," Michael glanced at his uncle who in his youth had been the best tracker in the Lapwai band of Nimpau.

Vision Seeker made a sign that he agreed, but otherwise kept his thoughts to himself. Everything was turning out far differently than he had expected. He did not like being involved in chasing down a party of white men, but perhaps his presence would make an impression on US Marshal Meek. Joe said Meek was a cog in the legal system. From the way the man spoke, *he was* the legal system.

The youth who had deserted the vigilantes and reported the intentions of Short's band of renegades, also agreed with Michael's estimate of the number in the party. "If I'd stayed with 'em, the total would've been 17," he said.

"All right, so we've located the lynchers. Now what are we to do?" Meek asked. "What about those Cayuses? You say they were camped over yon ridge of hills. Do we track down Short and his lynchers or go after the Cayuses?"

"Maybeso, we should move a leetle closer to the portage an' see what happens," Deacon suggested. "It's the prisoners both these outfits're after. Short's gang're so busy makin' nooses fer the lynchin' party they're probably blind ta anythin' else. I'll betcha me hat against one of yer poisonous jugs those wily Cayuses are sure ta know where they is an'll be on 'em like a cat on a mouse.

"It's them vigilantes, not the prisoners thet's gotta be saved. It'd be jest like thet redheaded ignoramus to git hisself an' his lot bushwacked. On top of the Whitman Mission killin's, thet ain't gonna set well with white folks."

Marshal Meek pulled on his nose. "Yep, for onct I think you're right. If Short and his gang git wiped out there'll be more than a hangin' to worry about."

Undecided what to do, Meek swore. "Keerist! What a mess. I reckoned on this a simple case of roundin' up some disgruntled farmers, spankin' them good an' sendin' them home with their tails 'tween their legs. Instead, this could turn into a nasty, bloody fracas."

"Consarn it, Joe. Don't be takin' the good Lord's name in vain," Deacon scolded. "He might turn agin' us. We're gonna need every bit of help we kin git."

XIV

When we were close, someone yelled, "Let us go!
This is a good day to die. . . ."
Fire Thunder, Oglala Sioux

Sergeant Coombs quietly listened to Governor Lane issue orders for protecting the column during the portage crossing, but didn't like what he heard. In the Mexican War General Lane had been noted for making rash decisions. This could be another one of them. Getting caught in the middle of the portage in the black of night was about the worst place one could be. Scrambling around in the dark would make these dog faces as jumpy as newly sheared sheep. The sergeant scowled. He was on the spot. Colonel Loring, who held the key to his future, would be furious if the prisoners were not delivered safely to Oregon City. He had to get them there even if it meant going against the governor's orders.

When informed of the sergeant's misgivings, youthful Lieutenant Addison, who had made the crossing of the "Big Open" with Coombs and relied on his judgement, took the sergeant's fears seriously. In fact the whole escort business had been a nightmare for young Lieutenant Addison.

Unaccustomed to dealing with Indian people, he had made one blunder after another. He had refused to smoke the ceremonial pipe when passed to him, saying he promised his mother never to let tobacco or strong drink touch his lips. True, he had not observed this promise completely, but he was not about to break it with these heathens. Who knew what diseases smoking the same pipe with them might bring on. They ate dogs, snakes, grasshoppers, snails and who knew what else.

Then, in his haste to escape the Cayuse hordes on departing The Dalles, he gave orders to push the boat away from the landing before the Klickitat pilot had completed his morning prayers. The men had to jump into waist deep water and pull the clumsy craft back to shore so the somber-faced Indian could get aboard.

"Let's put the matter before the governor," Lieutenant Addison finally told Sergeant Coombs. He had no wish to get crosswise with the governor again. "Let him decide what we should do."

"Ah!" scoffed Governor Lane, already fed up with Lieutenant Addison's foibles, "don't tell me Sergeant Coombs, the veteran of 20 years, has cold feet? I learned my lesson in the Mexican War. Don't give the enemy the slightest hint that we're weak. Sure as shooting that'll give them heart. We'll just have to brave it out. There's no turning back. These prisoners must get to Oregon City."

Sergeant Coombs, who overheard, started to retort but the expression on the governor's face told him there would be no changing of his mind. "All right, sir. May I have permission to speak to the men and prepare them in case we run into trouble?"

"Of course, but do so on the double-quick. Before we know it, it'll be dark."

Sergeant Coombs saluted and turned away. He studied the landing. A derelict, lightening-struck tree with deep veins of pitch running through it, acted as one of the mooring posts, the other was a tall stout fir. "Ha!" Coombs muttered to himself. He seized two burly troopers by the arm.

"Take your hand axes and chop this pitchy tree into stout kindling lengths, the more pitch in them the better," he said to the two men. Sergeant Coombs motioned to a third trooper. "Get someone to help and fetch two kegs of powder from the boat," he ordered.

The five Cayuse prisoners watched the activity with fear in their eyes and started chattering among themselves. Surely, these Blue Coats had not brought them all the way here to roast them at the stake as some eastern tribesmen said they might do. Even the governor stopped supervising the unloading of the Mackinaw to see what this crazy sergeant of his was up to.

After a sizeable stack of pitchy sticks had been cut, Sergeant Coombs gathered the men around. "Now, my good fellows, there's an old saying, 'He that can make a fire well can end a quarrel.' We're going to find out if this old adage is true. Bash in the head of those kegs," he said to the men who had unloaded the powder barrels.

"I want every one of you to a grab a pitchy stick and thrust it into these kegs of powder," Sergeant Coombs instructed. "Get as much black powder on the sticks as possible. -- No! -- Plunge the pitchy end into the powder. Of course you'll get a bit sticky, but your lives may depend on how much gunpowder you have on these sticks."

"What the devil is he doing?" the governor asked Lieutenant Addison.

"I don't exactly know, sir. Coombs claims he has a backup plan to deal with attackers."

"Playing with gunpowder is dangerous business," the governor exclaimed. "If a spark falls into one of those open kegs we'll be blasted to kingdom come. Besides, we may need that powder before we get home, and if we don't what's Colonel Loring going to say? He's already short of powder in Oregon City."

"Yes, sir. I'll caution Sergeant Coombs."

"Don't caution him. Order him to stop. We don't have time for this sort of foolishness. It's obvious you're new to this military business. Noncoms are like mules. To get them off the mark you have to let them know who's boss. Our mission is to get these prisoners to Oregon City. Now crack the whip and get these men on the move."

Sergeant Coombs who overheard, quickly motioned to his men. "Take a pitch stick in one hand and your rifle in the other and start pushing on this flat-bottomed contraption called Mackinaw," he ordered. "Heave ho! To Oregon City we go!"

The troopers grumbled and the governor scowled but, with the boatmen pushing and tugging, the Mackinaw began to move.

Gradually, the detachment picked up the chant. "Heave ho! To Oregon City we go!" Lieutenant Addison cringed. Everyone from the portage to Fort Vancouver would hear them coming. The Cayuse war party probably was following their progress every step of the way.

Much to the chagrin of Governor Lane and Lieutenant Addison, Sergeant Coombs called for a rest stop and then another. During the pauses only hard breathing and sighing of the wind in the trees could be heard. As they stopped for the final pause, darkness had fallen.

This was too much for Governor Lane to take. He marched forward and gave the order to keep moving. Just at that moment a raven uttered a squawk and swooped out of a tree to disappear into the night. The stolid-faced Klickitat pilot thrust his two hands skyward and uttered a bloodcurdling shriek. Everyone stopped in their tracks.

"What's the matter with him?" Governor Lane demanded of the half blood interpreter.

"These river people hold the belief a lone raven or crow flying over camp is a sign of death," the interpreter replied.

"They bloody may well be right," the governor exclaimed. "If we don't get cracking we'll likely perish right here at Cascade Portage."

XV

Sufficient unto the day is the evil thereof.
Matthew 6:34

Tension at Oregon City also was near the breaking point. No one seemed to know what was going on. The governor and the detachment of riflemen had marched north to escort the Cayuse murderers to the city for trial. An ample amount of time had passed for them to make the round trip journey to The Dalles. Yet there was no sign of them and no word when they would return.

To make matters even worse, US Marshal Joe Meek had collected a few men and also had marched north on the same trail. Joe Meek's harassed look and hurried actions sent a clear message something had gone awry.

"Ah! These blistering lawmen, they think they're better'n anyone else. Why can't they pull their heads out of the clouds and tell us what's going on?" Bill Morgan, Lucille Morgan Coombs' father, said in exasperation. "Those friends of ours, Joe and his Indian brother, are no better than the rest. They could have hollered over and told us what was going on. Instead, they hightailed it with the marshal like their tails were on fire."

"Don't get your dander up," Mrs. Morgan cautioned. "You know what that does to your stomach." But she, too, was worried. Her missing son-in-law was undoubtedly mixed up in this Cayuse prisoner business. She had gone to a lot of trouble to get her daughter safely married to a good solid man, then he disappointed her by rejoining the army and now was probably doing battle with a bunch of heathen savages.

Mrs. Morgan glanced at her daughter, Lucille. She looked so unhappy her mother grimaced. The poor child had to pull out of her blue funk. So that handsome Joe Jennings had reappeared. What was done was done. You couldn't unring a bell. The seat of the whole problem was that daughter had no more sense about keeping a husband happy than a cloistered old maid. Sergeant Algeron Coombs was a lusty man, not one that took to coddling and pampering like a pet poodle.

Mrs. Morgan shook her head. She had done her best to instruct her daughter, but the well-intended advice went in one ear and out the other. Now, just as she was trying to get husband and wife together again, Joe Jennings appears looking as dashing and handsome as a knight of King Arthur's Round Table. How could she have known he would escape from the savages and had inherited the takings from a gold mine. She had relied on the old adage, 'Better a sparrow in hand than a pigeon on the roof.' "Aagh!" she groaned. "Now, even the sparrow has flown the coop."

"Bill!" she snapped at her husband who had taken his wife's advice and was relaxing by watching the family in the next camp trying to pen a newly purchased shoat. His attention was particularly taken by the shapely wife who stood spraddle-legged trying to entice the grunting animal with a kettle of food. "Quit gawking and pay attention to family matters."

"What family matters?" he retorted, but he knew good and well what was eating on his poor mate. She had pushed her daughter into a shaky marriage and now was trying to hold it together. She should have known better than go against the whims of the heart.

"We shouldn't be kept in the dark like this. Somebody should go to army headquarters and find out what's going on," Nancy Morgan declared. "Since you haven't anything better to do than ogle the female neighbors, that would be a good job for you."

Reluctantly, Bill Morgan got to his feet. Nag-nag-nag. It had been this way ever since Son-In-Law Algeron left the farm to reenlist. Dammit! That wife of his was worse than a Willamette Valley mosquito. When she wasn't drawing blood, she was buzzing around keeping his nerves on edge.

"Now don't you start gabbing with those enlisted men,"

Nancy Morgan instructed. "Go right to the top. We don't care about those Cayuses. Find out what's happened to Algeron. For all we know . . ." She snatched up the skirt of her apron to stifle a sniffle and wiped her eyes. "After all, we can complain all we want, but we've given Algeron short shrift." She glanced accusingly at her daughter.

Bill Morgan was stunned. Underneath that nag-nag exterior, his wife of 25 years had feelings. "She actually loves that big lug," he muttered to himself.

Bill Morgan's experiences with army posts was limited to the fortifications encountered on the Oregon Trail, mainly Fort Laramie, Fort Hall, and Fort Boise. These forts were substantial edifices made of adobe with high walls encircling living and trading quarters and block houses guarding the approaches. Here there was nothing that resembled those sturdy defensive structures. The ramshackle frame buildings, flimsy corrals and absence of bulwarks came as a shock.

"This can't be," Morgan uttered in disbelief. He turned to a stern-faced noncom who was overseeing platoons of drilling troopers. "Is this where the Regiment of Mounted Riflemen is quartered?" he inquired.

"Yep," the trooper answered. "All right, git those laggards to work," the noncom shouted at a platoon that passed. "If yuh cain't tell yer right foot from the left we'll put a burr in one shoe. That'll larn yuh soon enuff."

The noncom turned back to Morgan. "Yuh should've seen the place last fall . . . six frame houses to barrack over 300 men, most of 'em no better than covered over chicken roosts. On top of that we had to make room for offices, sick bay, gaol an' storerooms. Yep, we marched across the country to save these souls from the Injuns an' they provided fer us like we was a herd of hogs. All right you men! Double-time 'round the track."

"Hmm!" Morgan grunted. He couldn't believe his eyes. Algeron left a comfortable home to put up with a dump like this? The military camp was little better than a slum. Nancy was right.

Their daughter hadn't taken care of her wifely duties as she should. For a moment he watched the men trot around the drill area, perspiration dripping off them like rain.

"The men're sure working hard," he sympathized with the puffing troopers. "What're you training for, running a steeplechase?"

"We don't discuss military exercises with strangers," the noncom brusquely answered. "If yuh haven't business here yuh better push off."

"I came to see the top dog," Morgan said, suddenly remembering why he had come. "I got business with him that can't wait."

"If yer meanin' Colonel Loring, I reckon he's in his office yonder, but yuh better go through the duty officer first. The colonel don't like people bustin' in on him unannounced."

When finally Bill Morgan was allowed into the colonel's office he was in for another shock. The Mounted Riflemen were led by an officer with one arm!

"Well! What did you find out?" Nancy Morgan demanded upon her husband's return. "From the look on your face it must not have been good."

"Don't start nagging me, woman," Morgan retorted. "We've got to pack up and get out of here. If you want to know, the military camp is a bunch of shacks. We are as exposed as ducks on a pond. We'll be a lot safer back at the farm. The troop we've been counting on to protect us are misfits from the colonel on down. They don't even know their right foot from the left."

"Ah! You must be daft. Algeron wouldn't have rejoined unless it was up to snuff."

"Quit arguing, and do as I say. I'm telling you the gospel truth. Those people are more in the dark than we are. The head cheese did say Algeron was away on a mission. When I asked him where he was and when he would return, he just sat there scratchin' on an arm that ain't there."

XVI

I am tired of talk that comes to nothing.
It makes my heart sick.
Chief Joseph, Nez Perce

Five Crows and his band of warriors were ready for battle. Already a sense of victory permeated the air. Everything seemed to be going their way. They were delighted at the way Cayuse elders had kept Governor Chief Joe at The Dalles for two lengthy days. Young Chief and the others had drug out the ceremonial smokes and council meetings as long as they could. Ostensibly it was done to demonstrate how deeply the loss of the five prisoners was felt by the tribe. But it also gave tribal leaders in the uplands time to organize their forces. Five Crows firmly believed when word was received that the captives had been rescued, warriors from many sympathetic tribes would join with him in opposing Governor Lane and his Blue Coats.

Five Crows' scouts had followed the progress of the river boat carrying the five prisoners from The Dalles all the way to the landing at Cascade Portage. Every single thing about the prisoner escort was noted: number of men, rifles, short guns and barrels of powder. Five Crows rubbed his hands together in glee. This was going to be easy. The hired Indian boatmen would not fight. The small number of Blue Coats would fall like ripe fruit in a high wind.

Of course there were the white faces with the redheaded leader to consider. He would keep an eye on them. As long as they did not get in the way he would leave them be. Nothing was going to distract him from rescuing the five Cayuse captives.

As the Mackinaw approached the portage landing, Five Crows and his painted warriors gathered in a circle. A shaman led them in prayer. Afterward the shaman addressed the gathering in a lengthy, impassioned speech.

"This is a battle of honor," he declared. "We do not need to kill, plunder, steal or count coups. We have come to rescue our brother tribesmen . . . keep them from the white man's hanging noose.

"Our leaders, Young Chief and Stickus, tell us Governor Chief Joe promises to treat our people good, give them what they call fair trial. Why is it then the prisoners must travel into this dark land where rain falls all the time . . . into villages where our people are not allowed to live? Why is it necessary to take our brothers away from the people and places they know to do this thing called justice? The crimes it is said these men have committed were done in the lands of the Cayuse, why should not justice also take place there for all our people to see?

"The Governor Chief says by giving up our five brothers we are making things right. The five men will go before many hairy faces in the council lodge called courthouse. There they will speak of the bad things our brothers are said to have done. If our brothers speak with a straight tongue and did no wrong, they will go free. Those of our brothers that did wrong will hang by the neck until they cannot breathe. When these things pass, Governor Chief Joe says we will live side by side as one family. No matter what the skin color, red - white, together we will share this land.

"How can all this be so? Our people do not speak the white man's tongue. Our people live in round, not square lodges. Our people worship a different god. The missionaries tell us we are heathen savages. They say they must sprinkle our heads with water or place our bodies under water before we will become civilized.

"The hairy faces befuddle us with many rules and laws. The Blue Coats march into our lands and say to live in peace they must build forts, lodges and trading posts which they arm with monstrous guns.

"The homesteaders who come with lodges on wheels tell us the Indian has more land than we need, we must share so they can plow and seed. They measure what they want of our pastures and hunting grounds and say the land is theirs because they put on it a claim with a paper called 'deed.' How can they claim ownership of the land? Like the air we breathe, land was made free to all creatures of Mother Earth.

"Some don't bother with these things called 'claims' and 'deeds.' They take our land, shoot our people as though ridding Mother Earth of pests, saying 'the only good Indian is a dead Indian.'"

The shaman thrust his hands skyward. "The Great Mysterious watches these things happen. He reads what is in the hearts of men. He will see what we do is right. Go into battle. Bring back our tribesmen. They must not die by the white man's rope."

Hardly did the shaman conclude his long harangue when a scout galloped into camp. "Red Beard is on the move," he breathlessly reported.

The news was greeted with a wave of excited chatter. Youthful warriors seized their weapons and mounted their horses. "Hey! Hey! Today is a good day to make coups," they chanted. Five Crows motioned for quiet. The shaman ordered the youthful horsemen to dismount.

Five Crows had had a day and night to size up the red-headed man and his group of horsemen. The hairy faces had spent much of the time lolling about, drinking and playing games with little white bits of paper and tossing buffalo dice. They posted guards who slept most of the night, but a few did keep careful watch on the river and the Cascade Portage crossing.

At first Five Crows believed talkative Short and his men had come to guard the portage from hostile attack, but their lack of discipline, dearth of scouts and lackadaisical guards led him to believe they had other intentions. If that was so, what did they plan to do? They acted much like the group of volunteers that marched up river to do battle at Sand Hollows where his friend Gray Eagle had been killed and he had been wounded. The thought made him grind his teeth. After rescuing the prisoners he would like to slaughter the hairy faces down to the last man. Others in the war party felt the same. They had wanted to sneak up in the night and cut the throat of the red head and everyone of his followers. The shaman would not allow it. They had come to rescue the prisoners -- not go on a frenzy of killing.

"It is not wise to solve one problem by creating a larger one," the shaman had cautioned.

Fortunately, the hairy faced raiders were careless. The guards they posted saw nothing. A group of men went to scout the portage and stumbled back half drunk. The strange behavior of the hairy faces baffled the Cayuse. They carried a great coil of rope which they cut into lengths. When they were not drinking and playing, they practised making fancy knots in the rope ends.

"Oh-hah!" A warrior who had traded with coastal tribes exclaimed. "These people are making hanging ropes. They plan to seize the prisoners at the portage and hang them. Brother Shaman is right. The governor chief speaks with crooked tongue. He has no wish to see our tribal brothers stand trial. It takes much money and gives much trouble. He wants our brothers dead before they reach Oregon City."

Five Crows mentally reviewed all this information. The pesky man with hair the color of fire was a nuisance he hadn't counted on. If he attacked Red Beard's party now the noise of battle could very well alert Governor Chief Joe and his Blue Coats. They would turn back and all would be lost.

Five Crows finally spoke. "We will wait -- follow Fire Beard and see what he does."

XVII

A man surprised is half beaten
Thomas Fuller, "Gnomologia"

Loudmouth Short and his men were in good spirits. Their plan to kidnap the Cayuse was on schedule. Far as they knew their presence had gone unnoticed, and they were having a roaring good time away from wives and families. To help keep them happy, the German settler, Hoage, who in his spare time distilled potato spirits on his Rickreall farm, had brought along a goodly supply of his product. The bung of the barrel of potato liquor was knocked out and the barrel's contents sampled freely. While half in their cups the men prepared the hangman nooses and joked about how the hanging would be done.

After the prisoners were in hand the men were to divide into teams and vie to be the first to get their man hanged. Judges were selected and prizes designated. They set aside a jug of Hoage's fermented potato juice to toast the winners. Another jug of potato alcohol was saved for pickling victims' ears and other body parts to show off when they arrived back in Oregon City.

"Yeah!" the scrawny-necked Short chortled. "Yuh can bet'cher life when word gits out we sent these Cayuse murderers swingin' higher'n kites, Injuns all over the territory'll think twice afore mixin' with the whites."

"They's roundin' the bend," a lookout shouted. "Thet Mackinaw'll be pullin' in afore yuh know it. Do we hit 'em early on or do we wait 'til dark?"

"We'll move ahead while we can still see," Short said, making for his horse. We'll hev more'n 'nough trouble findin' our way without runnin' into a mess of brush an' trees. Check your weapons. After all the bother we've gone to, we don't want to make a hash of it now. Let's go. We'll show those yellow-livered stay-at-homes we don't need traps and fences to take care of the two-legged coyotes and wolves thet're stealin' our stock."

Down the slope Red Short led his followers, sending deer, rabbits and other forest creatures skittering out of the brush. From a thick stand of trees a flight of crows cawed and flapped into the night. Only the roar of the river and the breeze whipping through the tall evergreens saved the vigilantes' advance from being heard by the escort of mounted riflemen who had started marching across the portage.

When the vigilantes came in sight of the shoreline, flaming redhead Short held up a hand. They were slightly ahead and above where the Mackinaw was being pushed and jerked along. "We don't want to be responsible for killing any of our own people so just fire to scare the pants off them," Short advised. He held up a red bandana and brought it down for the signal to fire. The volley of shot was louder than expected. A vigilante's mount reared and neighed, then, with a great jerk of its neck and head, broke away and thundered back up the hill.

"What's the matter with you galoots?" Short scolded, uttering a sharp screech. "Hold onto those animals. We sure don't want to be set afoot."

Barely did the words leave his mouth when dead ahead a line of fire set the forest ablaze. "What the hell!" an attacker yelled. The flames flashed through one bush and into another, then leapt into the trees. Horses snorted and stumbled over their hooves to get away from the rapidly advancing wall of flame.

"Get out! Run for your lives. Every man for himself," Short shouted. He put his foot into the stirrup to mount his horse. The animal skittered away. "Whoa! Whoa! Yuh stupid animal." The horse snorted, jerking the reins out of Short's bony hand. The skinny vigilante leader threw his rifle away and ran after his mount. He tripped and fell. He scrambled to his feet to find himself running alongside a bear, an elk and two deer.

"Oh! My Gawd!" Ahead were a dozen or more war painted Indians. Some of his men fell. Short cursed. The fire was the trick of those murderin' heathen! They had trapped him and now were cutting his men down like stalks of corn. Short closed his eyes, waiting for the tomahawk to descend. It was the end -- never again would see his wife, Gertrude.

Instead of the whack of a tomahawk, all Short felt was a terrible heat on his back. His coat had caught fire. He screamed. He tore off the burning garment and started to run. Smoke and cinders got up his nose and into his eyes. Racing on either side of him were hideously painted bodies, matching him stride for stride. If he didn't know better he would have sworn he was in hell.

#

Down by the riverside Sergeant Coombs glanced proudly at his men whose faces glowed in the bright firelight. Everything had worked out to perfection, better than he had expected. Governor Lane hardly had finished his scolding for cutting pitch sticks and coating them with powder when the first flurry of shot whistled down the hillside and thudded into the planks of the Mackinaw.

Sergeant Coombs was ready. "Fire up your sticks," he calmly ordered. "When I say heave, throw them up the slope as far as you can." One torch after another flared until the river bank was bright as midday.

"What the hell . . . !" the governor spluttered.

"Heave!" Sergeant Coombs shouted. An arc of flame shot into the brush and trees. For a moment the torches lay sizzling in the undergrowth. Breezes off the river fanned them into life. Higher and higher the flames rose until they were shooting from treetop to treetop.

The roar of the fire, the crash of bodies threshing through underbrush and hysterical yells of the fleeing enemy made Sergeant Coombs and his riflemen laugh and shout until Governor Lane stopped them. "Shut up! Listen! Those cries are not Indian. They're white people. How can that be?"

Sergeant Coombs had no answer. He was just as mystified as Governor Lane.

#

On a nearby hilltop Marshal Meek and his band of volunteers watched in amazement as the fire, roiling, snapping and leaping through the thick virgin forest, lighted the terrain bright as day.

"Look! Look!" the ex-vigilante who had delivered the message of Short's intentions, cried. "Short's gang an' the Cayuses're goin' at it tooth an' nail."

"They'd both better skeddadle or they'll be gittin' their tail feathers scorched," Deacon observed.

From the watchers' vantage point it was difficult to see what actually was taking place. Smoke, flame and cinders obscured their vision, but it soon became clear both parties had little stomach for fighting. There was only one thought in the minds of warriors and vigilantes, and that was to save themselves from the fiery hell hot on their heels.

The fleeing white men shouted and cursed. The red men were just as intent on saving themselves but did it more quietly. Some were able to mount horses and ride into the clear. Most were afoot, ploughing through brush, dodging trees and, where possible, taking to game trails. Mixed in with the men were horses, rabbits, squirrels, two bear, a covey of quail and a small herd of white-tailed deer.

"Tarnation!" Deacon exclaimed. "Ol' Joe Lane sure knows the sojerin' business. Who'd a thought he had the smarts ta smoke out the vigilantes an' Cayuses in one fell swoop. Look at 'em, the gangs thet was so hell bent ta give the guv a threshin' hev thrown their weapons away . . . red men an' white men runnin' side by side as if racin' fer a prize."

"Yeah!" Joe Meek said sourly. "The governor's as lucky as a flea in a hen coop." He was so disgusted he spat on his horse. What an ass he had made of himself. He had raised a great stink with Colonel Loring over the danger that faced the prisoners and the fierce fighting that would occur, and here the business had been handled without a shot being fired. For all the good he and his volunteers had done they might as well have remained in Oregon City.

XVIII

The woman cries before the wedding and the man after.

Polish Proverb

Much to his chagrin, Sergeant Coombs' imaginative tactics to keep the prisoners from falling into hostile hands, received little credit from the powers to be. Governor Lane claimed if word of the escort's narrow escape got out it would increase unease among the citizenry. US Marshal Meek, who was piqued by his fruitless efforts in the affair, agreed with the governor. "The less said about it the better," he said.

To keep peace among those responsible for law and order, Colonel Loring said nothing, but Sergeant Coombs could tell by the way he nervously massaged his stump the colonel thought it unfair. To make Sergeant Coombs' return even more bleak Colonel Loring informed him while he was away his father-in-law came to inquire of his whereabouts.

"Aagh!" the sergeant inwardly groaned. In his dismay over losing a commendation he knew he should have received, the Morgan family visit had completely slipped his mind. Even before arriving back in Oregon City he had assumed they would have returned home. His father-in-law was not one to needlessly waste time. It was the old lady that had kept them in Oregon City. She had made up her mind come hell or high water, her daughter's marriage would succeed.

"Why don't those damn in-laws leave me alone?" Sergeant Coombs said through clenched teeth. He had reenlisted to get out of their sight. Now that they were acquainted with the pitiful army post and its one-armed commandant, they would hound him until he returned to the fold. Old Bill was all right, but that wife of his was a harridan. As soon as the wedding bells quit ringing, she saw to everything, even making up the nuptial bed the following morning so she could examine the sheets.

"You're dismissed." Colonel Loring's jarring voice broke into Sergeant Coombs' grim review of his marital status. "If I were you, Sergeant, I would crack around and square things up with your family. From the way your father-in-law spoke, he's under the impression I pressured you into returning to duty and am more or less holding you against your will."

Sergeant Coombs was speechless. He snapped the colonel a salute, wheeled about to blindly stumble down the headquarters building steps. He could kill those Morgans. Not only had they interfered in every aspect of his marriage, now they had the gall to queer him with his commanding officer.

He hurried to the barracks to clean up. After he showered and shaved he discovered he didn't have a clean change of clothes. The man in charge of the laundry service had gone over the hill.

"The damn fellow," Coombs swore. "He probably wore my best uniform when he took off." Thus, Algeron Coombs was not altogether in the best frame of mind as he went in search of the Morgans. In fact he had half a notion to remain in the barracks, but if the colonel found him there he would be worse off than ever.

Sergeant Coombs had little trouble in locating the Morgan camp. As soon as he crossed Main Street Nancy Morgan's shrill voice could be heard berating her husband. He stopped short. The last thing he wanted was to walk in on a family quarrel. He had better reconnoiter first.

"Why is it whenever I give you a chore to do you make a mess of it?" the shrill voice demanded. "You come back with a cock-and-bull story that we've got to pack up and go home; the city is in danger of being overrun by Redskins. We hardly get packed and we find the Governor is back and the Cayuse murderers are safely under lock and key."

Bill Morgan growled something Sergeant Coombs could not make out, but whatever her husband said it did not stop the flow of shrill words. "Unhitch those horses, and be quick about it. We don't want Algeron to know we were running away like a flock of timid turkeys. Lucille, start unpacking. Get the rocking chair. Algeron will be tired and want to rest."

Sergeant Coombs wished he could sink into the ground and disappear. It was quite evident, Nancy Morgan was in her "patch up the marriage" syndrome. She would fuss around him all evening: "Algeron are you comfortable; Algeron are you getting enough to eat?" To make the situation even more impossible, before he could make a move Joe Jennings and Michael Two Feathers rode up.

"Sergeant Coombs, my hat's off to you," Joe greeted. "You managed the portage crossing perfectly. You should receive a medal."

Mrs. Morgan, who overheard, shouted, "Halloa! Algeron! We're over here. Bring your friends. Seem's like we've been waiting donkey's years for you to return."

Lucille scurried around to remove her apron and adjust her hair. She was so flustered she didn't know which way to turn. Even after more than six months of marriage, the sight of Joe Jennings made her heartbeat quicken. Why had she been so hasty? It was her mother's fault. She had been so afraid her daughter would be an old maid.

Sergeant Coombs submissively shrugged his shoulders and forced a smile but inside his stomach was tied up in knots. The irony of the situation was almost too much to bear. His thoughts were much the same as those of his wife, Lucille. Right from the start of the journey across the plains, Lucille had favored Joe Jennings over him. But he did not give up. As luck would have it, when disaster struck he was on hand and rival Joe was absent. In fact, at the time, it was rumored Joe Jennings had been killed.

For weeks afterward, thoughts of the drama that now unfolded made Sergeant Coombs wish he could dig a hole and bury himself forever. It was the presence of that damned Joe Jennings that made the situation impossible.

"How nice to be together again," Joe said, doffing his hat as though greeting royalty. He shook Bill Morgan's hand and in turn took Mrs. Morgan and Lucille by the hand and bowed low, charming them with his white-toothed smile. Mrs. Morgan placed the hand he touched on her heart as if she'd received a blessing. Lucille especially acted silly, blushing and fluttering her eyelashes like a damsel on a first date. Bill Morgan had to put in his two cents worth by reminiscing on the times they had spent with the brothers while crossing the plains. He invited the brothers to sample a blue berry pie, which Sergeant Coombs knew had been baked especially for him.

The pie was cut and coffee served, Mrs. Morgan cooing like a mourning dove. The brothers wolfed the food down, licking up every crumb like hungry dogs. Mrs. Morgan served them more. Since learning Joe Jennings possessed untold wealth and his people came from New England's upper class, she could talk of nothing else. One of the main reasons he, Algeron Coombs, had reenlisted was to get away from his mother-in-law's constant hints of how much better off her daughter would have been if she had married Joe Jennings rather than him.

Sergeant Coombs groaned. The whole business was disgusting. Like so many of the lonely men he had known, he had jumped into the marriage bed without realizing the consequences. If only he could have taken Lucille away where they could have set up housekeeping on their own, the marriage would have worked. But the Morgans clung to their only child as though, without her, they would shrivel up and die.

XIX

. . . All men were made by the same Great Spirit Chief.
They all are brothers . . .
Chief Joseph, Nez Perce

The day broke cold and gray, as if it had donned an early cloak of mourning. A shroud of mist hung over the river and spread into the foothills. The site where the matter of life or death for the five Cayuse prisoners would be decided was nearly hidden from view.

Vision Seeker, dressed in weatherworn buckskins with a fur cape thrown over his shoulders, stared blankly at the white blanket that covered the valley below. Although it was the Season of Tall Grass, he shivered. Accustomed to the plateau highlands, he disliked the fog and drizzle of these lands where white people loved to build their wood and stone lodges.

He raised a lean, tanned hand to wipe away the moisture that coated his hair and readjusted the lone feather he wore. Why did he stay when he so desperately wanted to return to Lapwai? A rider had brought word his sister, Raven Wing, had journeyed up from White Bird country to take Quiet Woman to live with her, but the fate of Lone Wolf and his buffalo hunters still was unknown.

Vision Seeker caught sight of Cut Lip who continued to have hopes his brother Kia-ma-sump-kin would be freed. Vision Seeker sighed. He had let poor Cut Lip down. His last hope had been to seek help from US Marshal Meek, but his efforts had gone for naught. The former mountain man appeared to avoid him. Why should he do that? Vision Seeker thought back to the days of trapper rendezvous. He had seen Joe Meek at several of them but never had gotten to know him.

Actually, the mountain man had repelled him. Always he seemed to have a jug of firewater in one hand and was fondling an Indian maiden with the other. Meek's first mate, a Shoshone named Mountain Lamb, had been killed in a fight with the Bannock, an arrow piercing her heart. Meek's next mate was a Nez Perce woman he acquired at the Ham's Fork rendezvous in 1837, who had born him a girl child . . . a daughter, Helen Mar. Meek had named her after a story book character he fancied. Helen Mar had died of illness after the Whitman Mission tragedy while prisoner of the Cayuse.

Meek never especially had been welcomed by the Nez Perce. He had married into the tribe but never settled in the homeland of his wife as had Red Craig, his fellow trapper. Neither had he accepted the responsibility of husband nor father.

"Hmm!" Vision Seeker thoughtfully grunted. Did Meek avoid him because he felt guilty over the way he treated the Nez Perce mother of Helen Mar? It was said she had run away from Meek's lodge while he lay senseless with drink. She took the child only to have Meek later seize Helen Mar and give her to the Whitmans to rear. Did memories of how he treated mother and child haunt him? Did her death while prisoner of the Cayuse cause him to hate all Indian people? Vision Seeker grimaced. Regardless of the source of his attitude toward Indian people, the prisoners could expect no mercy from US Marshal Meek.

Gradually, the fog over the river lifted. From his vantage point high above the river, Vision Seeker's keen, dark eyes began to make out the buildings that made up the white man's village called Oregon City. Along the eastern river bank a double line of buildings faced onto a muddy roadway. Beyond, a crest of white marked where the river waters gained speed to pitch over the rocky drop off that formed the Falls of the Willamette.

Below the falls a rocky point of land thrust itself to the surface dividing the river, creating an island. On the island, half hidden among the rocks, brush and scrub trees, sat a low, dark structure. Around it armed sentries marched back and forth. Here the five men accused of murder were housed. Even though shackles left them helpless, the populace still wanted them as far away as possible, yet easily accessible for trial and execution.

Although garrulous Red Short's band of vigilantes had been disbanded and sent to their homes with a scorching reprimand from Governor Lane, the mood of the city and surrounding countryside remained tense. Rumors were rampant that other lynch mobs were ready to take the place of Short's vigilantes . . . storm into Oregon City, overwhelm the apparently inept Mounted Riflemen, and make off with the Cayuse prisoners.

To add credence to this belief, immediately after the prisoners arrived Colonel Loring's command began lengthy drills. The official explanation was that the men were preparing for transferring the accused from prison to courtroom and guarding them during courthouse proceedings. The plan was, still shackled with irons, the prisoners would leave the low, dark structure, cross a bridge onto the eastern bank of the river and march to a large building that would serve as the courtroom.

For brief moments the closely guarded men would enjoy a breath of fresh air, but quickly would discover themselves imprisoned by walls more threatening than those left behind. The roadway would be lined with hostile, jeering faces, for it was said the trial would attract people from the length and breadth of the valley. Old and young, male and female, were inflamed by the macabre desire to catch a glimpse of these monsters accused of committing the infamous Whitman Mission killings.

From the second story balcony of a building commandeered for the occasion, US Marshal Joe Meek watched with satisfaction as people converged on the city. Makeshift shelters filled every available open space. Pasture grounds were thick with horses and oxen. From every campsite came excited chatter, sometimes so shrill it hurt the ear and made dogs whine and howl. The smoke of dozens of campfires rose above the treetops to mingle with the shroud of fog.

Opposite the island where the prisoners were incarcerated and in the shade of stately fir trees, a small cluster of Indian tipi lodges stood bleak and lonely. They intentionally had been erected well away from the camps of the curiosity seekers. These were temporary shelters for family members of the prisoners and those who had come to speak on their behalf. The presence of the lodges and their occupants presented an additional object of curiosity. Residing here were members of the tribe flamboyant reporters had labeled the "Murderous Cayuse."

Because of his facial deformity, Cut Lip drew special attention. Worry over the possible execution of his brother had caused him to neglect his appearance. His hair was wild and tangled. Circles beneath his dark eyes gave his face the appearance of a death mask. A white youth putting on a show of bravado shouted, "What did you do, tomahawk yerself?"

At that moment Vision Seeker had stood and strode forward, whetting his long-bladed hunting knife. The white youth and his companions, took to their heels. The incident did not bother Cut Lip. His mind was on the fate his brother faced.

"Chief Joe is good. He will not hang an innocent man," he said to Vision Seeker after the knife sharpening episode.

Vision Seeker turned away. Why did these people torture themselves? They, like himself, had come on a futile journey. It did not take a person with vision to see no words, no actions -- nothing would change the outcome. The crowds that had swarmed into Oregon City demanded blood. They would not accept any verdict but guilty.

Yet, deep inside, Vision Seeker knew exactly why he remained. He could not tear himself away. For all Indian people present, it was like being in a dream world where nothing was real. They could not conceive what was taking place. Yes, five of their brothers were about to die, but all living things on Mother Earth passed to the Great Beyond. The unreality was the manner in which these brothers would be forced to make the crossing.

Death should be a journey of dignity, like a warrior traveling home after a triumphant battle. Death by dangling from a rope around the neck was inconceivable. It tarnishing the greatest moments of life -- that wondrous journey into the hereafter.

XX

*Law is like a mousetrap: easy to enter
but not easy to get out of.*

Arthur J. Balfour

Although he had accomplished what he had set out to do
-- bring the five Cayuse prisoners safely to Oregon City, Governor Joe Lane was not a happy man. Some blowhard had gotten
wind of the narrow escape at the Cascade Portage and blew it all
out of proportion. The fact he had attempted to cover up the near
disaster gave his detractors even more ammunition. So far he
had warded off the criticism, but the incident left him furious,
primarily with himself.

He had survived a close call. If the prisoners had been
captured by either Five Crows' war party or the vigilantes, he
would have had to leave Oregon Territory in disgrace. What galled
him even more was the inept way he had handled the affair. A
mere sergeant had saved the day. Sergeant Coombs deserved a
commendation for his actions and he, Governor Joe Lane, deserved a good kick in the britches.

As if that was not humbling enough, people were now
questioning if he had brought in the right prisoners. Two of them,
Tiloukaikt and Tomahas, had obviously taken part in the killings,
but the guilt of the other three was in doubt. Witnesses of the
crime were not certain that one of these men even had been at the
mission on that fateful day.

Joe Lane got up from behind his desk in the governor's
office and stared out at the dark timberlands that lined the
Willamette River bank, his clean shaven face pale in the gloomy
light. The Whitman Mission tragedy had shocked the nation.
The trial and possible execution of the culprits would be carefully watched and reported. If the culprits got off lightly the local
citizenry would be irate. They wanted blood and would have it

even if it had to be that of Governor Joe Lane.

On the other hand, if innocent people were executed there well could be a hue and cry from Washington. Many members of Congress had no wish to take on the task of wedding the eastern states with the wilds of the west. Now, if a case of bungled justice should occur, he could well lose all the support he had worked so hard to acquire. Before his political career hardly got off the ground it could end in the ash heap.

He shouldn't have been in such a hurry. Instead of asking for five Cayuse prisoners, he should have demanded they root out all of the murderers. Survivors of the massacre were already asking where was Joe Lewis, the most vicious murderer of the lot? How could justice be rendered without his presence in the dock? Where was Waie-cat, the son of Tamsucky? He had taken an active part in the bloodletting. Were the authorities going to allow both of these villainous creatures to go scot-free?

Trouble was, Joe Lane had started too late. Shortly after the first of the year he received word that he had been replaced by an appointee of the new administration. As soon as the new man arrived he had to turn over the reins of government. Lane groaned. Political life was cruel. Regardless of how well or badly a person performed, when a new administration came into office old political appointees had to go.

Of all the challenges he faced on his arrival in Oregon Territory, establishing law and order in the region had been his top priority. He had pursued it as diligently as he thought prudent, but when it came to the Whitman Mission case, his efforts had fallen short. He had waited for the arrival of the Mounted Riflemen, believing he should show a strong show of force.

"Aagh!" What foolish thinking. When they did arrive the Regiment of Mounted Riflemen were about as useless as knotholes in a board fence. Bringing the prisoners from The Dalles to Oregon City for trial was a task that should have been handled by the military, but judging by the way Colonel Loring commanded the Mounted Riflemen, it would have been just like him to lose the prisoners on the way back to Oregon City.

Of course, that was not the only reason he preferred to bring in the prisoners on his own. His responsibilities as territorial governor also included that of superintendent of Indian affairs. In the latter capacity he felt it was incumbent on him to meet with the Cayuse people one last time. He had begun the peace process. For his own peace of mind he had to make certain it would continue after his tenure of office ended.

While at The Dalles, he once again had made it quite clear to the Indian leaders that all peoples of the region must obey the laws of the land whether they liked them or not. By the time he departed he was satisfied they understood that once the prisoners were in Oregon City their fate depended on the stories they told of the Whitman Mission tragedy, and they had to be prepared to pay the penalty for their crimes. The meeting ended on the right note. To indicate there was no ill will, the Cayuse rounded up a sizeable herd of horses, 50 in all, to pay for the defense of the prisoners.

So far things had proceeded pretty much as he envisioned, but he hated to think of what the future might bring. As soon as his replacement arrived he had to turn over the reins of government. It was a galling predicament. Upon vacating the governor's chair the Whitman Mission tragedy business was out of his control. Then there was the fuss between the Klickitats and Rogue. He had wanted to settle that before he left office, too.

Territorial laws were another problem he had hoped to sort out. Rather than write a code of laws of their own, the Provisional Legislature adopted the 1839 *Statutes of Laws of the Territory of Iowa* and later *The Revised Statutes of Iowa of 1843*. The acceptance of these laws of another state, raised serious questions that had yet to be answered.

Were these laws appropriate to the Territory of Oregon? If so, did they apply to Indian people? Were the aborigines to be considered citizens of the United States of America or were they outsiders to be dealt with as subjects of a foreign land? The irony

of the situation made Lane grimace. These were examples of the
legal quandary purveyors of justice would face in preparing for
the murder trial that would draw the attention of the nation -- a
conundrum with so many complexities King Solomon in all his
wisdom could not have sorted it out.

#

George Curry, editor of the local newspaper, probably had
a better knowledge of the legal snares and pitfalls that lay ahead
than anyone in the territory. For months the Territorial Legislature had fiddled with the statutes they had initially adopted, making changes willy-nilly. Many were noted on scraps of paper filed
hither and thither, or if together, shuffled like cards in a deck,
waiting for some one to put them into proper order and send them
to the presses. George Curry was singled out to do the job.

Curry, an open-faced man with a skimpy beard covering
his jowls, already was hip-deep in the task. He knew how important it was for everyone taking part in the rendering of justice to
know and go by an established and approved set of rules. The
pressure of the pending trial filled him with dread. The lives of
five men could well depend on the laws he published.

Making order of the legal morass was a nightmare. Statutes, edicts and minutes written in the handwritings of legislature
clerks were not always legible and the language was unclear or
couched in fuzzy legal terms. For days George Curry, along with
his partner in the task, Bill Buck, had struggled to make readable,
understandable copies of what the lawmakers had intended.

George Curry laid aside a sheaf of papers and rubbed his
tired eyes and sighed. Regardless of how well the statutes were
stated, there would be differences of opinion. Lawyer J. Quinn
for example, would go over the laws with a fine-toothed comb.
The pompous man was known to spend hours debating the meaning of an everyday word.

Curry grimaced. He had to do the best he could and let
the chips fall as they would, and God help those in the dock.

THE CRY OF THE COYOTE

XXI

'Tis better to have loved and lost,
Than never to have loved at all.

Tennyson

Upon their return to Oregon City after the portage affair, the brothers, Michael Two Feathers and Joe Jennings, found themselves living in a small Indian enclave made up of three large tipi lodges. Joe, the only all white man, felt somewhat out of place but for politeness sake remained. Although they had been together for the past three years, he still felt he really didn't know his Indian half brother. Yet, when emergencies occurred hardly was there a time when they didn't act in unison. It was almost as if one knew what the other was thinking.

Their uncle, Vision Seeker, who moved in with them, still was a stranger. He kept to himself and said little. An invisible barrier seemed to surround him that at times made Joe uncomfortable. The dark eyes took in everything. The flip of a squirrel's tail, a swan on the river, the caw of a crow, a deer on the hill; there was nothing that missed his sharp eyes and ears. In spite of his keen observations, Vision Seeker left the impression his thoughts were elsewhere. He was seeing these things in a setting privy only to himself.

Once in a great while Vision Seeker would relate stories of his youth, telling of great buffalo hunts when horizons were black with the huge beasts. He spoke of fields of whispering buffalo grass that undulated in the wind like ocean waves. He said when that happened the spirits of thousands and thousands of buffalo that had died on those hunting grounds were speaking. They kept repeating, "We are Mother Earth's creatures just like you. We have as much right to be here as do you."

Vision Seeker's tales were so filled with mysticism they left Joe in awe. Even Michael watched his uncle with diffidence.

Joe doubted if anyone knew the taciturn Nez Perce well. As a result of the tone set by Vision Seeker, their tipi lodge had an aura of mystery that caused Joe to wonder if Vision Seeker's buffalo spirits hadn't taken up residence there, too.

Joe found the spiritual quietness almost as disturbing as the bustling buzz of Oregon City streets. He felt out of place. In fact he did not feel comfortable in his sister's Willamette Valley home, either. Tildy's and her husband's hospitality overwhelmed him, and there was hardly anything he could do in return. More than once he thought that getting married and settling down was the answer to his restlessness.

Seeing the Morgans again had revived that thought, but Lucille had married . . . "Agh!" . . . He didn't have the guts to get married. What was the good of thinking about it? As Granny Jennings was fond of saying, "Faint heart never won fair lady." He'd had his chance with Lucille and bungled it. He could tell by Bill Morgan's long, warm handshake and Mrs. Morgan's apologetic smile, they were embarrassed at the way things had turned out. If they had their druthers he would be their son-in-law and Sergeant Coombs knew it.

He sympathized with the sergeant. The presence of Joe Jennings at the Morgan camp could not have been pleasant for him. If he, Joe Jennings, really loved Lucille, the kind thing to do would be to leave the valley and never return. And actually the best thing he could do for himself was to carve the memory of Lucille from his heart.

Joe stared into the evening mist that rose from the Willamette River and shivered. If he was going to leave he should do it right now. Before the trial was over he probably would run into Lucille again. Bill Morgan had made it quite clear that they intended to stay and see the red savages tried and hanged. Then there would be Luke Olafson and family . . . Bithiah, his first love, and her kids. They probably would show up, too. From what he had heard his first love had added two children of her own to the two she had adopted.

Again, Joe audibly groaned. If he left where would he go? He had no desire to go east. Now that the Jennings family had settled in the Willamette Valley there were no kin left there. Deacon and he were the last of Buck Stone's trapping brigade so the trapping fraternity had no pull on him. He could strike out on his own, but was he up to it? He stood and flexed his stiff leg, the one he nearly lost while prisoner of the murderous Tomahas. It was a good thing he and Lucille Morgan didn't marry. She deserved better. In his crippled condition, as husband and lover, he would have disappointed her.

Michael watched as his brother shuffled off into the evening mist. He knew the source of the troubled restlessness that had Joe in its grip. Ever since learning of Sergeant Coombs' and Lucille Morgan's wedding he had feared for what might happen. Still the meeting of Lucille, Joe and Sergeant Coombs went well. All three of them kept their composure. Only gossipy Mrs. Morgan and her pushy ways nearly brought the matter out in the open. At least her blueberry pie was delicious.

Michael had watched Joe's friendship with the Morgan girl grow into love. Joe never would admit it, but right from the moment Mrs. Morgan introduced them to her beautiful daughter on the river boat, San Francisco, it was love at first sight -- an extraordinary moment neither one of them would ever forget. Michael uttered a deep sigh. The Great Creator worked in mysterious ways. Why had Sergeant Coombs been provided this beautiful mate while the two true lovers were torn apart?

In fact he'd had a personal reason for hoping that Joe and Lucille Morgan would have wed. For the longest time his own secret love, Morning Star, the daughter of Deacon Walton, had had her eye on Joe for a mate. Morning Star had captured his own heart like no female had since the bright-eyed Cayuse maiden, Little Fox, daughter of Beaver Head.

For a while he had high hopes he would have a chance to ask for Little Fox's hand. He knew she liked him, and he would have turned Mother Earth upside down to possess her. Then she had shockingly disappeared one night with Tiloukaikt's first son, Edward. Now Edward was dead, and his father would soon go on trial and undoubtedly follow his first son to the grave, but what had happened to Little Fox? The last time he had seen her was the night before she disappeared.

Over and over he thought of plans to rescue her from Edward Tiloukaikt's lodge. Then word came that Edward had been killed by the murderous Joe Lewis who took everything Edward possessed. Did that mean Little Fox was taken too, or did she die along with her mate? As far as he knew no one ever had seen her again. There was talk of tracking Joe Lewis down, but he had disappeared into The Land of Many Smokes. Even the Blue Coats, who wanted him for the Whitman Mission killings, decided it was fruitless to try and bring him to trial.

Michael scowled. He was getting as bad as his brother Joe, mooning over lost loves. Where had Joe gone? Michael leapt to his feet. Joe had been gone entirely too long. His brother's leg still had not completely healed. In the mist and slippery underfooting he might have fallen and was unable to get up.

Michael strode in the direction Joe had taken. Not far away he came upon an open space where a dozen or more inquisitive out-of-towners had set up camp. In the deep shadows was Joe, leaning against the trunk of an evergreen with his eyes fixed on a campfire on the far side of the camp. There two women, Mrs. Morgan and her daughter Lucille, were bustling around preparing supper for their husbands who sat nearby waiting to be served.

THE CRY OF THE COYOTE

XXII

*If I give up my men that killed the settlers, to let them be tried
by your law, will you give up your men that killed our
women to let them be tried by our law?*

Captain Jack, Modoc

On May 21, 1850, the prisoners were marched through
the omnipresent mist to a building that, before the outlaw of dis-
pensing alcoholic beverages in the city, had been a tavern and
dance hall. This place was deemed the only public edifice in town
authorities believed adequate to hold the trial. Hardly did the
doors open before several hundred men and a dozen women
crammed their way inside, packed against the walls and each other
as tightly as sardines in tin. Disgruntled latecomers waited outside in the mist that soon turned into a drizzle.

They had good reason to be upset. The wet weather had
turned the ground to gluey mud that stuck to footwear like thick
coatings of tar. Fearful of dirtying their skirts, ladies hoisted them
to reveal shapely ankles, much to the enjoyment and hilarity of a
few rowdies.

"I say, ain't thet a bit of dainty flesh," a perceptive canvas
cloaked man, slyly, but loudly, observed.

Yet, it was all done in fun. The mood in the city was one
of gaiety -- not unlike that of an opening day at a county fair.
This was a historic event, an occasion that would be remembered
and talked about for a lifetime.

The onlookers were not disappointed. The curtain lifted
on the first act promptly and with color. Sergeant Coombs, with
the buttons on his uniform polished to perfection and the stripes
on his arms gleaming, marched the security troop up the street,
through the crowd and into the courthouse. Like a band conduc-
tor, Sergeant Coombs, swinging his arms and in a low voice, kept

his charges marching in harmony by repeating a field drill chant: "Right-left, right-left, one-step, two-step, backs straight, eyes ahead, sound off! We're the Mounted Riflemen."

Shortly after Sergeant Coombs posted the courtroom guard, US Marshal Meek, resplendent in a uniform made especially for the occasion, appeared with the prisoners and their armed escort. Here was the spectacle everyone had come to see -- the five Cayuse -- who had been hunted for two and a half years, and had kept the white populace shaking in their boots all the while.

Spectators fell silent as the prisoners shuffled in to occupy the space set aside for them. Except for the clanking of the prisoners' chains, a few whispers and shuffling feet, the courtroom was as still and disconcerting as a haunted house on Halloween. Awed by the presence of these savages who had carried out the bloody crimes at Whitman's Mission, onlookers stood on tiptoes to gawk. Those conducting the proceedings were subdued by the responsibility that faced them -- the lives of five men were in their hands.

There was a short wait while court officials assumed their positions. The scribe, George Curry, sat at a table and scrupulously set his writing tools straight and flexed his fingers. There was a lot of handwriting to be done. The eyes of the country were upon these proceedings. The official record was to make it clear everything that occurred here strictly adhered to the laws of the land. Interpreters and defense lawyers gathered near the prisoners. They had a long work table before them, as did Prosecutor Amory Holbrook and his assistants.

Judge Orville Pratt entered in a black robe, taking his place at the head table. US Marshal Meek yelled in a voice that could be heard by all who waited in the misty drizzle outside. "All rise! The Judge has arrived!"

Everyone one except the Cayuse prisoners and Cayuse visitors, sprang to their feet. The first hitch in the proceedings had occurred. The interpreters had remained mute. They had not understood the meaning of the marshal's command.

Judge Pratt scowled and aimed his gavel at the seated men. He would not take his chair until courtroom protocol was observed. Prosecutor Holbrook frowned at an assistant. The assistant murmured to an interpreter. Finally, the message got through. The seated men clambered to their feet. The judge took his seat. The wheels of justice now were ready to grind.

The first order of business was the reading of indictment number one, a lengthy document of closely spaced handwritten scrawls. It began with a confusing preamble and continued on and on in the same vein:

"... in the year of our Lord one thousand eight hundred and forty seven, at Waiitatpu in said county, the said place being then and there in Indian country certain Indians ... with force and arms, in and upon one Narcissa Whitman, she not then and there being an Indian, feloniously, wilfully, and of their malice aforethought, did make an assault, and that the said Indians, certain guns, muskets, and pistols, each of the same then and there being loaded and charged with gunpowder and bullets, which guns muskets, and pistols, they the said Indians in their hands then and there had and held to, against, and upon the body of the said Narcissa Whitman, then and there feloniously, wilfully, and of their malice aforethought did shoot. ..."

The charge of shooting the missionary lady was not enough. The indictment went on to charge the murderers with employing other assault weapons:

"... the said Indians, with certain knives, tomahawks and other weapons as yet unknown to said Ju-

*rors, which said knives, tomahawks and weapons, the
said Indians then and there in their hands had and held,
her the said Narcissa Whitman, in and upon her head,
neck, shoulders, breast and back, then and there feloniously, wilfully and of their malice aforesaid did strike,
cut and thrust. . . ."*

The reading was so wordy, lengthy and repetitious the
courtroom audience was stunned. How could anyone make sense
of this gibberish? Sitting alongside Nancy Morgan, a bearded
man chewing viciously on a cheek full of tobacco, swore under
his breath, spittle spewing from his lips.

"I've heerd many a long-winded storyteller in me day but
this fella beats 'em all. He's got more ways of sayin' nuthin' than
hairs on a dog. He's shot and knifed the poor mission lady, what
method of killin's he gonna pin on these Cayuses next?"

A short while later an audible groan was heard from another quarter. Afterward it was said it came from George Curry,
the courtroom clerk, who would have condensed the whole business down into one simple sentence: "The five men in the dock
are charged with the premeditated murder of Narcissa and Marcus
Whitman."

Yet, many of those attempting to follow what was said,
thought the wordy legalese was far from complete. Why didn't
the indictment describe the murders of all victims of the massacre? Some were incensed because Joe Lewis, the most cold-
blooded criminal of the lot, and who it was rumored to have been
the instigator of the terrible bloodshedding, had apparently been
overlooked. He was not in the dock nor was he mentioned.

Ignoring occasional derogatory remarks, the reading of
the document continued. The clerk, stumbling over the awkward
wording, the droning voices of three interpreters who valiantly
struggled to make sense of the legalese and translate it into a

language where legal terms did not exist, and the rustling of the restless crowd, seemed to go on forever.

Vision Seeker, who learned the English language at the feet of Buck Stone, a Harvard College graduate, could feel his face grow hot from the anger that welled up to nearly choke him. How could the prisoners defend themselves when the proceedings were conducted in language so obtuse even those trained in law were confused?

Furious by what he had seen and heard, Vision Seeker pushed his way through the crowd and out the door. The fresh air, though moist with mist and a light rain, refreshed him but did not take away the fury in his heart. His poor Cayuse friends had to be more befuddled than he. What was to become of them? They had suffered through one calamity after another. The devastating white man's diseases had ravaged their ranks. For more than two years they had been harassed by volunteer and regular army troops, forcing them to abandon their homes and possessions. Now, they were being overwhelmed by a legal system they could not comprehend. When and how would it all end?

#

Marshal Joe Meek also looked on the courtroom proceedings with disfavor. Why were these idiots wasting so much time? His head ached and his stomach growled. The previous night he again had attempted to get the best of that old mountain goat Deacon. Instead, on the eighth, or was it the tenth round, he reached for another jug and fell into a spittoon. After that he remembered little until his wife met him at the door with a broom stick.

"Go away! Sleep with the dogs. You smell worse than the carcass of a skunk that's laid in the sun too long," she had lashed out, giving him a couple of severe pokes in the gut that nearly had made him throw up.

The marshal groaned. Nothing was going right at home or in the courtroom. That blasted Sergeant Coombs had Colonel Loring eating out of his hand. The colonel had made Coombs' promotion to sergeant permanent, and also had placed him in charge of the prison detail. Already Sergeant Coombs had them performing like trained monkeys. As US Marshal, he had marched the prisoners in, but it was for show, to impress upon the people the proceedings were being conducted according to official rules. That blasted Coombs had drilled the prisoners so well when an order was given they looked to the sergeant before lifting a finger. The very thought of the way Loring and Sergeant Coombs had taken over made Meek's blood boil. He had complained only to receive a reprimand. "Everything is going smoothly. Don't rock the boat," Judge Pratt had admonished.

"Marshal! See that the prisoners are removed. We have to prepare for the afternoon session," Prosecutor Holbrook ordered, interrupting Meek's dour thoughts. "There are more indictments to be read -- the killings of the Sager brothers, the butcher, cabinetmaker. . . . You know the list."

US Marshal Meek didn't bother to look in the direction of the prisoners. He knew by the sound of dragging shackles Sergeant Coombs already had them smartly on their way.

XXIII

He who decides a case without hearing the other side, though
he decide justly, cannot be considered just.

Seneca

The prisoners arrived back at their dungeon-like quarters, tired and confused by their courtroom experience. Even usually placid Tiloukaikt, who expected to pay the supreme penalty for his crimes, was out of sorts. He sat against the wall and stared into space. His beaky nose, shiny with droplets of rain, gave him the appearance of a sharp-shinned hawk. He had told Big Chief Lane he was guilty and was ready to pay the price. So why did these people have to talk-talk in a language neither he nor his fellow prisoners understood? What did they have to gain when already they had made up their minds to execute them? His Cayuse friends should have saved their 50 horses. Among all the words uttered that morning, far as he knew, not one was said in the prisoners' defense.

Tiloukaikt did not disclose his troubled thoughts to his four tribesmen. He had sat through many meetings with the white man, none, of course, as wearisome as this. These civilized folk from beyond the River of Many Canoes liked to hear the sound of their voices but did not like to listen. Right from the beginning all they did was talk-talk-talk.

"Put away all your wives except one," the missionary preachers said. "Worship our God. He is the only true God." They listed their Ten Commandments. Don't do this . . . don't do that, many of the things Indian people had observed since the beginning of time. Not once did these teachers of the white man's religion ask about Indian gods or about Indian religion. What the Indian believed was not important. They were pagans, uncivilized savages. Their way of life led straight to hell.

The Cayuse leader brushed away a swarm of gnats and mosquitoes that buzzed around the prison enclosure all day and through the night. They didn't bother him, but the lice that had appeared to nest in his hair nearly drove him wild. There was one thing his people and the missionaries agreed on, that was their proverb, "cleanliness is next to godliness." But how many of these hairy faces observed these worthy words? The courtroom had an odor like that of a den of hibernating snakes. As near as he could tell it came from the badly or unwashed bodies of these white folks who called themselves civilized.

Tiloukaikt scratched at the lice crawling in his hair. It did little good. Like a disturbed ant hill, the tiny creatures scurried to new homes to bed down. Now he knew how lousy camp dogs felt, unclean and unwanted. What he wouldn't give for a lengthy stay in a sweat lodge and afterward a refreshing dip in the river.

Except for the mountain men in their midst, their white captors probably were against sweat baths. The dash from the sweat lodge to the river was done naked and undoubtedly viewed as sinful. Reproductive organs were not to be seen - might excite unholy thoughts in ones called members of the opposite sex.

Tiloukaikt grimaced. It was a wonder these pious people didn't clothe their horses, cattle, dogs and pigs who ran around naked as the day they came onto Mother Earth. And what did these people do when four-leggeds mated? Did they turn their backs and pretend it wasn't happening? The thought brought a rare smile to Tiloukaikt's face. Doesn't the white man know the planting of seed is the miracle that keeps renewing all living things on Mother Earth, that without seed planting Mother Earth would become ugly and barren?

In contrast to Tiloukaikt's earthy meditations, Tomahas, who sat cross-legged beside him, was wrapped up in thoughts of revenge. Big Chief Lane had said if the murderers gave themselves up, it would bring peace to the plateau. The Cayuse people could return to their homes and live as they had before. Tiloukaikt and the other prisoners believed the big white chief's heart was good and his tongue straight. How foolish could his people be? The white man could no more change his ways than a skunk could remove its stripes.

"Baagh!" This new white chief was only repeating the same lies that they had been told before. Tomahas glanced at Tiloukaikt's hawklike visage. The man never should have been leader of the Waiilatpu band. He gave the missionaries every thing they desired. When they claimed more and more land, he did nothing. He watched the fences go up, the skin of Mother Earth torn to bits, trees chopped down and game shot and left to spoil. Tiloukaikt even encouraged the missionaries by putting his own people to work tearing at the skin of Mother Earth. In the Season of Turning Leaves instead of hunting, the men did the work of women and children, harvesting corn, potatoes and squash.

Tomahas' thick lips tightened in an expression of disgust. If anyone deserved to hang it was Tiloukaikt, not because he had murdered the missionary doctor, but because he had allowed these missionary people to change the way the Waiilatpu band of Cayuse lived. A true leader would not permit such a thing to happen. When people lost their traditions it left them unsure of themselves, wandering around like a wolf pack that lost the scent of its prey.

Tomahas' thoughts were as black and venomous as the back side of the black widow spider that dangled from its web overhead. He had taken part in the mission killings and reveled in the thought. If he had the opportunity to do it again, he would create more havoc than ever. He should have given the white man even more reason to bring him to trial. Tomahas' cruel lips twisted into an evil smile.

Kia-ma-sump-kin, Cut Lip's brother, sat to one side. He had been present when the killings had taken place but had not taken part. The terrible bloodshed left him too weak even to run away. After it was over he had been drug aside by the treacherous half-breed, Joe Lewis, and Tomahas. They threatened that if ever he named a single killer they would cut off his head. To emphasize the warning, Tomahas took his knife and drew the sharp point down his cheek, leaving a wound that took ten sleeps to heal. When the five men were chosen to surrender to the Blue Coats, Tomahas had pointed to him. He had been too frightened to resist.

The dark dungeon called prison, appalled him. The crawling insects and rats that bounded about at night made goose bumps rise on his skin. Even snatches of sleep, more like periods of stupor, were filled with horror. He was riding through a dark forest. There were steep cliffs on either side shutting out the light of Father Sun. Suddenly from a dark stand of trees a man waving a knife, lunged into the trail to seize the horse's bridle. It was Joe Lewis. The murderous man jerked him from the saddle. His clammy hand caught him by the throat.

"Men without tongues do not talk," the evil Lewis growled.

Kia-ma-sump-kin struggled and for a moment broke free. He screamed for help. The clammy hands seized him again and forced his mouth open. He could feel the cold bite of steel. . . . At that point he always awakened, the dream so real he would sit shivering for hours on end.

Invariably, his nightmarish shrieks and violent struggles aroused the other four prisoners. Tiloukaikt would attempt to calm him, but Tomahas would be furious. "You are a Cayuse warrior," he would say in his ruthless manner. "Quit sniveling like a frightened child."

#

A short distance from the dungeon-like prison, the Cayuse contingent that had journeyed from the high country to be with their imprisoned tribesmen had made camp beneath a stand of tall evergreens. They, too, were shaken by the courtroom scene. The fear that sorrowed their hearts, the crowd, the smell, the droning talk, the seats that cut one's legs in two and the officials looking down on them as though they were dirt, had made it an agonizingly bitter experience that would live with them the remainder of their days.

Vision Seeker, always attuned to the feelings of his fellow man, could see his Cayuse friends were so deeply distressed they hardly knew what they were doing. He had to find a way to comfort them, but how? He invited them for a smoke. When the pipe was placed back in its pouch, he spoke. "In times like this we need to look to our ancestors -- the laws, religion, how to live and die -- the wealth of information they created and preserved."

The Cayuse glanced at one another and murmured their approval. "There is no better place to start than what we learned at our mother's knee," Vision Seeker continued. "When we cried she put her fingers to her lips and told us the importance of silence. I still hear my mother say, 'Be quiet, my child. The spirits speak to you. Listen to what they have to say and your troubles will go away.' When I was young I would do as Mother said, but all I would hear was the whisper of the wind -- the chatter of birds -- the rushing waters of the Kooskooskie.

"I heard no spirit talk. I would squint up my eyes to cry again. Mother would put her fingers to her lips and point to the blue sky, to a squirrel scampering up a tree or to the rocks that lay on the banks of the creek. 'All these wonderful things have been put here for you to enjoy,' she would say. 'Do you want to make them feel unwanted?'"

Vision Seeker glanced around the circle of expressionless faces. He spoke of childish things but his plan was succeeding. He had diverted the men's thoughts, but he had to do more for his friends' depression was dark and deep.

"When I said look to our ancestors, I meant we should remember the teachings of our mothers, fathers and their forefathers, even the more ancient ancestors. They had a plan for living that has served our people well. The ancients recognized the spirit of creation. They drew spiritual power from the sun, the stars, the trees, the animals . . . they knew The Creator had linked all these things together. The Eternal Being watched over everything placed on Mother Earth and all things in the skies surrounding her.

"The Supreme One is never forgetful. He is with his children wherever they may be. Unlike the white man, our people do not need to set a day or a meeting place to be with this Supreme Being. Indian people regard all days as holy. The sky above and the four horizons are the walls of our cathedral. Neither do we need preachers nor missionaries to explain what The Great One has to say. The deity whom often we call The Great Mystery, walks with us wherever we go, speaks to us by day and by night. The voice is the whisper of the wind, murmur of the brook, hoot of brother owl, the howl of hunter wolf and cry of trickster coyote. Every drop of rain and snowflake brings a message from The Holy Being. . . ."

Vision Seeker paused, astounded by the many words he had spoken. What was the matter with him? He was preaching like Reverend Henry Spalding, going against what he had said about Indian people not needing an intermediary to interpret messages from The Holy Being. He attempted to explain but the words that had flowed so smoothly, now failed him.

Stickus, who had adopted the Christian faith and had been a friend of dead Missionary Whitman, rose to his feet. He placed a hand over his heart and swept it upward toward Vision Seeker, the sign for good, and then spoke.

"The words of our Nimpau friend are wise and well said. He reminds us of the spiritual power who put us on Mother Earth. He tells us to have faith in this wondrous being to whom we have given many names. Yet, as the Christian people say, there is only one Almighty God to whom all people should worship. The white man's God and the red man's God are the same. As we go forward let us place ourselves in the hands of this Supreme Being. He has guided our people through many tragedies. He will not forsake us now."

XXIV

A good husband should be deaf
and a good wife blind.

John Milton

The spectators who experienced the first morning's courtroom proceedings also returned to their houses and camps exhausted and dissatisfied. Many had left homes and other property unguarded. Others turned the care of livestock and homes over to hired hands. As disgruntled out-of-towners straggled from the courthouse they debated if remaining in Oregon City was worth the risks they were taking..

Certainly, the first morning of the trial was a total loss. The cramped, crowded space set aside for spectators, thick with fetid air, actually made some people sick. Even those who had the advantage of front row seats where the air was better, grumbled as they left for the noon recess. They had expected to see five wild looking brutes in the dock. Only the thick-lipped, brooding countenance of hulking Tomahas had given the crowd the shivery thrill they sought.

In spite of his prominent beak, Tiloukaikt, the leader and the one who it was said wielded the axe that killed Marcus Whitman, had the appearance of a kindly grandfather. The other three, dressed in fringed buckskin pantaloons and hunting shirts decorated with bone and beads, looked more like young men returning home from an unsuccessful hunting trip rather than vicious murderers that for more than two years had terrorized the territory.

No one was more disgusted than Mrs. Nancy Morgan whose sensitivities had been offended by the distasteful courtroom atmosphere. She and Lucille had sat next to the bearded, tobacco-chewing character who complained about the lengthy indictment. She swore the man hadn't bathed or changed his

clothes for years. Between sending juicy squirts of tobacco splattering on the rough floor planking, the uncouth old timer kept up
a constant flow of chatter, his breath as foul as if coming from an
open sewer. When she attempted to lean away, he shifted nearer
to whisper in her ear, his odoriferous breath nearly gagged her
while drops of tobacco spittle spotted her freshly washed and
ironed gingham dress.

"Bill, I don't know why we stay here," Mrs. Morgan complained after they were outside in the clean, damp air, tramping
through the mud. "Enough's enough. I feel as dirty as if I had
been rolling in the dirt with pigs. I've ruined a good pair of shoes.
My skirt is spattered with that dirty fellow's tobacco expectora-
tions. I've had just about all I can take. We've had our visit with
Algeron, such as it was. We've seen the poor prisoners. It's time
we returned home and acted like civilized folks instead of staring
at those Cayuses like they were creatures in a zoo."

"But-but my love," Bill Morgan stuttered, "the trial has
just begun. "Algeron'll be disappointed if we leave. He and
Lucille hardly have had a chance to say hello. Anyway, as good
citizens it's our duty to see justice done."

"Justice!" Nancy Morgan exclaimed. "That bearded brute
next to me said three of those prisoners may be innocent. They
were tricked into giving themselves up. But they'll hang anyway,
he said, as if it was a foregone conclusion. Is that what you want
to see, innocent men executed?"

"Is that so? Everyone I've talked to seems to believe
they're guilty as hell. What do you think, Daughter? Has that
sergeant husband of yours mentioned innocent prisoners?"

Lucille, accustomed to frequent wrangling between her
parents, ignored the question. She was in too much of a quandary to worry about the fate of five heathen savages. Over the
past few days she had made a shocking discovery, one that she
could not reveal to her parents, yet one that she just had to share
with somebody. She audibly groaned. That husband of hers,
why did he have to reenlist? Since coming to Oregon City she

and Algeron hardly ever were alone. How could they possibly sort out their marriage if they never were able to talk?

"Daughter, I have been speaking to you," her father said. "Are you all right?"

"I'm fine," Lucille hastily replied. "Algeron doesn't talk much about his job. I did hear him say there's a question about the guilt of at least one prisoner that bothers him."

"Hmm!" Bill Morgan thoughtfully grunted. "The sergeant ain't one to get upset over trifles. Maybeso, that bearded guy is right. Except for that mean-looking Tomahas, and the old guy with the parrot-like beak, they appear about as dangerous as docile sheep.

"But you never know about these people. They may look tame, but they've been reared in the wilds. At a snap of the fingers they can revert to their wilderness upbringing. Look at the way they shot and tortured Joe Jennings and attacked us on the Barlow Road. Talk about a narrow squeak, they would have slaughtered us to the last man if Michael Two Feathers' gang hadn't happened along."

When Sergeant Algeron Coombs arrived to join his wife and in-laws, he shook his head when asked about the bearded man's story. "You shouldn't repeat rumors like that," he half scolded Nancy Morgan. "People might get funny ideas."

"Rumors are often based upon fact," Bill Morgan argued. "Are there any facts to back up this rumor?"

"No one at headquarters is talking, for no one seems to know exactly what happened. Rumor has it the Cayuse leader, Young Chief, promised the prisoners that if they surrendered and told the white chief what they knew about the mission killings and had no guilt, they would go free. When our officers arrived the five men who surrendered were seized and told they had to journey to Oregon City where their stories would be heard."

"That's downright underhanded. If what you say is true, guilty or not, they were led into a trap. An' there's that officious US Marshal Meek telling people all five prisoners are guilty, and five'll hang," Bill Morgan spluttered.

"That's why we're having a trial," Sergeant Coombs said patiently. "It will sort out the guilty from the innocent. Now, let's not say anything more about it. If it gets out I have been discussing the trial with you, it could mean my stripes."

"You mean you'd stand by and see innocent people hang just to save your stripes?" Bill Morgan's voice went up an octave. "That's not what I call playing the game right. What's going to happen to this society of ours if we bend the rules just to satisfy bloodthirsty people like blabbermouth Short and pompous Marshal Joe Meek? It's a disgrace. . . ."

"Sh-sh!" Mrs. Morgan hissed as the party in the next camp had stopped what they were doing to stare. "You don't want to get Algeron in trouble do you? Come, sit down. Everything is ready to eat."

When his mother-in-law mentioned they might return to their homestead home, Sergeant Coombs glanced at his wife. Was she leaving too? They scarcely had had a minute by themselves. There was a lot they should talk about, like why was she so quiet, looking like a mouse caught in a trap. What was the matter with her? Had that blistering Joe Jennings been around again?

Lucille, still stunned by her secret discovery, avoided her husband's eyes. In his dress uniform he looked so stern and formidable. At the moment she just could not bring herself to smile and act the welcoming, loving wife. She suddenly realized she hardly knew this man. Since the day of their marriage she and Algeron never really had had a heart to heart talk. Now, with him in uniform looking so hard and official, the distance between them seemed almost too broad to bridge. Lucille filled her plate and sat down beside her husband and attempted to eat.

Although Mrs. Morgan had cooked a tasty meal, Sergeant Coombs picked halfheartedly at the food and then shoved the plate aside. It was obvious his wife was keeping something to herself. It had to be that blasted Joe Jennings. He had a notion to seek that marriage breaker out and beat his handsome face in.

Sergeant Coombs groaned. Since coming to Oregon everything had gone sour. His marriage that held such promise, was on the rocks. Now, just when it appeared he had his sergeant stripes back, they were in jeopardy. Both Colonel Loring and US Marshal Meek were just waiting for him to stub his toe. They continued to feud over who and how the prisoners should be managed, and he, Sergeant Coombs, was caught in the middle. No matter what he did, he could not please them both.

Equally as exasperated by the impasse as Coombs, Meek had sought the help of the governor, demanding he issue orders placing US Marshal Meek in sole command of prisoner security.

"I'll think it over," the governor had said but had no intention of getting involved in the Loring/Meek controversy. With the prisoners safely in the Oregon City lockup, he turned to other items on his agenda. As soon as the trial was over Lane planned to lead a detachment to negotiate with the quarreling Klickitats and Rogues.

The thought of Governor Lane's peace efforts made Sergeant Coombs cringe. Because of his success on the prisoner escort detail, and because he was at the center of the Loring/Meek feud, it was very likely Governor Lane would chose him, Sergeant Coombs, to be in charge of the enlisted men that would be trekking into the lands of the Klickitat and Rogues.

If the expedition took place it would be best if the Morgan family did return home. With him away who would keep Lucille and that dammed Joe Jennings apart? Also, there was that big-bellied Teamster Beamer taking an interest in his marriage. Beamer was a friend of Joe Jennings. It would be just like him to approach Lucille and make the friction that seemed to be pulling them apart worse.

Sergeant Coombs ground his teeth. One disadvantage of marrying a woman half his age was having to guard her from youthful, virile males on the make. Then there were the busybody parents. They had the strange idea no one would take care of their precious daughter properly. Married life was far more complicated than he had imagined. When one married the daughter he married the whole damned family. Reenlisting had looked so appealing -- freedom from the constant presence and advice of his in-laws, but now . . .

"I have to be getting back and take charge of the prison detail," Sergeant Coombs said, abruptly getting to his feet. "If you're going home I'll say good-bye. If you're staying on I'll see you this evening."

"We'll be here," Bill Morgan assured him. "Now that you have told us about the possibility of skulduggery, I want to see how it plays out. I'm getting the feeling the shysters who locked the prisoners in the brig are as guilty as those facing trial."

"All right, I'll see you folks about supper time," Coombs said, glancing around at the adjacent camps where activity had stopped, the campers intent on listening to what the big soldier with the impressive stripes had to say. A group of youngsters sidled forward, watching his every move.

"Where's your gun?" a boy braver than others called out. "How kin yuh kill Injuns with no weapon?"

Not to be out done, the speaker's companion shouted. "Yeah! We seen yuh, marchin' with those murderin' heathens. If'n they didn't hev those irons they'd probably scalp yuh."

Sergeant Coombs turned on his heel and strode away. "The way children are brought up today is shameful," he grumbled to himself. They had no respect for their elders. He was thankful that Lucille and he had none. For certain Mother Morgan would spoil them rotten.

XXV

Every one can master a grief but he that has it.

Shakespeare, "Much Ado about Nothing"

Colonel Loring inspected the Mounted Riflemen's compound with Sergeant Coombs close at his side. What he saw did not please him. The men were tolerable for once, but the animals and equipment were in terrible shape. The quartermaster supply shed was nearly empty. The entire compound looked more like a slum than a military post. He completed the inspection and ordered the sergeant to dismiss the men and strode grimly back to his office.

It was the journey across the Cascades that was too blame, Loring thought, as he rubbed his stump and contemplated what should be done. That last 130 miles over the Barlow Road decimated wagons and animals. After the Battle of Shiny Mountain, as the Indians named it, the quartermaster detachment had fallen apart.

Initially, he blamed the officers and teamsters, but the supply train encountered terrible conditions. Besides the natural obstructions of a mountainous road, the air was thick with forest fire smoke. Fallen trees blocked the roadway, and for four days the animals marched without forage. All along the route animals, wagons and supplies had to be abandoned. It was a wonder any of the train completed the journey.

The colonel massaged his stump and stared out the window to catch sight of teamsters Stillings and Beamer walking casually in the direction of the city. What business did they have slouching off work in the middle of the day? If they were fit enough to stroll around town they were fit enough to do some honest work. There were those supplies buried on this side of the Cascades. . . . Loring started to call for his orderly but changed his mind. This was a job for Sergeant Coombs to organize.

#

Late in the afternoon the court reconvened. Spectators were few, which was just as well. The prisoners, the main attraction, had been left in their gloomy cell. Judge Pratt declared interpretations were too lengthy, and he doubted if the prisoners understood a word. The session opened with dispatch. More indictments were read. The proceedings went smoothly. No interpreters were droning, no governor present to impress. The court did its business and quickly adjourned. Except for notifying the public of the charges against the prisoners, which everyone was aware of anyhow, nothing had been accomplished.

Teamsters Beamer and Stillings, whom the colonel had seen strolling toward town, peeked into the courtroom. Actually, they were expected to remain on post. They had recuperated from wounds received in the battle of Shiny Mountain but still were on half duty. Now that Colonel Loring had seen them looking fit it was a matter of hours until their soft regime would end.

"Galloping Jehoshaphat! This place's as gloomy as a tomb," Beamer muttered, closing the courthouse door. "I figured we'd hev a leetle gabfest with our ol' mess mates, Michael an' Joe, but they sure ain't here. Yuh s'pose we got time ta hunt 'em down? If Sergeant Coombs sees us waddlin' 'bout town he'll find somethin' nasty fer us ta do, that's fer certain."

"Say! Ain't those Cayuse lodges yonder?" Stillings pointed a bony arm toward the circle of tipis. "Sure as shootin', Two Feathers'll be bunkin' with thet vision seekin' uncle of his'n."

"Stillins', yuh constantly amaze me," Beamer said. "Fer a creature thet looks like a grasshopper, yuh hev an alarmin' amount of brains. Sure thet's where the rascals'll be. The galoots might even be fixin' vittles."

Deacon was the first to spot them. "Tarnation!" he exclaimed. "If'n it ain't thet Beamer fella an' his grasshoppin' sidekick. He ran forward to get a better look. "Hey! Yuh ugly galoot," he hailed Beamer. "Ain't yuh off yer range? Heared yuh got inta a scrap an' were nicked a bit, but yer lookin' fit as a fiddle."

The two old timers clapped each other on the back and swore the other hadn't changed a wink. They knew they were lying but neither wanted to hurt the feelings of the other. "I swan, yuh ol' mule skinner, yuh look better'n ever. I think yuh've thinned a bit. Yuh used ta hev a gut bigger'n a washtub."

Deacon spoke seriously but was appalled. He thought his teamster friend looked horrible. Two of his chins had disappeared, leaving deep lines to mark where they had been. The slack mouth made it clear most of the teamster's teeth were gone and his hair was almost snow white.

"Yuh ol' varmit, yuh ain't lookin' so bad yerself," Beamer replied. "Must be those kids of yers're keepin' yuh young. Yuh married off thet daughter yet? I'll bet she's purty as a Jersey heifer in a patch of clover. Wished me son, Clay, was 'round. They'd a made a handsome team. Yuh couldn't hev asked fer a better son-in-law."

"Yeah! Yeah, he was a good lad. 'Member him well. He always did his bit," Deacon said. What was the matter with the old fellow? Clay Beamer had been dead nigh on ten years. If he was still alive, he'd be far too set in his ways for Morning Star. Perhaps the old man was getting senile. Of course that lead he took on the mountain didn't do him any good. From what Sergeant Coombs had said he'd been shot a dozen times. The old geezer was tough, there was no doubt about that.

"Seems as I git older thet boy of mine an' me git closer an' closer. Yer an ol' preacher. Tell me 'bout this God of yers. Up yonder will me an' Clay be tagether agin?"

"'Twouldn't surprise me a wit. God keeps an eye on everythin'. He knows how yuh've pined fer yer son. Yuh kin take comfort in what the Good Book says, 'Ye shall be sorrowful, but yer sorrow shall be turned inta joy,' *John 16:33.*"

"Those're mighty satisfyin' words. I shore hanker ta be with the boy agin. Whilst I was laid up I took ta carvin' a head marker fer Clay's grave. Before I kick off I jest want him ta know how much I've missed him. I cain't tell yuh what losin' thet boy meant. The missus went ta pieces an' I ain't done much better. Course I had me work thet kept me busy. The missus didn't hev thet ta fall back on. Bless her." Beamer paused to wipe his eyes.

"I'm worse than a weepin' willow these days. I guess thet lead an' arras I took on the mountain affected me nerves. Course, fer the longest time after thet shoot-out I reckoned I'd be leavin' this world, an' I wished I would. Anyways, gittin' back ta Clay an' his grave. I ain't never seen it. If'n I put up this marker, I gotta find it. I know it's in Blackfeet country an' thet's a mighty big place. Yuh an' Joe Jennings're the only livin' folks who knows perzactly where 'tis. I'd beholdin' ta yuh if yuh could make a map. . . ."

Deacon turned away to hide the mist that suddenly dimmed his sight. He knew the old timer had taken his son's death hard, but to sorrow all these years. . . . No wonder he had turned snow white. But what could he do? Beamer didn't have the slightest idea how dangerous and impossible a trek into Blackfeet country could be. It was nearly ten years since that day Clay and Buck were killed. The country could have changed. Besides, to keep animals and the enemy from savaging the bodies, they did their best to blend the graves into the terrain. They were so well hidden when they rode away and looked back, they couldn't see them. He glanced away to avoid the hopeful look in Beamer's eyes.

"Maybeso Joe an' I kin come up with a sketch," Deacon mumbled. "Those trails up thar ain't perxactly roadways. We kinda stumbled onta the place by accident. They was mountains here an' valleys there. Then ol' Buck Stone said, 'let's try this ravine.' A pocket in the hills opcned up an' there we was on the best trappin' grounds we'd ever seen. Yep, gittin' there ain't goin' ta be easy. A body kin git mighty turned about."

"Yeah, but I gotta try. I ain't jest thinkin' fer meself, but the missus might quit grievin' so much if she knew Clay's grave was marked. When the time comes fer the dead ta rise an' be counted, she shore wants her beloved son ta be there."

XXVI

Laws are like cobwebs, which may catch small flies, but let wasps and hornets break through.
Jonathan Swift

On the second morning of the trial the outlook for the Cayuse brightened. As the statutes approved by the Oregon Provisional Government decreed, legal counsel was assigned to defend the accused. Three men supposedly qualified in jurisprudence were given the task: Kintzing Pritchette, Major Robert Reynolds and Captain Thomas Claiborne. Of the three only Pritchette, a former Pennsylvania lawyer and Territorial Secretary appointed by President Polk, had practical legal experience. Major Reynolds and Captain Claiborne were Mounted Riflemen who at one time or another had been involved in court martial exercises.

US Marshal Joe Meek viewed the entire defense arrangement with a jaundiced eye. "This legal falderal's a complete waste of time and money," he informed his stony-faced wife. "If I were judge I'd rap the gavel fer order an' ask fer a show of hands. Those fer hangin' put up yer paws. I wouldn't have to go further than thet. Anyone thet refused I'd level me Hawken an' they'd soon change their minds."

However, neither prosecution nor the defense team were about to slight their duties. A trial that had the attention of the nation was an opportunity to make a name for one's self. Therefore it should not be conducted haphazardly. In the attempt to understand the people they were defending, the three defenders made a visit to the Cayuse camp.

The discussions were difficult. The Cayuse had little understanding of the legal system. The defense team had equal difficulty in understanding the people they were supposed to defend. They found themselves listening to the Nez Perce outsider, Vision Seeker, more than they did the Cayuse leaders.

"Is it fair to judge these five men in Oregon City, a hard three day ride from their homeland and where the crimes they are charged with happened?" Vision Seeker had asked, his words spoken with the clipped Boston accent learned from Harvard College educated Buck Stone. Ironically, the idea of administering Indian justice on their own tribal lands had been proposed by the deceased Marcus Whitman.

The defense team members glanced at each other in confusion. They were the ones who had come to ask questions. Who was this tall, dark-faced man who butted in speaking the King's English far better than they did? To further befuddle them, he appeared to have a nose for potential loopholes in the law.

"These people you have been chosen to defend are strangers in a strange land." Vision Seeker paused to let the meaning of his words sink in. It was his first opportunity to impress upon courtroom officials the men they were defending were intelligent human beings lost in a culture they did not understand -- overwhelmed by forces that had turned their lives upside down.

"Neither the prisoners nor the Cayuse speaking for them have sufficient knowledge of your language to comprehend what is happening. Only in the simplest of terms do they understand your laws or how they work. They are befuddled by recent tragedies. They have lost family members and friends through sickness, not even your own medicine men can cure. Their lands have been taken from them. Their herds and their homes have been destroyed. . . ."

Vision Seeker paused to glance at the three white men. He could tell by their expressions they heard the words but the depth of their meaning passed them by. How could they, who believed themselves on a much higher level than the Indian, understand how the Cayuse people felt, the obstacles they faced, the fear that was in every heart? It was too overwhelming for he, himself, with all of his learning, to grasp. So much had happened so quickly and catastrophically, the Cayuse had lost touch with their heritage. No longer did they know who they were or what their purpose was on Mother Earth.

In the old days the Cayuse were a great Indian nation. Marvelous horsemen, they freely roamed the lands between the Cascades and beyond the Blue Mountains. They feared no one because no one dared stand in their way. With the coming of the white man the Cayuse lost their land and herds. Above all, the intruders from the east took away their pride and dignity. They demeaned their way of life, scoffed at their religion . . . made them feel worthless and unclean.

"Aagh!" Vision Seeker grimly thought. The chasm between the white man and red man would take generations to bridge. Why was he trying to do it in one afternoon? Instead of helping his friends, was he making the situation worse? He could not decide. He glanced at Young Chief and Stickus. Their stoic expressions told him nothing. It suddenly dawned on him they were as ignorant of what his words meant as were the white men. He had spoken rapidly without sign language. His Indian friends hardly understood anything he had said.

But the defense team members had taken in far more than Vision Seeker thought. They glanced at each other in amazement. This tall Indian dressed in fringed buckskins was an oracle. He spoke with such eloquence and authority he could not help but impress the jurors, but how could they work him in? Judge Pratt was a stickler for the rules.

The tall Indian was not a Cayuse tribesman and had no legal experience. As far as they knew, he had never been to school. If he began to poke holes in the prosecution's case there would be hell to pay. To have an unschooled savage out of the Bitterroot Mountain foothills show up the lawyers and judges and in front of the crowd of spectators. . . ! Perish the thought. Likely as not, Judge Pratt would bar him from the courtroom. That didn't mean they couldn't make use of him. His arguments were solid -- well-founded. Only an Indian person immersed in the native culture could express such a heart-rendering view of the Cayuse cause. "All we have to do is raise sufficient doubt in the jurors' minds that this trial is rigged," Captain Claiborne said. "We can start by raising objections to the venue. That Nez Perce man is right; does a court in Oregon City have jurisdiction over crimes committed in Cayuse country? After all, the prisoners regard themselves as citizens of a nation -- Cayuse Nation. Why not write up what in legal terminology is called a demurrer -- question the jurisdiction of the courts of the United States over what took place at Whitman's Mission?"

"Hmm!" Lawyer Prichette murmured. "Why not make it stronger? Since these crimes were committed in Cayuse country, the offenders should be tried under the laws and usage of said Cayuse Nation."

"Excellent! We'll start with that. As a last resort we can fall back on the venue change," Captain Claiborne enthused. "If I remember correctly the Northwest isn't even classified as Indian territory. In 1834 Congress passed a law stating that Indian Country over which US laws had jurisdiction, ended at the Rocky Mountains. The location where these crimes were committed is far west of the Rockies. We can argue the court has no authority over these people."

The three men of the defense team, glanced at each other and grinned. Not one of them had wanted to get involved in this messy business, but since they were in it they might as well make it as exciting as they could.

"Let's get this down on paper," Captain Claiborne said. "Nothing I'd like better than to show these Oregon City legal slickers they can't trounce us without receiving a damned good punch in the nose."

"Now," Lawyer Pritchette said after the document had been written to the defense team's satisfaction, "To make this acceptable to the court, we have to have the signatures of the defendants."

Once more they sat with Vision Seeker and explained the

demurrer and the need for the paper to be signed by the five prisoners. Vision Seeker thoughtfully read what was written. The lawyers were shocked when the tall Nez Perce pointed out a spelling error.

Getting the prisoners' signatures was more difficult than the lawyers expected. Major Reynolds and Captain Claiborne assumed they could announce their mission to the sentry, walk across the bridge and be admitted into the island prison, but they quickly found out differently. They were stopped short at the bridge. Sergeant Coombs, in charge of prison security, had his men well drilled. No matter if Governor Joe Lane, himself, appeared, they were not to let anyone into the prison without the password.

Sergeant Coombs, who was well known to the two officers, had to be sent for. He arrived and saluted. Captain Claiborne took it upon himself to dress the noncom down. "This is preposterous. What makes you think you can keep two officers waiting? What is the password? We need to get in to see the prisoners, and we need to do it right now."

Sergeant Coombs glanced at Vision Seeker and frowned. This tall Indian who looked so wise, was a friend of the Cayuse. After that raid on the prison detail at Cascade Portage every Indian, no matter how intelligent he appeared, was suspect. From his 20-odd years in the service he had found officers were not the best judges of character. Had this Indian man given them a song and dance with a sly trick in mind?

"Sir, please state your reason. Colonel Loring has given strict orders not to let anyone pass without his or the court's permission."

"Look here, Sergeant, if you value your stripes you'll do as I say," Claiborne blustered.

Pritchette stepped between the captain and the sergeant. "We understand your position, Sergeant. You have your duty and we have ours. To make a document acceptable to the court we must have the signatures of the prisoners. If our Nez Perce companion is a concern to you, he is essential to our efforts. He has graciously offered his services as interpreter."

"Yes, sir!" Coombs clicked his heels together, saluted the two officers and did a smart about-face. "Follow me gentlemen." He had known all along he would be forced to let them do as they asked, but the opportunity to wield the power Colonel Loring had placed in his hands had been too good to let pass.

XXVII

*. . . I know nothing to support a contention that the Indian was
treacherous, and capable of breaking faith when
he had made a fair engagement.*

James McLaughlin, "My Friend The Indian"

With the introductory formalities over, the long awaited
confrontation between prosecution and defense brought hordes
of people to the courthouse. Again, the space reserved for spectators was crammed to capacity with people sitting and standing
on the stairs leading to the second story that under normal cir-
cumstances served as the tavern dance hall.

Vision Seeker, who managed a seat alongside the Cayuse
leaders near the front of the crowd, could feel the tension mount.
He felt uncomfortable himself. Although everything appeared as
it should, a threatening sense of doom seemed to press on his
nerves. When his Cayuse companions and he came in the people
edged away. "Don't let those murderin' savages touch me," a
boy cried out, expressing the general feeling of prejudice that
seemed to have infected nearly every citizen in town.

Judge Pratt entered to take his chair. After everyone was
seated he glanced at the defense table. "Is defense council prepared to present its case?"

Captain Thomas Claiborne, Jr. leapt to his feet. "Your
honor, we ask for this case to be dismissed. This court is not
following the rule of law," he stated in a loud and belligerent
voice. "This trial is illegal and against the Constitution of the
United States. By allowing the courtroom procedure to continue,
we are in fact committing a heinous crime by persecuting a people
whose rights have been ignored. In short, this body has no jurisdiction over crimes committed in the Cayuse homeland as that
region is not included in what is classified as Indian territory by
the Congressional Act of 1834."

The spectators stared. What was taking place? Why didn't Judge Pratt shut this asinine Mounted Rifleman up? Even the prisoners shifted uneasily in their seats, their chains making a menacing clanking. What kind of council did these white people conduct, any way?

Kintzing Prichette of the defense team shook his head. He could tell by the high color of Judge Pratt's face that any sympathy the judge had for the prisoners and those who defended them, had vanished into the thick courtroom air. Captain Claiborne had just wasted the defense's most powerful argument.

Prosecutor Amory Holbrook was immediately on his feet. "The conduct of the defense is reprehensible. Springing a charge on the court like this is against legal protocol. Besides, it is frivolous and only meant to confuse the people." Holbrook turned to shake a forefinger at the defenders

"Fie! Fie! The offences under question indeed were committed in Indian Territory and therefore under the jurisdiction of the Oregon Territorial Provisional Government. No one can say otherwise. I leave it up to the honorable judge to decide."

Judge Pratt ran a hand through his thick, graying hair. He was as stunned as anyone by the fractious manner in which the trial proceedings had been launched. Damn those pesky Mounted Riflemen. They were taking their brash barrack-like behavior into the sanctity of the courtroom. This, he would not stand for. His reputation was at stake.

He knew about the borders Congress had placed on what was called Indian Territory, but the boundaries had been set before the Oregon question had been threshed out with the British. Technically, the blustery army captain was right. But one had to think of the law's intent. Certainly, if the legislators had envisioned this crime they would have stretched the boundary to include the region where it had taken place.

Judge Pratt's deliberations with himself took so long the spectators became restless. Even Marshal Meek gave him an anxious glance. Prosecutor Holbrook leaned against his work table to steady himself. The defense counsel was looking pleased. Judge Pratt cleared his throat. The people came from all over the valley expecting to witness a trial. By gad, he was not going to disappoint them.

"It is the opinion of the court that these crimes were committed in territory that falls under the jurisdiction of the laws of the United States of America and therefore, indeed, are the business of this court," Judge Pratt proclaimed. "Let us not pursue this line of argument any further. We have wasted enough time as it is."

Defense counsel Pritchette got to his feet. "Please, your honor, may the defense approach the bench?" he requested. "This matter is too crucial to gloss over it. If need be we should get a ruling from Washington."

Judge Pratt's face turned crimson. "Is the honorable defense counsel questioning my authority? If so I want you to know I was personally selected by United States President Polk to assume the duty of Oregon Territory judge, and as judge I say this court is within its rights to conduct this trial. Now, let's get on with it. How do the defendants plead? Have them stand and make their statements. If the court clerk pleases, will he record each plea?"

One by one the prisoners stood and, with much mumbling with the interpreters, pleaded innocent. Court Clerk George Curry made his notes and nodded when he was finished. The judge acknowledged his nod and reached for his gavel. "If there is no other business the court will adjourn." Before Judge Pratt could rap his gavel, the defense team was on its feet. Captain Claiborne, the last to rise, still was writing furiously a statement to present to the court.

"Your honor, the defense wishes to submit a petition," Claiborne said, holding up the paper on which he had been writing.

"Yes, well what is it?" the judge demanded.

"Your honor, a change of venue is requested."

Judge Pratt stared in disbelief. "What do you mean, change of venue? No, don't read it. Bring it to the bench." Judge Pratt studied the document and grimaced. "Do you swear this is true and made in good faith? I will not permit it in the court record until you sign to that effect and the five defendants do so likewise."

"Of course it is true and presented in good faith," Claiborne answered. "All we desire is justice for these people. No one can object to that."

Claiborne signed his name with a flourish. He handed the paper to the interpreters. A mumbling with the prisoners took place. Each prisoner dutifully signed his X. Spectators murmured. The obstinate Mounted Rifleman was at it again, taking his job as defense counsel too seriously.

"If I war thet judge, I'd give him his walkin' papers," said the unwashed bearded man who again sat spewing tobacco juice on Nancy Morgan's ginghams. "Everythin' war 'bout ta git goin' 'til Blabbermouth Riflemen throws 'nother spoke inta the wheel. Look at ol' Pratt, he's fit ta be tied."

The document was properly signed and again presented to the judge. He examined it carefully and handed it back. "The petition shall be read and put into the record," he ordered.

The courtroom hushed, every ear strained to hear what was to be said. "Hear yea, hear yea . . ." Listeners were incredulous. In essence the petition charged the defendants could not get a fair trial in the county called Clackamas. Should the prisoners be acquitted several citizens of the county had issued death threats against the defense. In addition, influential citizens had employed their influence to sway the public mind against the defendants, creating a climate, that regardless of the trial's outcome, would lead to the prisoners' deaths.

"In short," the reader concluded, "the inhabitants of this county (Clackamas) are so prejudicial that an impartial trial in this courtroom is impossible. The request seeks the removal of the trial to the adjoining county of Clark."

Bill Morgan clapped his hands and nudged his wife. "I'm glad somebody in this crowd wants to see justice done," he muttered in a whisper that carried across the crowded room.

"Sh-sh!" Nancy Morgan admonished. "Keep your opinions to yourself."

Bill Morgan's utterance was like a spark touching off gun powder. Spectators craned their necks to see who dared take such an outrageous stand. A housewife shook a menacing finger. A man in the front row turned to glare. The bearded, tobacco chewing old timer sitting next to Nancy Morgan, spit in disgust. The judge rapped his gavel and called for order.

Before the audience fell quiet a rumble of protest rippled through the courtroom. The prejudicial charge was a sore point. They, the citizens, were being accused of being bloodthirsty avengers. According to this petition, if the finding of the court displeased them, they would take the law into their own hands. The thought was monstrous. A minister seated in the front row started to rise as if to speak, then sank back. The charge was true. Almost everyone, including himself, expected to have the prisoners condemned and executed, and would not be satisfied until it was done.

US Marshal Meek did jump to his feet. These damned Mounted Riflemen from Colonel Loring on down made a mess of everything they did. Judge Pratt hammered his gavel. Gradually the crowd hushed and Joe Meek sat down.

Vision Seeker, who continued to follow every word spoken, smiled to himself. The Blue Coat officer indeed had made a wise move. Moving the trial to Clark County meant it would take place across the Columbia River in a region settled by the employees and supporters of Hudson's Bay who would have far greater sympathy for the Cayuse cause. What would the courtroom chief do now?

Judge Pratt grimly stared at the defense lawyers. He had to admit the petition struck at a weak spot in the proceedings. If the trial was moved across the Columbia, where many of the residents were Canadians, the indicted men would face a more lenient public. A jury selected from the likes of those people could very well render an acquittal verdict. If that happened the citizens of Oregon City would never forgive him. The murmur of disapproval told him the restless crowd was on the verge of getting out of hand.

Trial Judge Orville C. Pratt pounded his table top. "Petition request is denied," he thundered. "Court is adjourned."

THE CRY OF THE COYOTE

*I have seen my freedom disappear like the salmon going
mysteriously out to sea.*

Dan George, Coast Salish

Judge Pratt's denial of the change of venue request cast a pall over the occupants of the Indian camp. Cut Lip, who had scarcely uttered a word since arriving in Oregon City, climbed the escarpment that overlooked the city to pray for his brother's life. Stickus, Young Chief, and other Cayuse leaders sat in council. In silence they smoked the sacred medicine pipe, seeking guidance from The Great Mystery. The sawmill powered by the waters of Willamette Falls started up. The saw blade, inching through a log, began to whine and screech, causing the meditating council members to glance at each other in annoyance.

The prisoners, locked in their cell on the island in the river, and much nearer the screeching sounds, clasped their hands over their ears. "These white people are very clever," Tiloukaikt said during a break in the noise. "They know many ways of torturing their enemies."

Vision Seeker, who had sat with his Cayuse friends during the courtroom proceedings, was not at all surprised by Judge Pratt's verdict. During the legal maneuvering he had studied the actors in the drama much as he would the antics of a newly discovered animal species. The workings of Judge Pratt's brain were as easy to read as carvings on a tree. His thoughtful deliberations were a sham. Before the petition even was read the judge had made up his mind as to the response he would make.

The thoughts of the spellbound audience were obvious for all to see. When the verdict was announced the white faces turned to each other with smiles, eyes bright with delight. They were not to be denied. The trial would proceed as planned. From within their ranks a jury of 12 men, who would decide whether the prisoners were set free or condemned, would be chosen. Judge Pratt was to be commended. He was carrying out his duties well. There was no doubt in their minds, in a matter of days the killers of Marcus and Narcissa Whitman surely would hang.

Spectators who had breathlessly awaited Judge Pratt's verdict, were not the only ones elated by the outcome. The following morning US Marshal Meek arose early, whistling a bawdy tune he had picked up at some fur trappers' rendezvous. He trimmed his side whiskers and took extra special care with his attire. On reasonably good terms with his wife, he asked her to press a crimson sash he decided to use as a cummerbund for his already resplendent uniform. Not at all impressed by her husband's finery or his high position, she ran a cold iron over the cloth leaving it more wrinkled than before.

"Woman, this is an important day," Meek scolded. "Before sunset the curtain surely will fall on this legal falderal. Don't you see, the people will expect me to be in full fig? Warm up the iron and press that cloth right," he ordered. "Please," he added as her dark eyebrows furrowed into a frown.

Colonel Loring also was relieved by Judge Pratt's decision. Moving the trial to Clark County presented all sorts of problems. It would mean sending the prisoner and courtroom guard detachment, along with transport and supplies, to the new location. The move would further fragment his command. Already he had troopers stationed at The Dalles, Fort Vancouver and Astoria. Governor Lane informed him he intended to travel south to meet with the Rogue and Klickitat with a complement of troopers. This, also, would be a drain on his command. Then there were the supplies and gear cached on the Barlow Road. The snow in the foothills had melted; it was time to send a detail after them.

"Hmm!" Loring grunted, rubbing his missing arm's tingling stub. He had intended to order a column of wagons under Sergeant Coombs to collect the abandoned materials. Now, that was out of the question. Coombs would be tied up until after the trial and punishment of the Cayuse prisoners had occurred. With Judge Pratt and Marshal Meek pumping up already inflated egos by playing to the crowd, that could take a long while.

Colonel Loring glanced through the skimpy roster of available troopers. The names of Beamer and Stillings met his eye. "By gum!" It was time those lazy slackers went to work. "Noonan!" he shouted for his orderly. "Round up Privates Beamer and Stillings. Tell them to report to me on the double-quick."

Noonan, recognizing that his superior was in one of his irritable moods, ran outside to call Field, the acting quartermaster corporal. The regular corporal had been one of the lucky deserters escaping to California's rich gold diggings. Field, still unsure how to handle his new noncom responsibilities, shouted for the two teamsters. When they did not respond he sent a runner to the barracks. The runner returned to report Beamer and Stillings had not been seen since morning chow.

"Damn those no-good louts," Corporal Field swore. "Yuh'll have to report to the colonel they're AWOL."

"I can't do that. The colonel is in high temper. He'll eat me alive," the orderly moaned. "Maybe they're in the pasture tending the horses and mules."

As was their custom, shortly after answering morning roll call and eating a substantial breakfast at the cook house, Beamer and Stillings quickly did the limited duties assigned to them, then slipped away from camp. Sometimes they sauntered down to the pool hall to while away the day, other times they went fishing. On this day, they stopped at the public stable. The farrier, deluged with orders from out-of-towners, had previously offered them pay to help shoe horses and mules.

Unaware of the commotion their absence was causing, after the shoeing chore the two teamsters collected their pay and sauntered toward the army post, debating on ways to spend their earnings. As they passed the building where the trial was taking place, the courthouse doors were flung open. The noisy crowd spilled into the street. Beamer and Stillings quickly turned away, making haste for a hiding place. If regimental officers or non-coms caught them downtown they would face embarrassing questions that could land them in the brig.

"Hey, there! Hold up!" An authoritative shout stopped the teamsters in their tracks.

"Of all the blisterin' luck," Beamer groaned, turning back, but instead of a member of the regimental staff it was Deacon Walton! "Yuh ol' scoundrel, what're yuh still doin' 'round heya? Thought yuh'd be half way ta the Sweetwater."

"Yuh 'member me ol' sidekick, Stillin's," Beamer said turning to his lanky partner.

"Yeah, he was with yuh the other day, fella thet does the grasshopper hop. Why're we hidin' in this alley, anyway? Why don't yuh fellas come over to me camp. Maybeso, we kin round up a snort an' cook some vittles."

"We're sorta dodgin' the law," Beamer confided. "We's 'sposed ta be in the regimental compound. If we're caught wanderin' 'round out here, we could wind up in the hoosegow alongside the Cayuse."

"Well, someun should be keepin' 'em company. They'er sure gittin' the dirty end of the stick," Deacon growled. "Don't know how I'll be able ta look me Indian people on the Sweetwater in the face again."

"Yeah," Beamer agreed, glancing sympathetically at his old friend. "I 'spect it does go agin' the grain, yer hevin' a Cheyenne family."

#

As usual, Sergeant Coombs marched the prison detail back to the prisoners' dank dungeon and made certain his Cayuse charges were securely locked in and guards posted. Satisfied no detail had been overlooked, Sergeant Coombs hurried to regimental headquarters to fill out the evening report Colonel Loring demanded. He was in an especially great hurry because he had been promised a pass to spend the night with his wife. All day he had schemed a way where they could be alone, which, with the crowded conditions in the city, wasn't easy. He finally practically commandeered a room that was little larger than a broom closet. This business of having a beautiful wife without being able to be near her, fondle her . . . Ah! It was driving him crazy. How could Lucille and he possibly work out their difficulties without getting off by themselves?

Much to his chagrin, Sergeant Coombs found the headquarters office in turmoil. The orderly greeted him breathlessly.

"Thank goodness you're here. The colonel's havin' a fit. He's got it in his noodle we've gotta go after those supplies left beside the Barlow Road on the double-quick. He can't find hide nor hair of the teamsters. Apparently Beamer an' Stillings have gone over the hill. He wants you to run them down. He told me to send you right in." The orderly motioned with his head toward the colonel's office door.

"Oh, no!" Sergeant Coombs groaned. His carefully planned evening with Lucille was ruined. The colonel would not rest until Beamer and Stillings were found and punished. As soon as he caught sight of Colonel Loring's glowering face he knew he was right. The colonel didn't even return his salute

"Those blistering slackers, Beamer and Stillings, have disappeared. We let them have soft duty because of their wounds and look at what they do. I want you to take your prison detail and track them down. I don't care if it takes you all night."

"Sir, the men just came off guard duty and have to be on the job in the morning," Coombs objected. "Why not send Corporal Field? He knows the city as well as I do."

"Wagh! Acting Corporal Field couldn't find his backsides with both hands. Now, quit arguing with me. If you want to keep your stripes, get after those teamsters straightway."

Sergeant Coombs drew himself up straight and snapped a salute. He would kill those two bloody teamsters. They had given him trouble every step of the way across the plains. Now this, when he had gone to great trouble and expense to have an intimate few hours with his wife. To lose out because of these two teamsters was too much to take.

"Bloody murder!" he exploded so vehemently Colonel Loring flinched.

"Control yourself, Sergeant. You can handle these fellows."

"Yes, sir." Sergeant Coombs snapped a salute and wheeled about so smartly he nearly fell. Then, at the office door he turned back. "What do you want me to do with them, lock them in the guardhouse?"

"No, get them back here and put them to work. I want two wagons ready to roll in the morning. It's time we got those supplies left abandoned on Barlow Road."

"Yes, sir." Sergeant Coombs saluted again and cursed under his breath. Not only did he have to find the two AWOL teamsters, he also had to put them to work and make certain they did it. He audibly groaned. The night with his wife was lost. The disappointment was almost too much to bear.

Sergeant Coombs strode away, kicking at lumps in the road. To butter up Mrs. Morgan he had told her of his plans. She had been delighted. She would start the evening off by cooking a festive dinner and see that Daughter had her overnight things ready.

Lucille's reaction even was more satisfying. "Oh!" she had trilled. "It will be a second honeymoon -- only better . . ." She had blushed, remembering the first frustrating weeks of their marriage when his manhood failed him. The pink face framed in hair the color of gold made her appear more desirable than ever before.

"Damnation!" The sergeant gritted his teeth until they ached.

XXIX

*Better to have a friend on the road than gold or silver
in your purse.*

French Proverb

Beamer and Stillings, the AWOL Mounted Riflemen, were having a pleasurable visit. Teamster Beamer, who liked nothing better than an audience, related tales of his days upon the road. Deacon and the Jennings brothers listened more out of respect than of interest. Most of the stories Beamer told they had heard before. Vision Seeker, who had not heard them, sat silent, his face expressionless. The man had an endless flow of words. Yet he was fascinating. His bright eyes, bearded cheeks and quick movements reminded Vision Seeker of an overlarge prairie dog. His bragging, blustering talk covered a heart as large as his belly. But today Teamster Beamer, after reminiscing about the past turned the conversation to the present.

"I tell yuh, fellas, after all the things I did, it's got me ta wonderin' why I'm stuck in this place called Oregon City. I've jest 'bout had the army up ta here." He raised a big hand level with the top of his head.

"I ain't been home ta see the missus in over a year. Now some folks hev a hankerin' fer this kinda life, but thet ain't me. I've been over too many trails ta hev some young officer who ain't got sense enuff ta come in outta the rain, tellin' me perzactly what ta do: when ta sleep, when ta eat, when ta git up and when ta do what yuh hev ta do. Now yuh take Serjn't Coombs he ain't comfertable . . ."

"Hsst!" Joe interrupted, motioning with his eyebrows. Sergeant Coombs stood not 10 feet away, hands on his hips. His nose pointed toward Beamer and Stillings like a hunting dog that had spotted something unpleasant.

"Dad blast it," Beamer said quickly. "Me an' Stillin's scoured town fer a spare set of butt chains an' ain't found a single one" He glanced up at Sergeant Coombs.

"Hi, Sarge," he continued, giving the belligerent noncom an amiable glance, "pull up a chair and make yerself at home. I was jest tellin' these gents 'bout the sorry state of our equipment. Hitchin' up's worse than hevin' yer teeth yanked out one by one. Harness leather's so dried and cracked a good pull'd tear most of it in half. Then there's the weak reaches, tongues, single trees, double trees an' brake beams. The whole lot 'twouldn't make a decent batch of kindlin'."

"Listen, you old wind bag," Coombs exploded. To be invited to sit with these lunkheads who were costing him a cozy night with his wife was the last straw. "Come to attention! You two no-goods have taken the business of annoying me an inch too far. So you don't like being told what to do. Let me tell you something, I'm going to make you like it or you'll be spending the rest of your enlistment in the stockade. Trouble is you've had it too easy, too long. Your period of rest and relaxation is gone. The colonel wants you heading up the Barlow Road at first light in the morning."

Dawn found Sergeant Coombs waiting impatiently for Beamer and Stillings to appear. He was in a foul mood. The previous evening he had arrived at the Morgan campsite long after dinner had been prepared and served. When he made his excuses, Lucille broke down in tears. Mrs. Morgan glowered as if she was about to explode. Dad Morgan puffed on his pipe, his expression one of a dog with a nose full of porcupine quills.

Deacon, Joe and Michael, who had come to see their teamster friends off, stood well to one side as Sergeant Coombs berated the teamsters and gave them final instructions.

"Now get out of here," Coombs ordered. The wagon rumbled away, the creaking wheels squelching ruts in the mud. A pop of Beamer's whip and cheery "tallyho" rang out to echo back from nearby hills.

Sergeant Coombs turned to glower at the teamsters' friends. "What're you standing around gawking for?" he roared. "This is an army post, not a stage stop. If you want to see your friends off, go down the road and do it out of my sight."

The teamsters' three friends paid the sergeant no attention. Their eyes were on the wagons bouncing along the rough track to disappear into a growth of trees that grew down to the river bank. Deacon broke the silence.

"Yuh know ol' Beamer's gittin' too long in the tooth ta be herdin' a bunch of mules. I swear those long eared critters hev gotta sixth sense thet makes 'em downright ornery. When their handler ain't up ta snuff they sniff it out quicker'n a huntin' dog kin flush a covey of quail. I'll betcha a jug of firewater afore the trip's over they'll giv Beamer as much trouble as he kin handle."

Deacon took a chaw and spit in Sergeant Coombs direction. "I don't like it at all. At this time of year thet trail inta the hills is gonna be straddled with wind fallen trees an' washouts thet could swalla team an' wagon. Besides, there's thet worn-out equipment."

The three men rode back to camp. Michael built up the fire and Deacon started to cook breakfast. They ate in silence until Deacon laid his tin plate aside and gave his tobacco stained beard a swipe with the back of his hand.

"Cain't git Beamer an' Stillin's off me mind. Think I'll tag along in case somethin' happens. Time I was takin' off fer the Sweetwater, anyhow." The ex-preacher began to roll up his blankets and tie them behind the saddle that perched precariously on the striped mealymouthed mule he rode. For a moment the brothers watched, then began to throw their packs together, too.

On his way to roust out the prison guard Sergeant Coombs was surprised to see the squat mountain man with the tobacco stained beard and the Jennings brothers ride away on the trail Stillings and Beamer had taken. Sergeant Coombs' dour mood brightened. How could he be so lucky? He had rid himself of the two troublesome teamsters. If the teamsters' three friends had left too . . . ah, with all the troublemakers gone now was the chance he needed to patch up his marriage.

#

The Morgan family also noticed the departure of the Jennings brothers and the defrocked mountain man. Their feelings were mixed. Bill Morgan breathed a sigh of relief. Lucille's loves were as upsetting as a house full of fleas. She had a good man. She had better come out of her blue funk and make the most of it. Of course the previous evening's disaster didn't help. All day Daughter Lucille had been as jumpy as a long tailed cat under a rocking chair. After waiting hours for that sergeant husband to appear, when he finally did arrive she virtually fell apart.

Mrs. Morgan watched the Jennings depart with a catch in her throat. It seemed everything she did to bring happiness to her daughter ended in tragedy. Yesterday she'd had such high hopes that Algeron and Lucille would come to an understanding. Instead, the day ended in failure, if anything the gulf between them had widened. Now the love of her daughter's heart was departing, perhaps riding out of her life. She glanced at Lucille. The pain she suffered must be terrible. Lucille looked more pallid than ever. "Poor child! How hard it is to be young and in love and no one can do anything about it," she commiserated.

Lucille, who knew her parents were watching her, did her best to appear unconcerned. She did not feel at all well. It was the two men in her life that made her feel that way, pregnant by one and heartsick over the other. She was irate with them both. Her husband was more in love with his sergeant stripes than he was with her. Last night was a good example. They had waited and waited; only after they had given him up did he arrive and then sat stewing over some silly assignment the colonel had ordered him to do.

She was equally furious with the other man, Joe Jennings. He knew how she felt about him. His tender glances and sweet smiles had led her to believe he felt the same, that he was leading up to ask for her hand, but he never did. If he had said a single word that he really cared, even though it was rumored he had been killed, she would have waited for him. Now he rode off without a good-bye or a look in her direction.

"Oh!" she groaned. Men! They were all alike. They caused more trouble than they were worth. Look at Father. Never did he make one attempt to give advice. He went along with whatever Mother decided. He knew she had fallen head over heels in love with Joe Jennings but what did he really think about it? What guidance or encouragement had he given? Not one word did he say directly to her.

Lucille sniffed and blew her nose. "I must not let this get me down," she sternly said to herself. "Mother is right. I have a good man and I'd better be thankful, make the best of what I have." The thought did not ease the pain in her heart. She was so tormented she broke down and cried.

#

"Hiya!" Beamer greeted when Deacon and the brothers rode alongside. "Reckoned yuh an' thet Coombs fella'd be celebratin' our departure. Even though I saved his hide on the mountain, he jest don't cotton ta me. He's so all fired 'fraid of losin' his stripes, he cain't act natural. I'll betcha he'd brace his own grandmammy if he thought it'd make him look good in the eyes of the colonel.

"Anyways, it's good ta git outta his sight fer a while, an' mighty kinda yuh fellas ta catch up. At me day an' age yuh never know when ol' Grim Reaper'll come sneakin' over the hill. Now, thet we'er a good ways outta town, let's pull over an' make camp. We'll heat up a leetle beans an' bacon an' hev a bit of sup."

The wagons were pulled well off the track. Under a group of towering firs, Deacon, who had ridden ahead, announced it a good place to stay the night. The mules were unharnessed, horses unsaddled, rubbed down and staked in a meadow of tall grass. Michael built a fire Indian style, laying the sticks of wood in a circle and lighting it in the center.

Stillings took a Hudson's Bay copper pot, filled it half

full of water from a cold rushing creek and hung it from a make-shift spit over the flames. From one of the supply wagons came fixings for the meal, beans and a slab of bacon which Deacon began to slice into bits. Stillings stood to one side clucking his approval like a setting hen that had hatched its first chick.

Beamer sat by the fire, resting his big belly on his knees, looking pleased. "Yep," he said, "this's the life . . . off by our-selves with friends gathered 'round like a family."

After the meal, which Grasshopper Stillings had spiced with dry and green cuttings from a trail side bush, stories began to flow. For once Beamer quietly sat and listened as Deacon spoke of the days when Young Joe Jennings joined Buck Stone's trapping brigade.

"He was so green yuh could see grass sproutin' from his ears," Deacon began. He went on to tell how the lad had been rolled and robbed by the biggest tough in St. Louie, One-Eyed Link. "Yep, but the lad had guts. He an' Buck ran the one-eyed rascal down an' made off with his duds while he was entertainin' a hussy in a back room of Rocky Mountain Saloon."

The next morning the camp was somber. Breakfast was cooked and eaten in silence. The mules were harnessed and horses saddled hardly before a word was uttered. "Well, fellas," Beamer finally said. "So long until we meet agin'." He popped the whip and the wagon began to move.

Deacon merely lifted his hand and reined his mule up the trail. The two brothers retraced their steps to Oregon City and the courtroom trial.

XXX

*The white man's strange customs which I could not
understand, pressed down upon me until
I could no longer breathe.*

Dan George, Coast Salish

Joe and Michael arrived back in Oregon City to find themselves jostling for space in the courtroom. Muddy buggies, spring wagons, riding horses, and other means of transportation lined the streets. The atmosphere was much like Joe remembered of Fair Day that annually came the first September weekend to his old home town in Middlesex County, Massachusetts.

Once inside the courthouse the brothers glanced up to see that the group they had elbowed and jostled for space with, included Macon Laird, Tildy and adopted David Malin Laird. Their tall British brother-in-law, who towered over everyone, nodded a greeting. Tildy, half hidden behind a man's canvas clad burly back, gave them a rueful half smile and David waved a hand.

"Worse than getting Agnes in her stall," David shouted, referring to the old holstein cow that was his chore to milk.

Astonished by their presence, Joe pushed his way near. "Where's Granddad? Is he all right?"

"Granddad volunteered to stay home with Baby John," Tildy answered. "Besides, he's about the only one in the valley who isn't interested in the trial . . . says people are treating a deadly serious business like a picnic."

"Granddad is quite right," Joe said, making their presence appear even more ghoulish. Of course Macon had reason to be there. He surely would have died if it hadn't been for the Whitmans. His bloody, beaten body had been found one cold night on the trail to Fort Walla Walla. For weeks the Whitmans cared for him as though he was one of their own.

Tildy, too, had to feel strongly about the trial. During the campaign to apprehend the Whitman Mission killers, her first husband had been killed by the Cayuse. Also, she had taken great interest in the work of the Presbyterian missionaries, especially that of Marcus and Narcissa Whitman. She first met Marcus Whitman at a church social -- a fund raising event when he made the trek east in the winter of '42-'43. She would never forget the time or place. After the social she returned home to find Granny Jennings had passed on. She had been enjoying herself while her beloved grandmother, who had reared her as if she were her own daughter, had taken her last breath.

Young David? This was no place for a boy, or was it? After Helen Mar Meek and Mary Ann Bridger, little David was the third half-breed child the Whitmans adopted. Deserted by his father and discarded by his mother -- nearly naked, dirty and covered with body and head lice -- little David, hardly more than a baby, was presented to Narcissa Whitman. At first the missionary woman hesitated. How could she manage a third half blood, one so small and who needed so much care?

"I could not shut my heart against him," Narcissa had said. "I washed him, oiled him and bound up his wounds (some malicious person had burned his naked body with glowing campfire embers) and dressed him and cleaned his head of lice."

"Yes," Joe thought. There was no one in the courtroom more deserving to be there than David Malin Laird. He had witnessed the massacre, seen his adopted parents and other family members atrociously murdered, then been held captive for a month by the killers. After surviving these tortures he cruelly had been parted from surviving family members and playmate friends. McBean, Hudson's Bay factor at Fort Walla Walla, would not allow David Malin to leave with the other survivors.

After the Whitman tragedy captives were ransomed and began to board the flotilla of bateaux, McBean declared, "This lad's father is Canadian and a former employee of Hudson's Bay. He is a British subject and must remain with his own kind."

Joe swallowed hard. The memory of little David Malin

standing on the river bank, crying his eyes out as his friends and family members boarded the rescue bateaux and sailed away, always caused a lump to well up in his throat. His brother-in-law, Macon Laird, himself British, had saved the day by wrapping his arms around the sobbing boy. He placed him on his tall horse, mounted up behind him and rode away, telling the lad what a wonderful life they would lead together. Perhaps by giving his family the chance to witness the trial was another display of the man's kindly thoughtfulness. Seeing the criminals answer for their terrible deeds might wash away some of the terror that must linger in the recesses of young David's mind.

Suddenly the courtroom came alive. "Hear Yea! Hear yea!" Judge Pratt had entered. There was a clatter of scraping chairs and feet as the people stood, and a rustle of clothes and whisper of voices as they sat. The third day of the trial was underway. The courtroom fell silent; the crowd waited expectantly. The horrific nightmare that had taken place on the bloodied mission grounds would now be related and debated, but, for the moment, the crowd was disappointed. The minutes of the second day of the trial had to be read and translated.

The reading of the minutes finished. The expectations of the crowd again grew to fever pitch, but again the audience was disappointed. Defense lawyer, Captain Claiborne, jumped to his feet. "The defense requests a delay in the proceedings. A crucial witness has been found in the land of the Cayuse."

"Ridiculous," Judge Pratt uttered. "This court is not going to be held up for such frivolous nonsense. It's time we picked a jury and get on with our business."

Captain Claiborne would not give in. "Chief Tiloukaikt swears this witness, named Quishem, has a straight tongue. He will prove the late Dr. Whitman administered medicines to many Cayuse who afterward died, among them wives and children of some of the defendants.

"Furthermore, he expects said witness to prove a certain Joseph Lewis, who resided at Waiilatpu, to have been responsible for inciting the massacre. Lewis claimed the Cayuse were dying because the medicine Whitman dispensed was poison. Furthermore, Lewis overheard Dr. Whitman say that he would kill all Cayuse by spring -- he would then have their horses and lands. This witness, Quishem, will also prove it is a law of the Cayuse to kill medicine men whose patients die."

"I am surprised the defense even suggests that the court consider such a ridiculous request," Judge Pratt tartly replied. "The man Joe Lewis is a murderer and should be facing trial along with these other men. Whatever he is quoted as having said is worthless. I'll not have the legal process held up to subpoena a witness who has nothing but drivel to offer. If these delaying tactics continue the entire defense team will be charged for contempt. Marshal Meek, bring in the jury panel members."

Joe Meek strode across the courtroom and hollered through the open door, "Bring those fellas in and be quick about it." A sizeable group of men who Meek already had selected and had been cooling their heels in the morning breezes, straggled in. Many of those chosen to serve as jury members had relatives and friends in the crowd, prompting a wave of hands and a scattering of ribald greetings.

"Hey, ther, Sid, sho' 'em how this legal business oughta be done," a high squeaky voice rang above the rest.

Judge Pratt rapped his gavel. "That's enough of that!"

With the panel of jurymen seated, Judge Pratt instructed the audience on what was to come. "From this group of some 25 or so men picked at random from the citizenry of Clackamas county, 12 of these men will be selected as jurors. The names of these men are on slips of paper in a bag held by court clerk, George Curry. I now request him to take 12 slips from the bag. As each slip is drawn the name of the individual will be called. The person named is then to take a seat in the two rows of chairs reserved for the jury."

The spectators perked up. Perhaps a friend or relative would seal the fate of the five Cayuses? They smiled in pleasure or frowned in disappointment as one by one the names were read and the 12 prospective jurors took their seats. When the 12th juror dropped into his chair, the prosecutor stood. The audience breathed a sigh. The preliminaries were done. Details of the grisly crimes would now unfold. Instead, Prosecutor Holbrook began to question the jurors. Did they know about the killings at Whitman's Mission? What was their attitude toward Indians? Did they object to the death penalty?

"What's the matter with this bird?" a man in the audience muttered testily. "One would havta go ta the hinterlands of Mongolia ta find a body thet ain't heerd of these ghastly crimes."

Attitudes toward Indians were varied. "I seen some good Indians in me time," a bearded prospective juror replied. "Course yuh cain't rely on 'em. They may show up fer work or they may not. Then when yuh do git 'em on the job, they're apt ta slope off an' go fishin're somethin' like thet."

There were few objections to the death penalty. "The Good Book says an eye fer an eye. What's good enough fer God's good enuff fer me," was the bearded man's answer.

Holbrook finished questioning. The defense team took over, grilling each man with determination. To get 12 impartial jurors was an impossibility but the death penalty required an unanimous vote. The best they could hope for was to select at least one juror who would not succumb to public sentiment and would hold out for acquittal or a lessor penalty than execution.

One potential jury member after another was declared unfit to serve on what were called peremptory challenges. Judge Pratt fidgeted while the defense mowed prospective jurors down until the panel group was depleted. Still the defense was not satisfied.

"We need more panel members," Captain Claiborne declared. "We are entitled to three more peremptory challenges."

Judge Pratt looked disgusted. Marshal Meek scowled. "All right," Judge Pratt agreed. "Marshal Meek, round up a few qualified men. No, not from the audience -- bring them in from the outside."

While Joe Meek departed in search of additional panel members, the audience squirmed and whispered among themselves. A few got up and left. It was nearly noon. Perhaps when court took up again the legal wrangling would be over.

Soon Joe Meek returned with a few men who were obviously upset and for good reason. They were the ones who had departed from the courtroom in disgust. Judge Pratt pretended not to notice. "Proceed with the jury selection," he ordered.

Finally, with the jury selected, Judge Pratt had them stand for the "swearing in." There was a mumble of ayes as they agreed to "truly try and truly deliverance make between the United States of America and the prisoners at bar . . . so help me God."

"Gentlemen, take your seats. The jury is now impaneled," Judge Pratt instructed. He glanced at the prosecutors' table and nodded his head. Prosecutor Holbrook advanced on the jury.

"You are here to judge the prisoners at the bar. The crimes they committed have shocked the nation. It is your business, the business of this court, to see that they pay for these heinous crimes." He continued by repeating the indictments. The prisoners stoically looked on. The interpreters glanced at each other and shrugged. How could one translate with no words in the Cayuse language to make the meaning clear?

After opening remarks, Prosecutor Holbrook called his first witness, a Mrs. Eliza Hall. The crowd hushed. The prisoners came alive. Here was someone they remembered. She was the mother of five children. Her man had been working on the mission house when the killing began. The Cayuse attempted to shoot him. He dove into the Walla Walla River and escaped. The attackers searched for him but he was never found.

Eliza Hall stood to be sworn in. Judge Pratt glanced at his watch and rapped the gavel. "The court will break for lunch," he announced.

A wave of disgusted groans arose from the spectators. They had sat on hard chairs all morning and had yet to hear a single eye witness account of the Whitman Mission disaster.

THE CRY OF THE COYOTE

XXXI

*We ask that the same law shall work alike on all men. If an
Indian breaks the law, punish him by the law. If a white man
breaks the law, punish him also. . . .*

Chief Joseph, Nez Perce

The court reconvened with a sense of urgency. During a
break in the proceedings Judge Pratt advised Prosecutor Holbrook
he wished to complete the testimony quickly. "There is no point
in dragging this out. Every hour spent in court is costing the
Provisional Government money it does not have."

Prosecutor Holbrook nodded. There was news a ship had
passed Astoria on its way up the Columbia. Figuratively speaking, Pratt wanted to clear the decks for mercantile transactions.
Crates of merchandise consigned to the judge were probably in
the hold of the incoming craft. The quicker it was unloaded and
offered for sale, the greater the profit.

Holbrook scowled. Regardless of Pratt's desire to shorten
the trial, he would deal with the case as he saw fit. He had little
liking for the judge, thought him conceited and devious. Besides, they both had political ambitions and their beliefs were
miles apart. Pratt would soon push to be the next delegate to the
Democratic convention. Holbrook was leader of a political action group, the Know-Nothings, whose members pledged to com-
bat Catholicism by voting solely for native born Protestants.

Pratt and Holbrook agreed on one point. The trial of the
five Cayuse fit into their ambitions perfectly. It provided exactly
the right forum to impress upon the citizenry that they were men
on the move, men who could shape the destiny of Oregon Territory. With this thought uppermost in his mind, Prosecutor
Holbrook began to question the trial's first witness.

"Mrs. Hall, let us go back to November 29, 1847 when

the terrible Whitman Mission massacre took place. . . ."

The courtroom grew silent. This woman had been wid-
owed at the horrible event . . . seen the shocking killings, and had
spent a month as captive of the bloody Cayuse. The Cayuse del-
egation stirred uneasily. This woman was trouble. While in their
hands she never ceased ranting about the hardships she and her
fellow prisoners were enduring.

Vision Seeker, who sat alongside the Cayuse leaders, ignored the crowd of spectators. His attention was glued to the
proceedings. His thinking was simple. By taking note of every
move and every word judge, prosecutor and witness made and
said, perhaps he could discover what the white man called loopholes that might save the three innocent victims. Even if he could
not help save them it still was important to learn how the white
man's legal system worked. His instinct warned him this was not
the last time Indian people would find themselves charged with
crimes and have to stand trial.

Vision Seeker quickly understood the prosecution's tactics. The man called Holbrook placed the widow woman on the
witness stand first as she was certain to draw sympathy. The
jurors, who were so critical to the trial's outcome, would remember how Mrs. Hall looked and what she said. He leaned forward,
his eyes intent on both the prosecutor who asked the questions
and on the lady who would answer them.

"Mrs. Hall I understand on November 29, 1847, you were
staying at the Whitman Mission in Waiilatpu, is that correct?"

"Yes, my family was living in what was called the Emigrant House."

"Would you recount what happened that day?"

"It was the day of the killin's."

"When you say killings, do you mean the murders of Doctor and Narcissa Whitman?"

"Yes."

"In your own words tell us what you saw?"

"I heard gunshots an' went to the door. In front of the

Mission House an Indian man was strikin' Doctor Whitman with a hand ax."

"Is the man who struck Dr. Whitman among the prisoners?"

"Yes." Mrs. Hall pointed. "It's the man with the big nose called Tiloukaikt."

"You are certain that is the person you saw wielding the hand ax that killed Missionary Whitman?"

"I will see that cruel face until the day I die." The witness went on to describe the shooting of Narcissa Whitman and Andrew Rogers, the schoolmaster, and the murder of Jacob Hoffman who had been butchering a beef. The details were recited so vividly and precisely the audience leaned forward in their seats so not to miss a single grisly word. Widow Hall had to have relived the tragic experience until it was etched in her brain.

But to Vision Seeker the evidence did not ring true. Was the prosecution in such a hurry to convict the prisoners they had instructed the witness what to say? And if they did, who would stand up and question the truth of the widow's statements? Vision Seeker glanced at Stickus and Young Chief, who stoically watched the trial unfold. Even with the help of interpreters they had little understanding of the damning evidence the widow woman recounted.

Prosecutor Holbrook, feeling he had drawn as many damaging details as he could from the first witness, turned her over to the defense for cross-examination.

"I must commend you on your remarkable memory, Mrs. Hall," Captain Claiborne began. "You say you saw one of the accused strike Doctor Whitman."

"Yes, that is true."

"You were in what you call the Emigrant House and the crime took place in front of the Mission House?"

"Yes, that is what I said."

"How far apart are these two houses would you say?"

"Near enuff to see the murderin' heathens do their killin'."

"Make a guess," Claiborne persisted.

"Maybeso, a hundred steps."

"And you clearly saw this man hatchet the doctor?"

"Yes."

"Hmm." Claiborne shuffled the papers he held, debating whether or not to challenge the witness' statement. Pretrial investigations implied that Whitman was struck down in the Mission House kitchen, not in front of the Mission House. Rather than press Widow Hall, Claiborne sat down. It would do no good to badger this witness who obviously had the sympathy of crowd and jury.

Although short, the cross-examination gave Vision Seeker food for thought. A person's memory was fragile and often undependable. Certain things were remembered and others forgotten. Over time details become enlarged or diminished. Events that personally affected them were embellished.

In the case of Mrs. Hall, grief and prejudice would slant her memory. She wanted vengeance and hated Indians. The distance from the Emigrant House to the Mission House was a good example. From what he could remember it was a considerable distance and, unless she stepped away from the Emigrant House doorway, it was doubtful she had a clear view of Mission House.

That was the trouble of holding the trial so distant from the crime scene. As far as he knew, neither prosecutors nor defenders had been on the grounds at Waiilatpu. They based their arguments on artists' sketches and the words of others. The slipshod proceedings made Vision Seeker incensed. Hopefully, the next witness would tell a different story, one not so damaging.

Vision Seeker's hopes were dashed. Prosecutor Holbrook called twelve year-old Elizabeth Sager to the witness stand. Elizabeth Sager had lost two brothers and a sister during the Whitman Mission debacle. The brothers, John and Frank, were shot down. Six year-old Louise, who had been sick with the measles, died a week after the massacre while captive of the Cayuse. Sympathy for Elizabeth Sager would be far greater than that for Widow Hall.

XXXII

It will be recollected that this is the most difficult range
(Cascades) of the whole route.

Colonel W. W. Loring, Regiment of the Mounted Riflemen

The track that crossed the Cascade Mountains called the Barlow Road, was not one travelers took lightly. No one knew this better than did the detachment of Mounted Riflemen who accompanied regimental supply wagons and livestock remuda over the trail in 1849. Two-thirds of the horses and mules perished or were stolen by Indians. Wagons and supplies were abandoned or left by the roadside from one end of the 100 mile stretch to the other.

A cache of these supplies were the ones Sergeant Coombs ordered teamsters Beamer and Stillings to collect and bring back to Oregon City, not an assignment either of them favored. All winter and spring memories of the previous fall's journey haunted them. It began disastrously and ended disastrously. Badly wounded in the battle of Shiny Mountain, every jolting bump in the rough track had been torture beyond anything either ever before had endured.

Now, with high water flooding over stream banks and the ground slick with melting snow, every mile traveled had its dangerous moments. On the first day after parting with Joe and Michael, a wagon skidded off the track and into a creek. It took both mule teams along with Deacon, Stillings and Beamer working pry poles and a winching rope to get the wagon back on the roadway. Half a day was lost and the animals and their tenders were left exhausted.

That evening they celebrated by skinning a rabbit Deacon had killed and, along with roots and herbs found along side the roadway, Stillings, who took great pride in his culinary skills, cooked up a tasty stew. Deacon contributed a jug pilfered from

Joe Meek's illegal cache of spirits. Before the evening was over the day's tedious travel was forgotten and the remainder of the journey looked forward to as if the threesome were schoolboys playing hooky.

Beamer, never one to say one word when he could use two, began to reminisce on his early years while freighting on the Santa Fe Trail. "Yep, yuh wouldn't believe it but in them days I was 'bout as big as a half pint of beer. Had ta stand on me tiptoes ta throw a harness on a mule. I'm tellin' yuh, those Mexican mules was somethin' ta larn on. Yuh know how sly they kin be, an' mean, they was as feisty as new-sheared sheep."

Beamer paused to take a chaw and tuck it into his cheek. "From there I went ta freightin' up north, carryin' stuff fer fur traders an' the like. Brought goods ta most of the rendezvous: Pierre's Hole, Green River, Ham's Fork -- yuh name it, I was there, haulin' firewater, trade goods, flour, beans, bacon an' guns an' powder. Yep, knew all the big uns: Ashley-Smith, Sublette brothers, Charlie Bent, Manuel Lisa, American Fur Company . . . hauled fer 'em all . . . never slept in me own bed for six months at a time. Then came the last rendezvous in '40. Nuthin' was right agin."

Deacon nodded. "Yep, fur trappin' an' tradin' plumb went ta hell. When the market fer beaver skins died it was the end of the world. What could we do? All we knew was settin' traps an' skinnin' beaver. We saw it comin' but didn't believe it would happen. Even ejucated Buck Stone reckoned it would continue."

Beamer pulled a blanket wrapped object from his wagon. "I was tellin' yuh 'bout what I was fixin' fer me boy, Clay. Since yuh was there when he drew his last breath, I think yuh might appreciate it." He pulled aside the blanket to reveal a large cross made of cedar. Carefully carved on the cross bar was the name, Clay Beamer.

"I ain't got 'round ta carvin' in the dates. It's gittin' so me hand ain't steady. Maybeso, when I retire from this bloomin' job me hand'll hold still long enuff ta finish it."

"It's a mighty fine bit of carvin'. Didja do it all yerself?"

Deacon asked.

"Yep, every inch of it. Guess it's taken me six months --
started while in sick bay at Fort Vancouver. He paused, then said,
"Well, guess we'd better turn in. We've a long piece of travel on
the morrow. Thank ye fer the supper, Stillin's. I'd stack yuh up
against any cook in the West. 'Tis no wonder I'm fillin' out like
a prize shoat."

The following morning the threesome got off to an early
start. Beamer's hope was to hit the first cache of supplies before
dark. He snapped the reins and drove his mules away with a few
choice swear words learned as a youth on the trail to Santa Fe.
Stillings followed closely behind, and Deacon brought up the rear
riding his striped, mealymouthed mule.

They drove through tunnels of evergreens, flushing out
scampering squirrels, rabbits and birds: blue jays, magpies, spar-
rows, flickers and an annoyed screech owl. For once the sky was
cloudless and blue as the shell of a newly laid robin's egg. Circling hawks, eyes of the forest, floated on air currents high overhead. Abruptly the forest opened up to reveal a meadow so colorful it took the travelers' breath away. Every where multicolored rhododendrons were in bloom: pink, white, purple . . . every
color of the rainbow seemed to be on display. On the far side of
the open area white blossoms of dogwoods emerging from the
dark green evergreens and backed by the startling blue sky, provided an equally breathtaking sight.

"I swan, hev yuh ever seen anythin' as purty as this?"
Beamer asked in a husky voice. "No wonder Indian people worship Mother Earth. She produces miracles no human kin possibly duplicate."

Stillings cleared his throat as though to speak, instead remained silent. The beauty of the scene was awesome but in his
travels with Beamer they had witnessed many miraculous sights:
sunsets against the white peaked Rockies, the rugged red sandstone cliffs of Wind River, vast herds of buffalo on stark endless
plains, brilliant chained lightening over the River Platte . . . yet,

not once had Beamer carried on like this.

Finally, Beamer clucked his team into motion. They entered the dark forest, shutting out the meadow and its striking beauty. As if to reveal another side of Mother Earth, rocks and potholes filled the tracks, making the wagons rattle and bounce. Thick brush threatened to overgrow the trail. Here and there fallen limbs and tree trunks had to be laboriously cleared. Rivulets of water gushed out of hillsides, strewing debris and creating gullies that had to be filled. Finally, they came to a stretch where a rushing stream had carved a new channel that cut deep into the roadway. Beamer pulled his team to a halt and clambered down from the spring seat.

"Looks like we've come to the end of the line," Stillings observed.

"Yeah," Beamer agreed. "Maybeso, if'n the mules don't spook, we kin edge around it . . . move a few rocks an' I think we kin do it."

For an hour or more the three men labored, shoveling dirt, rolling rocks into the stream below and chopping brush. "Thet should do the trick," Beamer finally said, mopping his face. "I'll giv it a go." He clambered up on the spring seat, braced himself and snapped the reins. The mules snorted but would not move.

"Giddyup, yuh stubborn critters!" Beamer gave the lead team a pop with his whip. The wagon jerked ahead.

"Oh! My gawd! Stop! Stop!" Stillings shouted. The mules pulled up, but it was too late. An ominous creak came from the wagon, then the bank gave away. Mules and wagon flipped over and dropped bottom side up into the rushing stream below.

XXXIII

Your time of decay may be distant, but it will certainly come,
for even the white man . . . cannot be exempt from
the common destiny.

Seattle, Duwamish

Deacon and Stillings stared helplessly at the wreckage. The wagon, with wheels thrust skyward, looked like a turned over beetle, struggling to right itself. The cold, rushing waters buffeted it with a ferocity that left the two watchers stunned.

"Dammit!" Stillings swore. Everything had happened so suddenly and without warning neither man could believe his eyes. In a fierce display of power, Mother Earth had whisked wagon and team off the hillside track as easily as if they were toys.

Deacon recovered first. "Hey! We've gotta git down thar an' do somethin' afore Beamer an' those critters drown."

"What's the matter with me, standin' here like a blind fool?" Stillings ran to his wagon and brought back a coil of rope. He tied one end around his waist and handed the rest to Deacon.

"Hang on ta this. Let me slide down an' . . . no, yuh better wrap it 'round thet ol' stump. When I hit thet water like as not, it'll jerk me downstream like a shot. Aw' right, here goes."

With his long legs and arms flailing to keep himself upright, Stillings skidded down the embankment. At the edge of the stream he grappled for the bridle of a threshing mule. The animal let out a bellow and attempted to right itself but the wreckage shifted, pulling the mule into deep water alongside the other mules that had become dark mounds of skin, bones and flesh.

"Never mind the dad-blasted mules," Deacon hollered. "They're already dead're doomed. Git after Beamer. Hurry up! He's trapped under the wagon seat. Take yer knife. Cut those reins. Ah! His coat's caught. Cut it away. Quick! We ain't got all day."

"Quit yer damn shoutin'. I see him. Slack off on the rope. I cain't git at him with yuh holdin' me back." Stillings pulled the rope to him, took a step and went sprawling. The surging water banged him into a wagon wheel. A gangly arm reached out to grasp a spoke. He came to the surface spluttering like a landed fish.

Agonizingly, Stillings pulled himself across the upside down wagon box to where Beamer lay trapped. He grasped the teamster by the collar of his buckskin jacket and pulled his head to the surface. The movement made the wagon bed shift. A wave of water jerked the wreckage free from the creek bank. Down the stream it swept. Held fast by the rope, Stillings tumbled over to flop up and down in the surging riffles like an elongated cork.

Somehow, with Deacon pulling on the rope and Stillings scrambling, the lanky teamster got back up the slope. Dazed by the tragedy, the two men stared downstream where the wreckage came to rest, hooked on a boulder, the mules on one side and what was left of the wagon on the other side. Beamer's body was not to be seen.

"We gotta find Beamer an' git him outta there, but how do we do it?" Deacon finally said. "Maybeso one of us should ride fer help."

Stillings glanced up at the sun. "That's not the answer. Before yuh know it, the sun'll be down an' it'll be darker than the insides of a cat. If we don't find his body now he may be gone for good."

Beyond the wagon wreckage they found Beamer's body washed up on the far stream bank. The soaked buckskin clothing gave him the look of a miniature beached whale.

"There's extra rope in the wagon," Stillings said. "If yuh'll let me down again, I'll take it, tie it 'round Beamer an' we'll pull him ta safety."

"Yer in no shape ta go down there," Deacon objected. "Look at yuh, yer as trembly as a leaf in the wind. I ain't done nuthin' an' already I'm bushed. Besides, thet water's movin' faster'n a gallopin' horse. Yuh saw how it picked up thet wagon an' took it lickety-split down the creek."

"All the more reason why we should get Beamer out. If we don't do it now he may wash downstream an' we'll never find him. If I kin git a rope 'round him we'll hitch my team to the rope. Thet's the best way I kin think of gittin' the job done."

"Yeah, " Deacon agreed. "I'm so upset I'm not thinkin' straight."

Getting a rope around the big teamster was far more difficult than either man envisioned. Moving the slick buckskin clad body was like wrestling a greased pig. Stillings tugged and pulled but the remains of the big teamster would not budge.

"Thread the rope down through his shirt," Deacon hollered. "Maybeso, thet'll giv enuff grip ta pull him free."

Stillings waved a hand that he understood, but while he was forcing the rope down the dead man's shirt front a monstrous wave picked up the body and swept it away. Caught unawares and still tied to the rope that Deacon had cinched around a tree trunk, Stillings had his feet cut from under him and again found himself bobbing up and down in the rushing stream. Slowly, Deacon pulled him ashore. By now dusk had fallen. Still they searched for their fallen companion but to no avail. Hidden by darkness the deadly torrent raced along like a noisy, fast crawling snake.

#

The crowd stirred as young Elizabeth Sager took the witness stand. Her long, carefully brushed hair, held in place with a ribbon, gleamed in the dimly lit courtroom. Everyone knew the story of the seven Sager children orphaned on the Oregon Trail. Billy Shaw, who had captained the wagon train that brought them across the plains and delivered the seven orphans to the Whitman Mission, was in the crowd. As Elizabeth took the oath he stood as if to give her support. She did not need any. She had been through far greater trials than this one in Oregon City. Nevertheless, Judge Pratt reminded her as a witness she was under oath and the lives of five men could well depend on what she said. Prosecutor Holbrook gave Pratt a glance of annoyance. The silly man, always showing off, then he began asking innocuous questions.

"Elizabeth, where did you reside before coming to the Willamette Valley?"

The Sager orphan answered in a straightforward manner, her youthful voice carrying to the far ends of the courtroom. "I lived with the Whitman family in Cayuse country."

"How long did you live with the Whitmans?"

"I guess it was about four years."

"Do you remember the day they died?"

"I most certainly do. It was a Monday afternoon."

"Tell us what you remember about that day."

"There had been a lot of sickness in the Indian village. Many Indians had died, three of them on Sunday night. About eleven o'clock the next morning Father went to the cemetery to give the three bodies a Christian burial."

"By Father, you mean Doctor Whitman?"

"Yes, we called him Father and Mrs. Whitman, Mother."

"What happened after the burial services?"

"All was quiet until mid-afternoon. Then an Indian man came to the kitchen door and asked for Father. There was loud talking and shooting."

"Did they shoot Doctor Whitman?"

"I didn't see it, but he was wounded."

"Where did the talking and shooting take place?"

"In the kitchen."

"The shooting and loud talking took place in the kitchen, not outside in front of the Mission House?"

"It took place in the kitchen."

"What else happened?"

"Mother was wounded."

"At this time was anyone else hurt?"

"Mr. Saunders came and was knocked down by Tamsucky

and Ish-ish-kais-kais. A gun went off. The following morning Mr. Saunders was dead. My brother John had been killed and later brother Frank was shot and killed." Elizabeth's lips trembled. Prosecutor Holbrook stopped questioning.

Captain Claiborne slowly got to his feet for the defense. He was half a mind not to question the youthful witness. She had suffered enough, but there was one point she said that had to be clarified -- where was Marcus Whitman murdered? Mrs. Hall said in front of the Mission House where she had a clear view of the crime. Elizabeth Sager said she didn't see the attack on Father Whitman but did see him laying wounded in the kitchen.

"You say you saw Father Whitman laying in the kitchen wounded. Did you see who attacked him?"

"No, I only heard the shooting."

"Did the shooting take place in the kitchen?"

Elizabeth nodded her head and was asked to answer by voice. "Yes," she said.

Claiborne paused. At the time of the massacre the poor girl had been ten years-old. What a terrible shock it must have been to lose two brothers and foster parents within a few hours and in such a shocking manner. It was said the Delaware half-breed, Joe Lewis, ordered students of the mission school from their classroom and shot Frank Sager while they looked on. Was Elizabeth one of the witnesses?

"Was a man called Joe Lewis involved in any of this?"

Elizabeth did not answer, and Claiborne did not insist on one. After all, how much grief and terror could a twelve-year old bear?

Prosecutor Holbrook next called for Lorinda Bewley Chapman to take the witness stand. The crowd craned their necks to see this young woman who, while in captivity, had taken the fancy of several Indian men. It was said shortly after the massacre the murderer, Tamsucky, had raped her, committing the dastardly act while Linda's sick brother looked on. The following day the brother had been slain.

The Cayuse leader, Five Crows, also had had his eye on Linda Bewley. He sent a man to fetch her to his Butter Creek tipi lodge. Sick and terror-stricken, Linda begged Tiloukaikt to protect her. Tiloukaikt, who had lost control over the young men of his band, even his own sons, told her she should go. She would be better off in Five Crows camp than in Waiilatpu.

As it turned out, Tiloukaikt was right. Soon after she left for the lodge of Five Crows, Tamsucky returned to the mission with team and wagon and fellow murderer, Joe Lewis, planning to abduct Linda. Now that she had been raped she was open game to all who desired to ravish her. In the minds of these youthful hot bloods raping was an act of war in the same tradition as taking scalps. Tiloukaikt had saved her from this horrific fate.

Five Crows proved an unpredictable mate, treating Linda with kindness one moment and harshly the next. Her ordeal did not end until the tragedy survivors were rescued by Hudson's Bay's Peter Skene Ogden on December 29, 1847. Ten months later in the Willamette Valley Linda had married William Chapman.

All of this information came to Prosecutor Holbrook's mind as Linda took the oath. Yet, he had no reason to expose these embarrassing incidents. It was the murder of Doctor Whitman that he had to establish beyond a reasonable doubt.

"I am going to ask you about the day Doctor Whitman was killed. On the afternoon of November 29, 1847, do you remember where you were?" Holbrook asked.

"I was upstairs in the Mission House sick abed."

"Did you see or hear anything unusual?"

"Yes, I was awakened by loud, quarreling voices coming from the kitchen."

"The kitchen was right below you?"

"Yes, the stairs led down to it."

"Did you know who was quarreling?

"Yes, it was Doctor Whitman and the Indian man, Tiloukaikt."

"How did you know it was Tiloukaikt?"

"He often came to talk to Doctor Whitman, complaining, asking for medicine. . . . I would know his voice anywhere."

"What happened after the quarrel?"

"There were shots and more angry words."

"Was anyone hurt?"

"Yes, Doctor Whitman was carried upstairs bleeding badly."

"Did Tiloukaikt shoot Doctor Whitman?"

"I don't know. When Mrs. Whitman helped me downstairs Tiloukaikt was there, so were his two sons and Joe Lewis and Tamsucky." She shuddered as she uttered the name, Tamsucky. Taking a quick breath, she continued. "At the door they killed Mrs. Whitman and Mr. Rogers, the school teacher."

After Prosecutor Holbrook completed his questioning, Captain Claiborne rose for the defense. So far his cross-examinations had done little good. He could not hope to get Tiloukaikt or Tomahas off and he didn't particularly want to, but the other three . . . if he could only produce doubt in the minds of a few jurors, they might stand a chance. So far the only crack in the prosecution's case was the location of the attack on Doctor Whitman. Widow Hall said it took place in front of the Mission House. The others said it occurred in the Mission House kitchen.

"Did the altercation you overheard come from within the Mission House?" Claiborne finally asked.

"Yes. I heard it distinctly. It came from the Mission House kitchen," Linda Bewley Chapman replied.

"No more questions." Captain Claiborne glanced at the jury. The witness' response did not seem to make an impression.

Prosecutor Holbrook called one more witness, Elijah Osborne, who with his family had hidden in a crawl space beneath the Mission House. When night fell they had emerged from their hiding place and fled, crisscrossing the freezing waters of Mill Creek and Walla Walla River.

The next day they had hidden in the bushes while Indians traveled back and forth on a nearby trail. Nearly frozen by the cold winter weather, that night they pushed on until Mrs. Osborne finally fell from exhaustion. Osborne left wife and family to get help at Fort Walla Walla. In the past two and a half years he had relived that terrible time over and over until he knew by heart every detail of the torturous escape.

"From your hiding place could you tell what was going on?" Holbrook asked after a few preliminary questions.

"We sure could. The Injuns was murderin' Marcus an' Narcissa Whitman an' several others."

"What do you mean by several others?"

"When we crawled out that night we stumbled over the bodies of John Sager an' the young school teacher, Rogers."

"Did you recognize the voices of the killers?"

"Yes. They were the voices of Tiloukaikt, Tomahas an' Tamsucky."

"Are they in the courtroom?"

"Tiloukaikt an' Tomahas're right there," he pointed to the two prisoners who sat side by side. "I'm told Tamsucky is dead."

Holbrook glanced at the jurors. He had intended to put a half dozen more witnesses on the stand but what good would that do? He had proven without a doubt how Marcus and Narcissa Whitman had died and identified who had done the dastardly crime. "No more questions," he said and sat down.

The crowd grumbled. They felt cheated. Survivors of the tragedy, Eliza Spalding, Catherine Sager and Mary Saunders, whose husband was beheaded, had not been called on to testify. The court had proved the guilt of Tiloukaikt and Tomahas but what about the other three prisoners? They barely were mentioned. Were they doomed just because they had been surrendered by the Cayuse leader, Young Chief? And what happened to the main murderer, Joe Lewis? Why was he not standing trial?

Even US Marshal Joe Meek disapproved. He was affronted. The death of his daughter, Helen Mar, had been glossed over as if it had not occurred.

XXXIV

What we are told as children is that people when they walk on the land leave their breath wherever they go. So wherever we walk, that particular spot on the earth never forgets us.

Rina Swentzell, Santa Clara Pueblo

Deacon Walton and Teamster Stillings were up and about before dawn. They had spent a night they never would forget. At dusk a thick mist had fallen so densely they hardly could locate the remaining wagon and team of mules. Trees and bushes were coated with moisture, soaking their clothes through. They staked out the mules, but rain had turned the grassy area into a bog. The hungry animals stood up to their fetlocks in mud. The exposed roadway dirt had turned into sticky gumbo. Deacon attempted to start a fire, but even dead limbs and leaves were dripping wet.

"What a mess," Stillings grumbled. "Maybeso Beamer has the best of it after all."

Finally, they hunched beneath the canvas wagon cover, dug out a pot of left over stew and choked down a few mouthfuls of the cold, tasteless food. It was impossible to sleep, so they sat dozing and listening to the constant drip-drip of water drops falling from the canopy of evergreens overhead.

When the first light of dawn began to filter through the trees, stiff and chilled, they clambered out of the wagon and peered down at the rushing stream that had turned into an even greater torrent during the night. "Blast thet striped rumped ape, Coombs," Stillings swore. He had no business sendin' us on this fool's errand. He jest wanted to get us out of the way."

"Blamin' the sarge an' cursin' fate ain't goin' ta git us nowhere," Deacon said. "Somewhere in thet tangle of brush yonder is our friend, Beamer, an' we gotta find him. I suggest we git started. Right now creatures of the forest maybe makin' breakfast of the poor fellow."

Stillings shuddered. "Yeah, if only I could hev got a rope aroun' him an' held him fast. The way this water's tearin' along, he may be half way ta the Willamette River."

Keeping a sharp lookout for the body of their missing companion, Deacon and Stillings started plodding downstream. They passed by where they last had seen the wreckage. In its place was a pile of driftwood and a tangle of brush. Disheartened, they plodded on, each one carrying a coil of rope made heavy by the inclement weather.

"By gum!" Deacon uttered. "Ain't thet a mule?" They picked up their pace to see the body of a mule sprawled on the opposite side of the creek. Farther on they came upon the front wheels of the wagon chassis still linked together by the axle. Strips of canvas trailed away from it, rippling in the water like fish swimming upstream, but no sign of Beamer.

"The ol' teamster was tough as an ol' boot. Yuh don't suppose he came to an' walked off?" Deacon said hopefully.

"Are yuh crazy," Stillings scoffed. "I never saw a body deader than Beamer."

"Hey! What the heck's thet?" Deacon exclaimed. The men scrambled over a pile of rubble toward a planed board that only could have come from the wreckage of Beamer's wagon.

"Aagh!" Deacon groaned. "It's the grave marker Beamer was makin' fer his son, Clay. Poor fella, he'll never finish it now." The old trapper picked up the board and brushed away a crust of sand and mud. "Maybeso, I kin finish carvin' on it. I don't spose he'd mind."

The two men clambered up the slope, Deacon struggling with the grave marker. At the top Deacon had to take time for a blow. He glanced at the steep bank that rose on either side of the creek and shook his head. "I ain't in shape fer this scramblin' up and down these slopes like a bloomin' jack rabbit. Me ol' heart's beatin' like a churn. Say, ain't thet bundle yonder somethin' else from ol' Beamer's wagon? Looks like a bag of clothes."

Once again, down the slope they scrambled, skidding to a

stop almost on top of a mound of buckskins coated with silt and mud. Stillings knelt and lifted the top layer of clothing.

"Oh! My God!" he uttered and fell back to retch.

"What the tarnation!" Deacon took a step forward and stopped to stare. Two protruding blue eyes leered back. Where a human nose and forehead had been was a mass of exposed bone.

#

Josiah Osborne, the prosecution's last witness, was scarcely dismissed before Judge Pratt looked to the defense. "You may begin with your testimony," he declared. An audible sigh came from onlookers. It was getting late in the day. If the prosecution had completed soliciting information from witnesses, the excitement they had enjoyed was over. As far as they were concerned the court could adjourn. Most had no desire to hear the defense attempt to whitewash the prisoners. At least two of these uncivilized creatures were as deadly as rattlesnakes.

The jurors were equally ready to put the day to rest. Their minds had been bombarded with shooting, hacking, rape . . . tales of terror beyond belief. Nothing the defense would say could possibly erase these terrible acts from their minds.

The defense team also was appalled. They had requested a recess to prepare their rebuttal. How could they respond effectively to all the evidence thrown at them by the prosecution without a minute's respite? Besides, they knew the impact the prosecution's devastating evidence had on the jurors. They needed time to collect themselves before they could objectively deliberate the case.

Judge Pratt was adamant. He wanted testimony completed post haste. Each hour spent in the courtroom was costing the Provisional Government money that it did not have, he argued. The defense team had no choice but to call their first witness, the most well known citizen of Oregon City, Dr. John McLoughlin, formerly head of Hudson's Bay's Northwest fur trading empire.

The crowd hushed as the tall, stately six-foot-four inch figure, topped by a head covered with long snow white hair, strode

forward to take the witness stand. The defense team took heart.
Even the Cayuse prisoners, who had nearly fallen asleep, sat up
straight. Here was a man they could trust. His tongue was straight.
More than once he had befriended them. He had married an Indian woman and had sons with Indian blood.

The citizenry had mixed feelings about this witness. Although he had resided in the territory longer than any of them, he
did not fit into the Willamette Valley community of homesteaders. McLoughlin was not even a US citizen, and they did not
particularly want him to be. He had married a half-breed. He
was Catholic. He had built a fine house in town. He did not
suffer fools or charlatans. Except for appearances like this, he
held himself apart. He worked and dealt with various Indian tribes
most of his life. More than once he had kept them from going on
the warpath.

The people knew they owed this man a great deal. If it
hadn't been for McLoughlin's influence and generosity, hardly a
settler in the valley would be as well off as they were. McLoughlin
had done more to settle Oregon than anyone in the territory.

Perhaps Dr. McLoughlin's good deeds had worked against
him. There were many who resented his presence. Since the
boundary question had been settled, Oregon was United States
territory. Although McLoughlin had raised the first buildings and
mapped the streets and environs of the village that would become Oregon City, it was now a municipality of the United States.
McLoughlin had to come off his high horse and realize he was an
outsider, a citizen of the British Commonwealth. Even as the
trial was going on, movement was afoot to force McLoughlin to
forfeit much of the land he had laid claim to when the region still
was a wilderness.

Yet, in spite of the prejudice, the defense could not have
chosen a more powerful witness. McLoughlin's commanding
presence made Judge Pratt, Prosecutor Holbrook, US Marshal
Joe Meek and others appear awkward and unpolished actors in a
badly produced play. Kintzing Pritchette, Secretary of the Terri-

tory and second in command to Governor Lane and member of the defense team, rose to question McLoughlin.

"You were acquainted with Doctor and Mrs. Whitman?" Pritchette began.

"Aye, even before they established their mission among the Cayuse the Doctor and Mrs. Whitman visited my home in Fort Vancouver."

"At any time did you warn them of the dangers they faced in Cayuse country?"

"Yes, I most certainly did, particularly about practicing medicine among Indians. It was the native custom to kill medicine men who tended patients that ultimately died."

"So, in spite of your warning Doctor Whitman went ahead and practiced medicine."

"Aye, that he did. He had no fear. His life was in the hands of God, he said."

"Would you say Doctor Whitman was well liked . . . accepted by the Cayuse people?"

"Not by everyone. He was too busy to sit and parley. He expected the people to work as diligently as did he."

"Are you saying the Cayuse did not appreciate the missionary work Doctor Whitman was doing?"

"There are Cayuse people present. Why not ask them?" the man the Indian people called White-Faced Eagle replied.

"Thank you. We will," Prichette said.

Judge Pratt looked to Prosecutor Holbrook. "You may question the witness."

Holbrook hesitated. There were many things he could ask, but what did he have to gain? He had established Tiloukaikt and Tomahas as the murderers of the Whitmans and the other three prisoners had been seen on the mission grounds during the tragedy, and therefore obviously were involved. Even though McLoughlin insisted he had warned Whitman of the danger he faced, that did not condone the bloody killings that took place. "I have no questions," Holbrook finally said.

Prichette continued for the defense by calling the Cayuse leader, Stickus, to the witness stand. Wearing a long fringed buckskin jacket as though dressed for a winter hunt, Stickus looked as out of place as he felt. The rows of staring white faces made him forget what few English words he knew. The two interpreters who attempted to help him made matters worse.

Yes, he had been a friend of the missionary medicine man, Whitman. Two days before the killings the medicine man had visited his village. At the time he had warned medicine man Whitman not to ride back to the mission at Waiilatpu.

"Waiilatpu bad mens waited to kill," Stickus said, at last calling on his limited English vocabulary.

"Is it the custom of the Cayuse to kill medicine men whose patients die?" Prichette asked.

Judge Pratt rapped his gravel. "Irrelevant. We are not here to go into the various facets of Cayuse law."

"It is relevant," Prichette argued. "How are we to judge these people if we do not understand the rules they live by?"

Judge Pratt scowled. "You heard the ruling of the court. Proceed with your next witness."

"As you wish," Prichette said, his voice dripping with sarcasm. "Will Reverend Henry Spalding please come forward."

Michael, who sat between his uncle and half brother, uttered a grunt of disbelief. In his early years he attended Spalding's Lapwai mission school and had witnessed the whippings Spalding had ordered when members of his flock broke the Ten Commandments or disobeyed his orders. Spalding had come within an eyelash of being killed alongside Missionary Whitman. His daughter, Eliza, who had been visiting the Whitmans, suffered through the tragedy and its aftermath. What testimony favorable to the Cayuse could Reverend Henry Spalding possibly give?"

"You were present when Stickus warned Doctor Whitman. Do you remember the words he said?" Prichette asked.

"I was present," Spalding replied. "Not only did he warn Doctor Whitman, Stickus warned me as well."

"Would you say Stickus attempted to save both of your lives?" Prichette continued.

"Yes, you could say that. However . . ."

"That is all. Thank you. Your witness," Prichette said to the prosecutor.

Holbrook stood to cross-examine, but noticing the scowl on Judge Pratt's face, changed his mind. Given half a chance Reverend Spalding had the reputation for speaking long and loudly on the forces of good and evil. There was no time for that. Already it was late in the day. Judge Pratt was determined to wind up things and turn the case over to the jury. However, the judge was in as much need of relief as the audience and jurors. He felt rump sprung from sitting so long. The call of nature also was strong. He rapped the gavel and announced a short recess which triggered a mad rush for the doors.

Before court could reconvene, a wagon clattered into town. Sitting on the spring seat was gangly Teamster Stillings. Trailing behind the wagon came a rider astride a mule with striped withers. Sergeant Coombs, who sourly had watched the wagon and mule rider approach, scowled. From the way the wagon rattled and bounced it obviously was empty. Although the sergeant was in the process of herding the prisoners back into the courtroom, he couldn't contain himself. His orders to collect more supplies cached along Barlow Road had been ignored. He brought the prisoner escort detail to a halt. Then quickly moved to snatch the reins of the lead mule and pulled the team to a stop.

"What's going on? Why are you back with an empty wagon; where is that no-good Beamer?"

Stillings remained silent. Instead, he jerked a thumb toward the back of the wagon.

Still fuming, Sergeant Coombs stalked to the rear of the wagon and lifted the canvas flap. An oblong object wrapped in blankets met his eyes. "What the devil?" he uttered. "He pulled the blanket covering away. Beamer's cold, ravaged face looked back. Coombs gasped and hurriedly replaced the blanket covering, then staggered away as if drunk. Coombs' assistant, had to take over and march the five Cayuse men back into the courtroom.

Joe Jennings and Michael Two Feathers, who had taken a breath of fresh air and were about to reenter the courthouse, also had veered away to meet the wagon. From the way their two friends, Deacon and Stillings, acted, they immediately sensed something terrible had occurred.

When ashen-faced Coombs stumbled away and they saw the blanket wrapped bundle, they knew what they feared had happened. Joe uttered a heart-wrenching groan -- Teamster Beamer had gone to his reward. One more of the hardy frontiersmen who had played such an important role in his life was no more.

XXXV

Life is not separate from death.
It only looks that way.

Blackfeet Proverb

For a moment confusion reigned. The crowd was hushed. A wagon with a body in it brought with it a feeling of terror. Indians! There was no doubt about it they were taking their revenge. If the prisoners were found guilty and executed, this was the kind of thing Willamette Valley citizenry could expect. Away from the safety of home any one of them could be slain without provocation. Only when it was announced the dead man had met death through an accident did a semblance of calm return.

Judge Pratt was beside himself. He called for order, rapping the gavel on his desk top so violently a pitcher of water tumbled over and shattered on the floor. "Prosecutor Holbrook, will you kindly lead off with your summation," he finally croaked, his voice made harsh from shouting.

The prosecutor had his say and was followed by each of the defense team lawyers. Major Reynolds expounded for nearly an hour. Not to be out done, Captain Claiborne spoke nearly twice that long, pausing to rest several times to prevent his voice from cracking. There was not much Prichette could add so kept his speech short. Prosecutor Holbrook took the floor again to address the jurors. He repeated nearly the same words he said the first time but added a tirade against the defense team.

"My honored opponents have employed every weasel trick in the book to get the men they defend off, but they have failed. You heard from the lips of honest people who witnessed and suffered through the terrible Whitman Mission massacre that these prisoners who sit before you killed, killed and killed. What more evidence is needed? These people are guilty . . . every single one of them. Guilty beyond a shadow of doubt is the only possible verdict you can truthfully render.

The prisoners, unable to understand what the verbiage was all about, sat and stared at the crazy white man. In their homeland when people were tried for crimes, it was done with solemn dignity. The life of every creature on Mother Earth was precious, given to them by The Great Mysterious, a fact these white men ignored or chose to forget.

The prisoners also were physically exhausted. Irons enclosing their hands and feet had created sores that felt like rings of fire. The muscles of their backs and legs ached unmercifully. Their ears rang from the loud haranguing. They were not accustomed to long and loud speech making. They wished for the quietness of their village where even children at play did so unobtrusively.

Now, that the summation had been completed everyone expected the court to adjourn. Hours previously, darkness had fallen. A chill of the night air whistled in around the windows and doors. Spectators had experienced enough legalese to last them a lifetime. They were hungry, and like the prisoners, their muscles pleaded for relief from the hard, uncomfortable chairs.

Yet, Judge Pratt was not finished. He instructed the jurors not to speak of the trial, not even to each other until they met for deliberation. He issued orders to Marshal Meek to escort the jurors to a rooming house where they would be fed and bedded for the night but not allowed out or receive visitors, not even members of their families. In the morning they would be returned under escort to the courthouse to deliberate and render their verdict.

#

Joe Jennings and his brother did not attend the trial summation. The unexpected death of their friend and benefactor, Teamster Beamer, left them bereft. Just two days previously they had joked and supped with him. When they parted the last thing on their minds was that they would never see the big man again. He had been such an intimate part of their lives. Beamer had been far closer to them than had their own father. The preparation of the body for burial had been a gruesome task. Joe hardly could bear to look at the battered, water soaked flesh that had been his friend, Teamster Beamer. Deacon, who took over and did most of the preparation, gratefully accepted a pair of sheets the Morgans contributed. Deacon tore them into strips, then tenderly and carefully bound them around Beamer's body until it looked like an Egyptian mummy.

"Don't know why we're goin' ta so much trouble," Deacon said, fiercely blowing his nose. "This bound up thing ain't Beamer. The ol' fraud's off on some cloud lookin' down on us, laughin' hisself sick, an' here we's grievin' like calves with the slobbers."

"Yeah! Now thet yuh mention it, the ol' varmint found fun in most every situation," Stillings replied. "Wonder where he would like ta be buried? Maybeso, in thet colorful spot he liked so much. It'll take a powerful lot of diggin' but it kin be done. We could use the head marker he was carvin' fer his son, Clay. I'll betcha thet would make him feel good. He was always playin' jokes. What was his first name anyway? I never did hear him say."

Joe thought back. It almost was ten years to the day that he and the Beamers first met. Buck Stone's brigade of trappers was on the way to the Green River rendezvous. He had been standing guard when he heard the creak of harnesses and wagon wheels.

"Hey, you in the wagon," he had shouted. "Pull up and show yourself."

A string of oxen, plodding slowly along, emerged out of the darkness. Alongside them walked a barrel-chested man covered with dust and splattered with mud. "Name's Beamer," he said. "This's me son, Clay" He motioned to a bareheaded youth with blonde, dust-covered hair.

Joe choked down a lump in his throat and swiped at his eyes. Yes, that was his first glimpse of Teamster Beamer and his son, Clay. The meeting had been casual and commonplace, yet left an impact that neither he nor Beamer ever had forgotten.

"Yuh've known Beamer a long spell," Deacon said, bringing Joe back to the present. "What's his Christian name? Somewhere along the road he must've mentioned it?"

Joe shook his head. "Never." Yet in the back of his mind there was that conversation the two Beamers had when parting at the last rendezvous. "Take care of yerself, Junior," Beamer had said. "We ain't got much but 'member yer mom an' me're countin' on yuh ta carry on the family name."

"His dad called his son Junior so they both must have had the same first name, Clay."

"Perfect," Deacon said. "We kin carve in the death date an' the ol' rascal's grave marker will be jest right."

"No!" Joe said so sharply the sound of his voice startled him. "We'll make a special marker for Beamer Senior. More than anything in the world Beamer wanted to have his son's grave marked with that board he carved on for so long. I'll never be able to live with myself if I don't try to make Beamer's wish come true. I'm sure you'll want to come along."

"But-but," stuttered Deacon, "thet boy's buried in the heart of Blackfeet country . . . in one of ther sacred valleys. Besides, yuh kin betcher life those Blackfeets ain't fergotten us, sendin' a bunch of ther warriors to the happy huntin' grounds like we'uns did."

"We'll just have to be extra careful, won't we?" Joe dryly replied.

XXXVI

Far to the East, I see a pale-faced people pushing the red-man back to the setting sun. The red-men fight this onward march to no avail . . . Their dead lie strewn along the trails, their bones dry on the sandhills. . . .

From story of a Columbia River Indian Medicine Man

The hanging was over. North of the city the bodies of five Cayuse men lay in a mass grave. The people, many of whom attended both trial and execution, gathered in groups to engage in excited chatter. The thrills and excitement they had experienced had to be relived with friends and neighbors. They had come to see that justice was done and had not been disappointed. They had taught the heathen savages a lesson that never would be forgotten.

As Judge Pratt had wished, the verdict of guilty was handed down with dispatch. On May 24, 1850, the jury, only taking 75 minutes, condemned all five prisoners to death. After an even shorter period of deliberation, Judge Pratt set the execution for June 3rd, 10 days hence.

A motion for a new trial was immediately introduced by the defense. The principal reason for the appeal was that the crime charged in the Indictment: ". . . was not proved to have been committed within the county for Clackamas, the Territory of Oregon or the jurisdiction for the court."

In addition to the jurisdiction issue was the manner in which the defendants had been charged for the crime. " . . . there is no evidence before this court that the Cayuse nation had surrendered the Defendants as the murderers."

Prichette, the defender with the law experience, felt strongly about both points. It made him shudder to think of the way the convicted men had been lured into giving themselves up.

It was appropriate for Tiloukaikt and Tomahas to do so. They were guilty without a doubt. The other three's guilt was not clear cut. One jury member even said so, insisting Kia-ma-sump-kin was innocent. The other jurors scoffed and threatened bodily harm if he did not change his mind.

Once again the white man had said one thing and had done another. The prisoners had been promised they would have the opportunity to tell their stories. If they spoke with a straight tongue and had no blame they would be set free. Not a single one of the prisoners had been asked to stand before the people and tell their story. Of course, it would have done no good. These courtroom people in their high collars and fancy coats, only heard what they wished to hear. They had no time to sit and exchange talk with Indian people of any kind. The only good Indian was a dead one, and the quicker the prisoners were hanged the better.

The irony of it all left Vision Seeker weak with anguish. Only Lawyer Prichette and the juror that had been overruled seemed to realize that justice was not being served. But now they, too, were helpless. The legal process had gone down river too far. The verdict of guilty had been made. A motion for a new trial had been turned down. Governor Lane had signed the death warrant. Judge Pratt had set the date of execution. The citizenry waited with bated breath to witness a mass execution.

Suddenly the unbelievable happened. Governor Lane left to settle the Rogue - Klickitat troubles, assigning Prichette as acting governor. Pritchette had the power to do the impossible, pardon the Cayuse. Prichette struggled with his conscience until the night before the hanging, then approached Joe Meek, the executioner. Knowing full well the anger he would create among the populace, Pritchette courageously ordered the marshal to set the prisoners free. As acting governor, he had pardoned them. Joe Meek looked at him as though he had lost his mind.

"What's the matter with you, Prichette? I've been waitin' fer this day fer goin' on three year. I've got a death warrant signed by the real governor in my pocket thet says those five

Cayuses're goin' ta hang, an' hang they damn sure will."

The US marshal kept his word. A gallows was quickly constructed not far from Dr. McLoughlin's Main Street residence. As with the trial, people swarmed to see the strangling of the "bloody Cayuse." Showman Joe Meek, decked out in his finest regalia, gave the crowd their money's worth. In an orderly manner, he marched the convicted men up to the gallows. In deference to the clergy, he allowed priests to baptize the victims and give them the last rites.

However, Meek's compassionate act got him in trouble with the Protestants. "Why should these heathens carry the brand of Catholicism instead of Presbyterianism into the hereafter?" Reverend Henry Spalding irately asked. "These people are Protestant products nurtured by missionaries sent by the American Board of Commissioners for Foreign Missions to evangelize the natives. Why should Johnny-come-lately Black Robes, who take their orders from the Pope in Rome, have the right to instruct and baptize the condemned into their faith?"

Other minor matters caused the avid audience to murmur. Tiloukaikt refused to have his hands tied and Kia-ma-sump-kin pleaded to be killed by the knife. "Hanging is not a fit way to die," an interpreter explained. Meek abruptly ended the plea by shoving the innocent Kia-ma-sump-kin aside and, swinging his sharply honed hatchet, cut the rope that triggered all five trap doors, dropping the five doomed men into nothingness. Some complained afterward it was not a clean hanging at all. Three of the condemned died instantly but two struggled in choking agony: ". . . one danced fourteen minutes at his rope's end."

Although there were dissenters, most Oregon City citizens were proud of the quick, decisive manner in which justice had been done. Only later would it appear they had gone about this ghoulish business in a slipshod, inhumane manner. A noted specialist in Western history, writing of the event nearly thirty years later, referred to "the little nasty town of Oregon City, which had grown nastier over the years."

However, all was well with Oregon City in June, 1850. From the second story veranda of his home, US Marshal Joe Meek, puffing on a fat cigar, watched the comings and goings in the streets and camping grounds that had so recently been packed with people. All had gone according to plan, but it was a good thing he had been on hand, Joe Meek thought.

Actually it was his old friend, Joe Lane, who nearly threw a monkey wrench into the works. When he went off to chase down the Rogue and Klickitats, he should have assigned anyone other than Prichette as acting governor. Naturally, the shyster attempted to take advantage of the temporary power he had at his command. He had written and signed a pardon for the lot. He would have set all five Cayuses free to murder again. "Ha!" The thought still rankled. The killers of the Whitmans and those responsible for the death of Helen Mar would have laughed themselves sick at the gutless Pritchette.

US Marshal Joe Meek leaned on the balustrade and savored his victory. The only fly in the ointment was that blessed few folk realized the important role he had played in getting those bloody Cayuse hanged. He had a notion to shout at the people who still lingered on the streets and in the campgrounds.

"Hey! Look here. This is your marshal, Joseph L. Meek. I'm the one you should thank for riddin' the land of these murderers so you can sleep in peace."

Meek threw his half smoked cigar away and lit up a new one. If any day was a two-cigar day, this was it. Yet, he should not get carried away. He did not want to overplay his hand like that damned Prichette did. Perhaps he should drop a word to George Curry, editor of the *Spectator*. The way he thwarted Kintzing Pritchette from cheating the gallows certainly was a historic act, one that should be recorded for posterity.

"Hmm!" Joe Meek grunted, glancing toward the north campgrounds where Vision Seeker, the Jennings brothers and Deacon Walton were breaking camp. "Thet ol' mountain man an' his cronies hev finally got through ther thick skulls there ain't no place fer them in Oregon City." He let out a huge puff of blue smoke and hurriedly brushed it out of his line of sight. He had to see this, make certain that blasted bunch left the city for good. The defrocked preacher had guzzled so much of his booze there hardly was a jug of it left.

Then there was that Nez Perce Indian man. The fellow had an uncanny way about him. When it was all said and done, it was he that nearly got the Cayuse set free. He was the only one of those Indian fellows who knew what was going on, kept suggesting arguments for the defense team. It was the points the Nez Perce busybody made that softened Prichette into issuing the pardon writ. It was a good thing he was leaving. All Oregon City needed was a smart Indian.

#

US Marshal Joe Meek was not the only one to watch the Deacon Walton party break camp. Some distance away two ladies dressed in gingham, holding on to each other, watched the men roll up their possessions and strap them to saddles already in place on their mounts' backs.

"'Tis for the best, Sis," the older lady said. "With your child coming, what else can you do? Now, dry your eyes and make like a little mother. The baby will be here before you know it. It will take up so much of your time Mr. Joe Jennings will never enter your thoughts again."

"Yeah-yeah," Bill Morgan, the older lady's husband, snorted to himself as he hitched the team to the wagon. "Womenfolk!" But he had better start watching his P's and Q's. When gals were expecting babies they could turn upon a man like she-bears guarding their cubs.

Hardly was the Morgan wagon loaded when a trooper galloped up, bringing his mount to a skidding stop that raised a cloud of dust. He tipped his hat to the ladies who, with the help of Bill Morgan, hurriedly got aboard the wagon.

"Lucille, kiss Algeron good-bye," Mrs. Morgan instructed. The trooper replaced his hat and reined his mount close to the wagon. His big pair of hands plucked the younger woman from the wagon bed as easily as if she was a sack of feathers. He placed her in front of him on the saddle and, much to the consternation of the older lady, cantered away.

"Algeron! Quit your silly carryin' on. Don't you know that wife of yours is in no condition to ride astride a horse?"

"She'll be all right! Lots of army wives go riding while carrying babies. It's all part of the training. Like his father, this son of mine is going to be a soldier -- a future Westpointer. To make certain he makes the grade, he'll take his first breath on an army post. With my permanent sergeant rating comes a posting at Fort Vancouver, which includes furnished housing. We'll let you know when your grandson arrives." With that the big soldier gave a wave of his hand and a touch of spur to his restless mount and cantered away.

The Morgans gaped. This was a side of their son-in-law they had never seen. Through all their troubles the sergeant had treated his wife like a queen. Now, there he was, manhandling her like she was a sack of feed. The daughter was equally startled.

"Algeron!" she screamed. "What's the matter with you, you're acting like a ruffian."

"That's right! From now all these la-di-da days are over. You're going to be a housewife and mother," the sergeant replied in his drill field voice.

"Where are you taking me? I'll not go to that miserable, rundown army post. I can't possibly live there. . . ."

"Beeiill!" screeched Nancy Morgan. "Why don't you do something? Stop him. Why-why, anything can happen. Do you know she hardly has ever been out of our sight. How can she manage to live on a man-filled army post without our help? Beeiill! Aren't you going to do anything?"

Bill clucked at his horses and snapped the reins. "Yep, I'm going to take you straight home. Perhaps with Lucille gone we can begin living like man and wife again. At least we can try."

XXXVII

Remember that your children are not your own,
but are lent to you by the Creator.

Mohawk Proverb

Joe Jennings had arisen before dawn. He felt terrible. He scarcely had slept a wink. The trial had been torture and the aftermath worse. He had urged the others to leave days earlier. He had no wish to view the execution and was pleased to see Macon and Tildy had departed as soon as the trial had ended. He had ridden a short ways with them, which was a mistake. All the way Tildy kept pleading with him to remain in the valley.

"Take up a homestead and be our neighbor," she said. "We'll help you every way we can. Remember, Granddad won't live forever."

"Perhaps later," he had replied. "Deacon and I are traveling east to place a marker on Teamster Beamer's son's grave."

Tildy finally gave up. "I know, you would rather ramble around with that crusty old mountain man than settle down. He's getting a bit long in the tooth so maybe one of these days . . ."

"Yep, one knows not what tomorrow will bring," Joe said, reining his mount up and doffing his hat in a farewell salute. The very thought of a world without Deacon made his skin crawl. When that happened he, Joe Jennings, would be the last living member of Buck Stone's legendary trapping brigade.

Back at his camp, just as Joe pulled the rawhide saddle strappings tight over his bedroll, Lucille's tortured cry rose above the city noises. Automatically, Joe reached for his Hawken. He would have mounted up and galloped after the big sergeant who was struggling to hold his wife in the saddle, but a restraining hand pulled him back.

"Easy does it, lad," Deacon cautioned. "I'd sure hate ta

see yuh git on the wrong side of the law here in this berg. Yuh
sees how they deals with Injuns. I'd say home-breakers ain't
perzactly ther cuppa tea either."

"Yeah! Yeah!" Joe jerked free from Deacon's grasp. "I
was just planning to say good-bye."

"Yep, thet's what I thought," Deacon said. "Sometimes
good-byes git kinda emotional."

Joe went back to packing, his thoughts more grim than
before. When would he stop torturing himself with thoughts of
what he had lost? When it came to women he had to be the
dumbest man in the West.

As was his practice, Vision Seeker also had arisen before
sunup and said his morning prayers. He was in a hurry to get
home. There was no telling what Lone Wolf was doing or even if
he was alive. Word had come by a Blue Coat scout that a small
band of Indians had been sighted on the Bitterroot. Their leader
was a tall man astride an Appaloosa. The party appeared peaceful but the soldier still gave them wide berth.

Vision Seeker sighed. If this was his father's hunting party
Lone Wolf was ending life as he began it, on the trail. Words of
the Great Shawnee warrior, Tecumseh, came to Vision Seeker's
mind. "*When your time comes to die be not like those whose
hearts are filled with the fear of death . . . sing your death song
and die like a hero going home.*"

Vision Seeker ruefully grinned, something he seldom did.
He couldn't help but admire his father. He was living out his life
to the fullest. Although in the beginning he thought Lone Wolf's
idea of a last buffalo hunt was crazy, now it seemed the perfect
thing for him to do. If he fell along the trail or on the grasslands
of buffalo country he would be crossing to the next life triumphant instead of fading away in the stuffy long lodge.

Finally, the party broke camp and started north with Deacon Walton sitting the old donkey with striped withers leading
the way. Following close behind came the two brothers, Joe and
Michael. Vision Seeker brought up the rear.

They passed by the fresh earthen mound that covered the bodies of the five executed Cayuse. Cut Lip, who lingered beside the grave of his brother, mounted up and joined them. All the remainder of the free Cayuse had left shortly after the end of the trial. To stay and watch their fellow tribesman strangle like game fowls being prepared for the spit would bring the condemned men even greater shame.

Eventually, the small party left the areas cleared by homesteaders and wound their way through the virgin forest. Except for the sounds of Mother Earth, the travelers rode in silence, each one wrapped up in his thoughts of the grim Oregon City experience and what tomorrow would bring. Perhaps Deacon's thoughts were the most cheery of all. He was riding home to the family he hadn't seen since the Season of Falling Snow.

He hadn't worried. The family was in good hands. His Cheyenne woman watched as closely over the youngsters as Mother Quail over her chicks. His son, Left Hand, was old enough to go on hunts and see the family was fed. Of course there was Morning Star. That was the one he had to worry about. She was just ripe for the plucking. In fact he had journeyed to the west in the hopes of securing her a mate, and now he was returning home empty-handed.

He had set his mind on Joe Jennings but the obstinate fellow always evaded him. He would have to start thinking of someone else. Joe was brokenhearted over losing that silly yellow haired Morgan woman. It was a good thing she had married that army sergeant. From what little he saw of her, she needed someone like the big sergeant to turn her over his knee and spank that pretty bottom good and proper. She and her goo-goo eyes and that family of hers, would have driven poor innocent Joe to drink.

"Agh!" Deacon muttered to himself. The galoot was hopeless. He had no hopes of corralling him, and it probably was just as well. Joe was like his father, Little Ned -- loose-footed. Whenever news came of a rich beaver colony, Little Ned was ready to pick up and go. He also was a sly one. The character had kept two families going, one in the east and one on the frontier, and neither family knew about the other until after that Crow arrow put an end to his life.

Ah, yes, that Little Ned had been a good man but he had done some foolish things. He had married that she-cat, Raven Wing, the mother of Michael Two Feathers. Of course Michael had turned out well, had more sense than most half bloods.

Deacon turned in the saddle to study Michael Two Feathers. Perhaps he was the one Morning Star should marry. They were both half bloods. Michael was a solid lad who took life seriously. He had good training; the missionaries and his brother Joe had seen to that. And, if he remembered correctly, Michael had taken a shine to Morning Star. He couldn't say the same for her. Ever since she first met Joe, she only had eyes for him.

"Hmm!" Deacon grunted thoughtfully, "maybeso now that she cain't interest Joe, she'll come to her senses and be happy with his brother, Michael."

Deacon slapped the donkey's neck rein. "Come on, yuh striped-legged, creepin' creature, we gotta do some fast talkin' afore we hit Nez Perce country. Of course winnin' Michael over's only half the battle. Mornin' Star has a mind of her own."

Deacon rode along thinking of arguments he would employ on both daughter and prospective son-in-law.

XXXVIII

Indians saw the salmon running up the rivers each year. They saw those that reached the high waters die there. . . . They came to the conclusion that these fish were immortal. The fish swam voluntarily into the rivers to feed mankind (and bears), died and were reborn in the ocean.

Oliver La Farge, "The American Indian"

The party of travelers continued on the trail up the Columbia. They bypassed The Dalles and pulled to a stop to make camp at Celilo Falls where fishermen were preparing and packaging a harvest of fish. The travelers soon learned this was big business. Much of the packaged salmon would go to distant trading centers, possibly on ships that weighed anchor at Fort Vancouver bound for the Far East or other foreign destinations.

"By gum." Deacon exclaimed. "I've been along here a dozen times an' ain't seed this spectacle afore. They tell me the Injuns pack this fish so it don't spoil fer coon's years."

Even Vision Seeker, anxious to get home, put his cares aside and hunkered down to watch the skilled fish packers work their miracles. Dried strips of salmon were pounded into pulp and placed in baskets of grass and reeds lined with salmon skin. When a basket was filled, another layer of salmon skin sealed it. The baskets were then placed one on top of another and a matting wrapped around the lot and securely bound into place.

"Tarnation!" Deacon enthused. "I've a good notion ta take a bundle of those fishes home with me. Now, all I need is another pack animal." An alert member of the fishing tribe overheard.

"Man with much hair on face want *skookum* pack horse?" he asked. "I give - ten dolla." He pointed to a scrawny bay. "You like?"

"Criminy! I want a critter thet'll git me over yon Blues

an' through the Snake River Desert. A decent gust of wind an' likely as not, this poor beast'll blow away."

"Why don't you wait and bargain with the Cayuse," Michael suggested. "They should have a much better selection."

"Dad blast it, cain't yuh see? I need somethin' right now ta haul this pack of salmon I bargained fer. I aim ta git this bunch of fish to the Sweetwater'er die tryin'. Why don't yuh take a look-see at this critter. It's good fer a few day's travel, ain't it?"

Michael reluctantly got up to do as Deacon asked. Why was the pack of salmon so important to the old mountain man? From what he had seen on visits to Deacon's home there was plenty of game about, even a stream loaded with tasty trout just waiting to be caught.

Michael sidled up to the horse that began to back away. He held out his hand and said a few soft words. The horse flipped its ears. Michael waited, talking and holding out his hand. The horse moved its head to look at him.

"I'm your friend," Michael cooed. "From your looks you have not had too many of them." He took a step nearer. The nostrils flared open, but otherwise the horse did not move. "You want to be friends, don't you." He took another step. Before long he was rubbing the muzzle and scratching between the animal's ears. Even the horse's owner was surprised. "Yah! Yah!" His face split open in a toothless smile.

"What do yuh think, Michael. Will this critter carry this salmon packet all the way ta the Sweetwater?" Deacon asked.

"If you take care of him, he should. Right now he needs a good drink and a little pasture." While Deacon completed the fish and horse bargaining, Michael watered the horse, rubbed it down and staked it in a patch of knee high grass.

"I don't see why in the world you want to haul a bundle of salmon all the way into the hinterland," Joe said in exasperation. "I thought we had agreed you would help me locate Clay Beamer's grave."

"Yea! Yea! I won't let yuh down. I said I'd help yuh find

Clay Beamer's grave. This mess of fish ain't gonna be no bother."

"It's none of my business but if we expect to get a crowbait like this through Blackfeet country, we'd better think again. And that pile of fish. They'll smell us coming a mile off."

"Ah! They'll jest think we've got some powerful medicine. Probably'll be afeered ta attack us."

But Deacon was not as confident as he appeared. While bargaining for the salmon and horse he had completely forgotten his promise to find and mark Clay Beamer's grave. Joe was right, traveling through Blackfeet country was risky at best. An odiferous pile of salmon carried by a skeleton of a horse, was asking for trouble of the worst kind. Then there were the grizzlies and other varmints that would be attracted by the odor. From what he had seen, grizzlies liked nothing better than a good salmon feast.

"Blast it all, what was I thinkin' 'bout?" Deacon growled to himself. The thought of finding a mate for Morning Star had pushed all else from his mind. The salmon was meant to celebrate the wedding of Morning Star and Michael. A salmon feed and the elaborate marriage would be remembered in Cheyenne oral history forever. It would give Michael a standing in the tribe that otherwise could be gained only by battlefield coups. As usual, he was getting the wagon before the horse. He hadn't asked either one if they would agree to be man and wife. What could he do? He had the salmon and crowbait on his hands. He couldn't recant his bargain. The Indians might skewer him with their fishing spears. Deacon swore under his breath. He was stuck.

The travelers continued up the south shore of the Columbia River. Although it was early June, the weather was hot. An easterly dry wind blew dust and grit into their faces. An occasional band of Cayuse horsemen appeared to look them over. The first group had galloped away, scarcely noting their presence.

"They go to make known our coming," Cut Lip, who had been silent all trip, announced. "More will come."

Cut Lip's prediction was correct. In a few hours another,

larger band, rode over a ridge and pulled to a stop. Unarmed Vision Seeker rode forward, holding up his hand in the gesture of friendship.

"You come in peace?" the leader of the group asked. "Do Blue Coats come too?"

"No Blue Coats," Vision Seeker answered. "We all are friends." Vision Seeker motioned for the rest of the riders to join them. When they all had come together, clasped hands and made the sign, brother, the Cayuse leader reached for his pipe bag.

"Good time for smoke," he said. As if the words had been a command, the riders squatted in a circle to patiently wait for the pipe to be filled. After the pipe made the first round it was refilled and sent around again. All the while the Cayuse leader seemed to cock his head from one side to another as if hearing or seeing something that disturbed him. At the end of the smoke he cleaned the pipe and placed it in his bag.

"Is that fish you bring?" he asked Vision Seeker.

"Bearded man takes fish to his family."

"Must be large family."

"He has Cheyenne mate, perhaps many relatives."

"Governor Chief Joe see all men hang?" the Cayuse man asked after a long pause.

"Yes, all men hang," Vision Seeker replied.

"Hah-hoh! Hairy faces now come take land?"

"Not right away," Vision Seeker said.

"Where do Cayuse make home?"

Vision Seeker did not answer. Where were these people to go? The hordes of white people, more than one could count, would have their way. Who was to stop them?

Vision Seeker must have had a premonition. At the very moment he spoke the US Congress was working on legislation that would lead to the Donation Act of September, 1850, granting 320 acres to persons who settled in Oregon before December 1, 1851, and 640 acres to married couples.

XXIX

*We have come here to promote peace and happiness among
you, leaving behind all that was bad, bringing only that which
is good. . . . When you understand this then there will be no
difficulty, but we will all work together for the best.*

Joel Palmer, Superintendent of Indian Affairs speaking at Walla Walla Council, 1855

The travelers continued east, following the ruts made by
the wheels of homesteader wagons. They came to the rich pasture lands along Butter Creek, the domain of Five Crows. More
people rode out to inspect the newcomers, but Five Crows was
not one of them. It was said he was nursing burns received in the
attack on Cascade Portage. The party of riders came to the shady
banks of the Umatilla where they dismounted to rest while their
horses watered.

Michael flipped a pebble into the slow-moving water and
watched the splash form rings that quickly broke up to disappear
among the riffles. It was on the desperate march fleeing before
Colonel Gilliam's volunteers, who intended to cut them off at
Umatilla Crossing, that he unexpectedly had run into that merry-
eyed creature called Little Fox. The memory of that moment
came back as clearly as if it had happened yesterday.

"Where did you come from, Mission Boy?" Little Fox
asked, her voice as merry as her eyes. Almost for the first time
ever he hadn't minded being called Mission Boy. Striding alongside her was like walking on air. She wore a large hat so he had
to stoop to get a glimpse of her short round nose and cheeks pink
as a summer's rose. Her hair, of what he could see, was dark and
glossy as a blackbird's wing, but it was her voice that captivated
him. He loved to hear her speak. He tried to think of things to
say but while he mulled over proper words, the fleeing crowd
shoved them apart.

He didn't see her again until days later and only to say

hello. "Ah!" What bitter memories. Then the Tiloukaikt brothers had arrived. The next thing he knew she was gone. "Little
Fox rode away in the night," Straight Arrow, her brother had reported. "She has a mate, the son of Tiloukaikt. . . ." The dreadful
news still rang in his ears.

Michael was shaken out of his reverie as the men mounted
to ford the Umatilla and follow the trail over and around sagebrush covered hills. The valley where Cut Lip had the vision on
the night of the eclipse, appeared normal. The thought of that
night made him shudder. The brother he had seen hanging from
the end of a rope had turned into reality. He hoped never again to
witness such an awesome phenomenon. This one would haunt
him for the rest of his life. He glanced at Vision Seeker, who it
was said had foreseen many disastrous events in his day. How
did he manage to cope with the memory of them? No wonder he
talked and walked with The Great Mysterious. Without supernatural help he surely would go out of his mind.

The riders approached the camp of Stickus. Herders, keeping watch over a band of horses, raised a cry of alarm. Armed
horsemen soon bounded through the sagebrush to join them, their
mounts sawing and jerking at the rope reins that held them in
check. Vision Seeker rode ahead and raised his hand in the gesture of friendship. Even so the horsemen made no move to come
forward. Instead, their eyes were on the hairy faced riders, especially the bearded one on the mule leading the skinny pack animal. Almost in unison, they lifted their noses, sniffing like dogs
picking up a fresh scent.

"Fishes!" someone uttered. The horsemen put aside their
weapons and surged straight for Deacon. "Oh-Hah! Welcome!
Welcome! Hairy faced one bring gift of fishes?"

Deacon was suddenly surrounded. The lead rope of the
pack animal was taken from him. He looked on aghast as his
bundle of precious Celilo salmon disappeared over a ridge, the
new possessors hooting and shouting in their glee.

"That was a nice gesture," Joe observed. "So that's why

you brought the salmon, to gift to these people. You old scallawag, good for you. You certainly know how to make friends. These people will have a feast tonight that will go down in history."

"Yeah! Yeah!" Deacon said, hiding his chagrin. "I jest knowed they'd appreciate somethin' like this. After all these people hev been through, it's good ta spread a bit of cheer."

A festive air gripped the camp. The womenfolk busied themselves with pestle and mortar, pounding dried roots and seeds into a flour which they added to the salmon and baked tantalizing cakes. A drum began to beat, another one joined in. A group of girls gathered in a grass covered open space. Giggling and chattering, they began to sway back and forth, trying to make up their minds if their elders would take offence.

Michael idly watched them, his thoughts going back to the last time he had camped in this very same place. He had led Magpie down the slope to the nearly dry stream that supplied camp water. On the way he had seen the lodge with a beaver head painted above the entrance. It was the lodge of Beaver Tooth, the father of Little Fox. He had looked for her but she was not to be seen. Michael inwardly groaned. He had to stop thinking about the dark-eyed maiden that had captured his heart.

Deacon, still chagrined over the loss of his salmon, came and plopped down beside Michael. He might not be able to give Morning Star a fish feast on her wedding day, but that shouldn't stop him from bringing home a proper mate.

"Takin' yer ease, are yuh?" Deacon said, eyeing Michael's passive expression. For a short while he, too, listened to the drummers and watched the dancers start to move. "These people seem ta be enjoyin' theirselves, considerin' all the troubles they've seen."

"Yes, they live for today," the usually silent Michael replied. "They can't redo yesterday and tomorrow may never come, so they make the most of what they have today. They really mean it when they say any day is a good day to live or a good day to die. Whatever happens is part of the Great Creator's plan."

Deacon gave Michael a sidewise glance of astonishment.
"What's come over the lad?" he silently wondered. "All of a
sudden he's as windy as a patent medicine huckster. Maybeso,
while he's in this loquacious frame of mind is the time ta strike."
"Michael, with all this hangin' business behind us, ain't
yuh kinda foot loose and fancy free? Maybeso yuh'd like ta travel
along an' visit me an' my family on the Sweetwater. Yuh remember me sons, Left Hand an' Small Hawk, daughter, Morning
Star, an' sidekicks, Buffalo Nose an' Walkin' Eagle, all mighty
fine folk. We could do a bit of huntin', hoss racin', feastin', er'
jest sit an' watch the grass an' trees grow. . . ."
Michael let Deacon ramble on, turning over in his mind
the invitation to visit the Cheyenne camp. There was one person
he would love to see, Morning Star. If Joe didn't go along maybe
he would have a chance. He stared at the dancers who had made
their way across the open space. A lissome maiden was leading
the way . . . how graceful, how beautiful was her hair, shiny as a
raven's wing sweeping up from her brow. Did the mention of
Morning Star create this vision of her? He sat up straight to study
this apparition that was coming straight toward him.
"What yuh say, Michael?" Deacon asked.
Michael leapt to his feet. "Little Fox!" He ran to take the
lissome maiden by the hand.
Deacon shook his head in disgust. Everything was going
wrong. He lost the gift of salmon that he had intended for a wedding feast. Now, it seemed, he had lost the mate he had hoped
would play a major role in that feast. The joyous way the usually
reserved Michael greeted the slim, dark-eyed maiden told him
that she had a very special place in the young man's heart.
#
Not all members of the camp joined in the festivities.
Under the shade of a grove of locust trees a group of elders gathered. In spite of their tradition of living one day at a time, they
could not shake the fear of what tomorrow might bring.
"Will Governor Chief Joe keep the promises he made?"

someone asked.

Stickus glanced at Vision Seeker. This was a question that Vision Seeker also had been asking himself. He believed in Governor Joe Lane, but the man was leaving. His replacement, an Easterner named Gaines, was said to be a far different type of person.

Vision Seeker knew exactly the difficulty Stickus faced. He didn't want to tell his people that in the future they would have to deal with a different governor chief and that even the white folks were concerned about the way he would rule the land. Vision Seeker thought back to conversations he had overheard.

"I'm told the galoot thet's takin' over from Joe Lane's a pompous, pretentious ass," the bearded man whose spittle kept splattering Nancy Morgan's ginghams during the trial had declared. "In the hen yard he'd be the head rooster, peckin' everybody thet objected ta the way he was managin' the flock. What'll he do on the Redskin question, no one knows, not even hisself."

"Yeah, I'm told he's a politician through an' through," the bearded man's companion had added. "He'll say'er do anythin' ta git 'nother vote. Since the Injuns ain't got a vote, yuh kin betcher life he'll hev little're nuthin ta do with 'em."

Unfortunately, Vision Seeker thought, the judgement of these old timers was probably accurate. Until the new man started to deal with matters concerning Indian people, it was impossible to know what the future would hold. Vision Seeker returned Stickus' silent appeal for help with a wry shake of his hand, but he had to do more than that.

"My friends, there is much we do not know," Vision Seeker finally said. "The authorities in Oregon City tell us the bad times are gone, that from now on we will live in peace alongside the white man. Since the white man is here to stay, we must hope that this will come to pass."

"What kind of words are these?" a second elder asked. "Lullabies mothers sing to babies have more meaning. We need to know if our villages, herds and pasture lands are safe. There is talk all Indian people will soon be forced to leave the Willamette Valley and make their homes east of the mountains. Where will they live, in Cayuse country?

"Other talk is Blue Coats plan to build things called forts along the trail from Fort Vancouver to the city called St. Louis and will arm them with guns as large as tree trunks. Hairy faces who have been afraid to travel will then come over the big open like strings of ants."

Vision Seeker was shocked. "How did you come by this information?" he asked.

"The Black Robes tell us these things," the elder replied.

Ah, yes, Vision Seeker thought. Here was another problem to confuse the natives. The Protestant missions at Lapwai and Waiilatpu were either closed or destroyed. The Catholics, with the help of McBean, Hudson's Bay's factor at Fort Walla Walla, had seized the opportunity to take over the task of Christianizing the natives. Already they had established two missions: one at the mouth of the Yakama River and the other a few hours ride from Stickus' camp on the upper Umatilla.

Vision Seeker inwardly groaned. He could not remember a time when he had felt so foolish. No wonder the Cayuse elders thought the words he spoke were meaningless. On every side changes in the environment in which they lived were taking place. They wanted to know how they were going to cope, and he did not have the answers. How could these poor people, who for centuries had lived so simply, adjust to this new world that changed from one day to the next?

Vision Seeker gestured to Stickus and the elders and sat down. He might as well accept the inevitable, he thought. His time as foreseer was over. Yet, the fact that he could no longer read the future gave him a sense of relief. From now on he would live as a normal human being. People would not be looking to him to solve their problems. Maybe it was not too late to seek a mate and start a family.

THE CRY OF THE COYOTE

XXXX

Before white men entered our world bison numbered about 75 million. Near the end of the 19th century they were near extinction.

Field Guide to the North American Bison

The long grass that carpeted the Blue Mountain foothills undulated in the morning breeze. Here and there long spikes of blue Lupine, purple blossomed stalks of nettles and patches of brown headed bulrushes, added dashes of color to the carpet of green. Whistling notes of brown, yellow and black striped meadowlarks and quavering, reedy *conk-a-lee* of blackbirds vying with each other, serenaded the travelers as they continued their march eastward.

The only detracting feature of the colorful, musical setting was a series of zigzag scars that ran as far as the eye could see, finally to disappear in a dark green bank of evergreens. These were tracks made by the wheels of homesteader wagons that had come pouring down the mountains each Season of Turning Leaves.

Native horsemen hated these tracks, not only because they were ugly and damaged the beautiful grasslands, but because they were dangerous. During the Season of Melting Snow water drained into them, cutting even wider and deeper swathes through the strips barren of grass. The channels that were formed were like traps, snapping the feet and legs of their beloved horses, especially at night when herders' mounts had been badly injured by stepping into a wagon wheel rut.

Vision Seeker, who led the travelers away from the camp of Stickus, took great care to avoid the wagon wheel tracks. This was another thing Indian people would have to learn to live with, he thought, the gradual ruination of their beautiful homelands. The trail, not only marked by wagon wheel ruts, but abandoned wagons, various items of household goods, skeletons of fallen oxen, horses and mules, brazenly announced hairy faced intruders had passed this way.

Stickus, who had ridden along with Vision Seeker's party, stopped on the crest of a hill, hating to see the good man leave. It was Vision Seeker's ancestor speech that soothed the agony of the trial. His Cayuse brothers had done as he said, looked to The Great Mystery and found peace and hope. Because they had no churches, no preachers, no Sabbath day and did not bow their heads in prayer, the white man believed they had no god -- no religion. They completely failed to recognize the deep spirituality of Indian people who prayed daily . . . quietly, privately and directly to The Great Mysterious. Always they stood, faces upward and open for The Creator to see.

Why did white people never ask about these things, Stickus wondered. Of course, they were convinced Indian people were uncivilized. They possessed no knowledge that was worthwhile. Promise them anything -- lie to them -- do anything to keep the Indian in his place. Did they not know that lies always returned to haunt those who told them? The Great Mystery heard every word spoken. Indian people did not lie or make promises they could not keep. They knew whatever they gained was not worth offending The Supreme Being who placed them on Mother Earth.

The travelers who pressed on only were three. Michael had remained behind to be near Little Fox and Cut Lip, a member of the upper Umatilla band of Cayuse, had moved in with relatives. The small party made travel easier. With this thought in mind Vision Seeker decided to take an especially beautiful route to his home in Lapwai by passing through the Grande Ronde Valley and Wallowa Lake country.

Vision Seeker's companions, Joe and Deacon, made no objection. Joe's mind was busy with thoughts of his brother, Michael. He was not impressed with Little Fox. Even though Michael loved her, could he have made a big mistake? The Cayuse maiden had the timid look of one who was afraid of her own shadow. He had voiced his concern to Stickus. The village chief was reluctant to speak. But others were more forthright.

"She suffer much pain -- much bad things," Cut Lip had said. He, too, did not want to talk about her, but gradually Joe pieced together an appalling story. The murderer, Joe Lewis, had persuaded Little Fox's husband, Edward Tiloukakt, and his brother, Clark, to travel to the Great Salt Lake region where he insisted they would get rich trading with a religious sect that resided there. The brothers selected a prize band of horses and set out on the trail, Little Fox accompanying her husband. Near Fort Hall the party stopped to camp. They now were within a day's ride of the Great Salt Lake and soon would begin to trade. To celebrate they had a great feast and stayed up half the night talking about the riches they soon would possess.

Travel weary, Little Fox wrapped a sleeping robe around herself and fell asleep, only to be jerked awake by the gasping, struggling sounds of her husband and brother-in-law drowning in their own blood. Joe Lewis just had slashed their throats with a long-bladed knife. Before she could scream, a fist struck her senseless. When she regained consciousness she found herself gagged and strapped to the back of a horse. The remainder of the night and into the dawn, she bounced along like a sack of meal.

She was in Joe Lewis' hands only a few days before he tired of her and traded her to a band of Snakes. Little Fox never revealed the agonies she had suffered under Joe Lewis. Just the mention of the murderer's name sent her into a trembling fit that might last for days.

"What're yuh so down in the mouth 'bout?" Deacon asked, riding the striped mule alongside.

"I've been thinking about Michael and the girl, Little Fox. I don't know if that's a good match or not."

"Yeah! I've been wonderin' the same thing. Yuh know, I jest had Michael on the verge of agreein' ta journey with me ta Sweetwater country. I know'd if I got him ther, an' he stayed a while, he'd fall hook, line an' sinker fer Mornin' Star. Right when he was ready ta say he'd come, thet Little Fox danced right up an' put a kabash ta the whole business. Maybeso, thet Cayuse gal's got more smarts than we think. She seemed ta know that if she was goin' ta ketch Michael she'd better act fast. Poor Mornin' Star. When it comes ta matchmakin' her ol' man ain't worth a bucket of spit."

They passed through beautiful Grand Ronde Valley and into the Wallowa Mountains. Every morning Vision Seeker had them up and on the trail earlier and earlier. In these latitudes the days became longer and longer and warmer and warmer. By the time they made camp at dusk, Deacon and his striped mule were exhausted. They forded the Snake River and turned north to follow the Salmon River to White Bird Creek. Vision Seeker came to a likely camping spot and called a halt. His mother, Quiet Woman, and sister, Raven Wing, were in the vicinity, living with relatives of the White Bird band of Nimpau.

Vision Seeker invited his two white companions to accompany him while he located and visited with his mother and sister, but they declined. Deacon was exhausted and Joe had no desire to see Raven Wing, his dead father's widow, ever again. The last time they met she had attacked him with a knife and nearly put out an eye. All he had to do to remind him of that time was to look into a mirror. The knife wound had left a half moon scar dividing his left eyebrow.

If Deacon and Joe thought they would avoid meeting up with Vision Seeker's kin, they were badly mistaken. Near midday a noisy band of youngsters arrived to surround the two white men, chanting a welcome that neither man understood. Soon a cluster of adults appeared. Among them Joe identified his father's widow, Raven Wing. Beside her walked a tall silent youth who had to be Michael's half brother, Young Wolf, son of Michael's cruel stepfather, Francois.

Joe found himself staring at his Nez Perce stepmother. Raven Wing did not look a day older than the last time he had seen her, the day she nearly put out his eye. At the time she had been furious, believing he had poisoned Michael against her. Either she had forgotten the episode or chose to ignore it. Her beauty and charm was impossible to ignore. She smiled at Joe and acknowledged Deacon with a wave of her hand.

"My people send gift for you," she said, her English retaining the New England accent taught her by dead husband, Little Ned. She handed Joe a mat covered basket from which issued a tantalizing odor.

"Tarnation! Thet smells like finger lickin' vittles," Deacon exclaimed. "Mighty handsome of yuh, 'specially since we ain't laid eyes on each other fer a coon's age . . . guess the last time was when yer son, Michael, still was a pup. I must tell yuh, he's growed inta a mighty fine fella. Yuh must be proud of all the good things he's done."

Raven Wing, who had not seen her first son in years, smiled and, with a gesture of farewell, turned away. Without saying more, she and her party disappeared around the rocky bend in the trail. Deacon looked aggrieved. "Did I say somethin' wrong? I was jest gittin' started. I could've tol' her a whole lot of good things 'bout her son."

The next morning Vision Seeker appeared and they moved on. After visiting his mother and sister there seemed no point making the trip to Lapwai. Instead, Vision Seeker took his companions on a shortcut. They crossed the Kamiah and Weippe Prairie camas fields to the Lolo Trail and followed it into the Bitterroot. The party pressed on with Vision Seeker leading. He was in a desperate hurry to find out what had happened to Lone Wolf. They passed through Hellgate and along the Blackfoot. On either side the tall dark forest closed in until it was like tracking through a narrow canyon of whispering evergreens. Creatures of the forest, accustomed to the dim light, could be seen silently flitting back and forth or scurrying through the undergrowth and into the trees.

"Spooky, ain't it?" Deacon observed. "I guess that's what we should expect, bein' on kinda of a ghoulish mission. I hope to heck those Blackfeet ain't on the prod. We might end up hevin'

Clay Beamer's grave marker placed over our own dead bodies, don'tcha ever think of thet?"

Finally, they broke out of the thick evergreens and onto the plains. Vision Seeker hurried ahead. A mysterious force seemed to pull him forward along the trail to Sun River. At the crest of a rise in the trail Vision Seeker stopped to shade his eyes. Everywhere there was the thick, tall grass buffalo enjoyed, but not one of the shaggy beasts in sight.

Vision Seeker urged his mount on. Somewhere in these grasslands Lone Wolf had set up his hunting camp. Suddenly, there it was, looking much as it had in that long ago buffalo hunt. In front of the lodges lounged a group of men. When the travelers approached, one of them rose and strode toward them.

"Welcome, Son!" The voice was almost as strong as in the old days. Vision Seeker dismounted. With tears blinding him, he ran into his father's outstretched arms, marveling at their strength.

"How have you managed?" he was finally able to ask. "I see no meat hanging in the trees, no game on the plains. You can't have brought all your food in your packs."

"Ah, my son. Do not forget the words of the ancients. In spring and summer everyone is rich, even to the lowly earth worm. Mother Earth provides us with fish in the creek, roots in the ground, berries on the bushes and small creatures bounding about. Anyone with two arms and two legs and the sense The Great Mysterious gave us, will never want."

Vision Seeker stood back and studied his 80 year-old father. He looked better than he had for many moons. If this continued the old fellow would outlive him and his youngest son, Running Turtle, too.

"Tarnation!" Deacon, who had watched the meeting from a distance, exclaimed. "Look at the ol' timer, as agile an' bushytailed as a squirrel. Who said the Injuns're done fer. They'll probably still be 'round when all us white folks're dead an' gone."

XXXXI

Everything the power of the world does is done in a circle. . . .
Even the seasons form a great circle in their changing, and
always come back to where they were. The life of a man
is a circle from childhood to childhood, and so it is in
everything where power moves.

Black Elk, Oglala Sioux

Joe and Deacon remained two days and two nights at the Sun River hunting camp before moving on. Joe, who had spent little time in these rolling grasslands, was entranced. He loved to watch the thick luxuriant grass moving to and fro like ocean waves and listen to the rustle and whispers of the ever present wind.

The hours before dusk were best. The swallows came skimming out of their nests to begin their silent food quest. Rabbits and field mice would creep from hiding places, keeping cautious eyes on the sky where circling hawks dipped and glided, riding air currents, the setting sun making their wings glow like fireflies.

Oft times Deacon would join him and reminisce of the days when Buck Stone's trapping brigade first came to Sun River and met up with the Lone Wolf Clan.

"Yep, snowin' like blazes 'twas when we camped. Night had fallen, couldn't see yer hand in front of yer nose. I guess 'twas a mercy at thet. If'n we'd gone jest a leetle farther we'd've run right smack dab inta Lone Wolf's huntin' lodges. Thet ain't somethin' yuh do in the pitch dark if yuh wanta keep yer scalp." Deacon stopped to spit and brush drops of spittle from his already tobacco stained vest.

"Yep, the Lord works in mysterious ways. 'Stead of losin' our scalps we gained a bunch of friends. Yer ol' man, Little Ned, found a wife who giv yuh yer brother, Michael. 'Twas kinda good ta see Raven Wing agin. She's a stunner, no doubt of thet. Yuh kin sure see why yer ol' man fell fer her. Didja notice she was wearin' the elk tooth decorated dress Little Ned giv her as a weddin' present? It was thet elk tooth dress Little Ned picked up in Crow country thet sealed the bargain. She jest hadta hev it, even if it meant marryin' Little Ned." Deacon paused to spit.

"Yuh don't suppose Michael is bein' taken by thet Little Fox? Course I don't know anythin' of his'n thet'd ketch her eye 'cept thet Magpie hoss."

Deacon fondly glanced at his old trapping partner. "Maybeso everythin's turnin' out fer the best. Me an' yuh're the last of Buck Stone's trappin' brigade. I think ol' Buck'd like ta see us continue ta hang tagether. Now if yuh was ta come ta the Sweetwater . . ."

"You old dodger, quit your matchmaking," Joe scolded, but Deacon's invitation brought to mind Morning Star's limpid black eyes brimming with love. Perhaps he should reconsider. When they finished marking Clay Beamer's grave it wouldn't do him any harm to make the journey to the Sweetwater to have another look-see. He certainly could do a lot worse. As a wife Morning Star would bring joy to any man's life.

What would it be like living permanently in an Indian village? His father had done it; why couldn't he? Bear Claw's band of Cheyenne always had treated him with kindness and respect. With the country filling up with people from the east, he probably could help them adjust to what were certain to be difficult times ahead. But was he capable of settling down? All of his adult life he had hopped from one place to the next like a Mexican jumping bean. Joe shook his head. There was no point in making a hasty decision. First, they had to find and mark Clay Beamer's grave.

The following day Joe and Deacon said good-bye to Vision Seeker and Lone Wolf and his fellow hunters. It was an emotional farewell. For Deacon the parting with Vision Seeker was especially heart wrenching. He had known the tall Nez Perce man as a youth. Along with Buck Stone and Little Ned, he had taught Vision Seeker many things, including the Scriptures. To see him use that learning to help his fellow man was gratifying beyond measure. Then, because of Deacon's years, it was doubtful if ever they would meet again. When they finally tore themselves away, Deacon was so blinded by tears he had difficulty mounting his striped withered mule.

From Sun River Deacon and Joe wended their way southeast toward the Land of the Big Smokes. They carried their long-barreled Hawkens resting on the pommel of their saddles and made certain their hand axes and knives were within easy reach. Once they left the grasslands they came upon a trail that led them into the hills. This was Blackfeet land. Instantly, their senses became alert to the slightest sign of danger. Their eyes flicked back and forth like the heads of Great Horned Owls watching for prey and their hearing seemed to become more acute. Every movement and sound was instantaneously recorded and analyzed: the sudden scamper of chipmunk or squirrel, the flight of birds, . . . even a deep silence could be cause for alarm.

Thankfully, Lone Wolf and the members of his hunting party had said the Blackfeet had moved their camps north across the Canadian border in hopes of encountering one of the few remaining buffalo herds. Nevertheless, danger lurked around every bend in the trail. The Gros Ventre, Shoshone, and bands of Blackfeet that had not journeyed north, could jump them in the blink of an eye. The deeper they traveled into the wilderness, the more watchful they became and the more Deacon grumbled about the hazards that could befall them.

"I ain't likin' this at all," Deacon said one evening as they made camp. "All day I've had the feelin' we're bein' tailed. Yuh know these Blackfeet, they kin sneak up on a man like a bull snake slitherin' inta a nest of eggs."

"It's your imagination," Joe scoffed. "Anyway, we're just about at our destination. Don't those mountains yonder look familiar? I'm convinced we're close to the ravine that Buck led us through to that beautiful valley where we spent the winter after the last rendezvous."

"Hmm!" Deacon grunted. "Maybeso yer right, but thet don't take care of these hostiles thet may be tailin' us. Yuh know how mean those Blackfeet kin be. Once they been stung, they don't fergit 'till they git ther vengeance. I shore didn't take time ta count 'em, but when those painted varmints came stormin' inta the valley we sent a passel of 'em ta the happy huntin' grounds. I'm tellin' yuh, we'd better be watchin' our behinds're we'll be jinin' Buck Stone an' Clay Beamer permanently in these bloody mountains."

Two days later, just as it happened with Buck Stone, the mountains opened up and there the beautiful valley lay before them, the best trapping grounds Buck Stone's brigade ever had experienced. The last two members of Buck Stone's trapping brigade pulled their mounts up and stared. It was like stepping back in time. Except that now, instead of fall, it was spring and the white barked aspens were loaded with green leaves. Through the length of the valley ran the same sparkling, beaver-laden stream. In the background towered a circle of snow topped mountains.

"My," Deacon uttered reverently. "It's jest like paradise, ain't it? Everythin's so crisp an' clean. Yuh 'spose this is the way Mother Earth looked when The Great Creator first got done makin' her?"

There still was the problem of locating the grave. One group of aspens looked like another. The rocks that lay strewn on the ground were lichen covered. They all looked as if they had never been disturbed. Finally, Joe climbed up to the point where Clay and he first caught sight of the Blackfeet war party. He sighted along the rows of aspen. In his mind's eye he pictured the battle. Clay running across the swale to save the horses, Buck emerging from the trees to shout at him. . . . There it was, right below a hatchet mark on the white bark of an aspen.

The last two members of Buck Stone's trapping brigade

said little as they prepared a place for the marker Beamer had so carefully carved. Their thoughts were on the glorious winter they had spent here and its disastrous end. Deacon's eyes brimmed so full of tears, he had to stop and walk into the aspen grove where Joe could hear him talking to himself and violently blowing his nose.

"I was jest thinkin' of Buck," Deacon explained when he returned. "There wasn't a guy thet ever lived thet was better'n him. The day the Blackfeets shot him down, some of me died too. I thought by comin' back I would capture the part of me thet I lost, but it ain't workin'. When we leave an even bigger part of me heart will stay here with Buck."

The labor and emotion they expended in setting the head marker and cleaning the grave, left both of them exhausted. Deacon, who still feared that hostiles had trailed them, wanted to leave as soon as the work was done, but Joe dissuaded him.

"If the Blackfeet were tailing us they would have jumped us before now. Let's eat some chow, sleep a bit and then get an early start. You're so bushed you can't see and so am I."

After a cold meal of leftovers, the two men turned in, but neither one slept. They lay thinking of the departed ones who lay in the earth just a few steps away. Suddenly, Deacon sat upright and seized his Hawken. "Ssh!" he hissed. "Someun's comin'. Yuh hear those hoofbeats?"

Joe quickly threw back the covers and reached for his rifle and hand gun. Deacon was right. He also could hear the sound of hoofbeats, slowly coming toward them. The two men cocked their rifles and peered into a curtain of ground fog. The horseman certainly had to be following their tracks. The hoofbeats steadily approached, coming straight for their camp.

"Injun're whatever yer are, come a step closer an' we'll blast yuh deader than a mackerel." Deacon shouted into the fog.

The hoofbeats halted. For a moment there was silence, then a saddle creaked. The rider had dismounted. Both men swung their rifle barrels directly toward the sound. Then came a friendly birdcall. "Thet sounds familiar," Deacon whispered, "but I ain't fallin' fer it, those Blackfeets kin be mighty tricky."

"Come slowly forward and show yourself," Joe ordered. The lips of a horse fluttered. The muffled hoofbeats slowly moved nearer. Abruptly, a man leading a horse emerged from the fog. Immediately, the former trapping partners recognized horse and rider.

"Michael! What are you doing here?" Joe exclaimed, lowering his rifle.

"Yeah, yuh scallywag, yuh near got yerself killed," Deacon added. "Where's yer missus, Little Fox? Yuh got yerself hitched didn'tcha?"

"No, Little Fox is taken," Michael said. He removed the saddle from Magpie, rubbed him down and staked him out. "Now, that I don't have anything better to do, I thought I would ride a ways with you," he said before rolling up in his sleeping robe.

"Well, well, well, yuh know yer welcome ta ride with us all the way ta the Sweetwater," Deacon invited. "In fact we'd love ta hev yer company."

For a while the men fell quiet, listening to the sounds of the night: the stomping of horses' hooves, the gurgle of the brook, the whisper of the trees and the far off, lonely cry of a coyote. The thoughts of each man was on the morrow. Deacon was delighted. How lucky could he be? If he played his cards right he would be accompanied to the Sweetwater by two eligible males. Which ever one she chose, Morning Star would have a husband to be proud of. Ah! He could not wait to ride up to the lodge with these two stalwarts by his side.

Michael Two Feathers' thoughts were also on the journey to Sweetwater. He did not look forward to meeting up with Deacon's family again. He had just lived through one bitter experience and was in no condition to face another. Morning Star was certain to continue her fascination with Joe. To see them as man and wife would be more than he could endure. He should light out on his own -- go somewhere where he could start over.

Where would that be?

Michael glanced at his brother whose, face was hidden by shadows. Why was he going to the Sweetwater? It had to be because Deacon had talked him into taking Morning Star as a wife. Otherwise, why was the old mountain man so happy? Michael wrapped his sleeping robe around himself and closed his eyes. Vision Seeker always had said, "Why think of tomorrow. It never comes."

Joe's thoughts were on his half blood brother who had to be terribly disappointed. He had been captivated by Little Fox. What possibly had gone wrong? Of course, although Michael had not said so, tradition had stepped in. Once a Cayuse maiden married into a family she was married to it for life. If her husband was slain or died of natural causes, a brother took the widow for his wife. If he died, some other male member of the family filled in.

"Ah!" Joe inwardly groaned. Poor Michael. For the remainder of their lives he and Little Fox would remain as far apart as if they lived on two different planets.

Joe's thoughts turned to himself. What business did he have in making the trek to the Sweetwater? Was it just because he and Deacon were the last members of Buck Stone's trapping brigade that made it difficult for the two of them to part and go separate ways? Was Deacon holding that over his head to pressure him into marrying his daughter, Morning Star?

Joe glanced at the sleeping figure of his Indian half brother. Michael would make Morning Star a far better husband than himself. If he went along on the journey to Sweetwater, he would surely ruin any chance Michael would have in winning Morning Star's heart. The best thing he could do would be to disappear, leave the field open for Michael. With that thought in mind, he too, reached for his sleeping robe.

Dawn was just breaking when Deacon aroused himself. In his old age Mother Nature's call came earlier and earlier. He walked to the edge of camp, near where they had staked out their mounts. "Tarnation!" he exclaimed. Instead of three animals, there were only two, Magpie and his striped mule. Joe's high stepping black was gone. Michael came up to stand by his side. "Joe's horse is gone . . . those dastardly Blackfeet. Hey! Joe," Deacon called out. "Yuh better get outta the sack, some thievin' . . ."

Michael gave Deacon's sleeve a tug and pointed to the place where Joe had slept. The only indication his brother had lain there was a patch of flattened grass. Then Michael noticed a fresh blaze on the trunk of an aspen. Inside the circle of missing bark were two knife marks.

"What the Devil!" Deacon muttered. "It's a sign ol' Buck Stone taught us. Yer brother Joe's gone lookin' fer new trappin' 're huntin' grounds. In these days, with every blamed creature from beaver ta buffalo trapped're hunted out, where in the blazes could thet be? What's the matter with him? He knows there's no such thing. . . ."

Michael remained quiet and Deacon also fell silent.

Deep in their hearts they knew their companion, to avoid an emotional parting, had left during the night, leaving his mark to let them know that he had gone and would not be coming back. Still, Deacon could not accept the loss of his long time partner. He cupped his hands around his lips and shouted, "Hey Joe! Yuh cain't leave us. Come on back an' we'll hev breakfast."

The only reply to Deacon's pleading call was the whisper of trees, gurgle of the brook and lonely cry of a distant coyote.

HISTORICAL NOTE

The trial and execution of the five Cayuse was not the only questionable rendering of Oregon Territorial justice. Among the more grievous miscarriages took place on December 5, 1855. On that date Oregon Volunteers under the command of Colonel James K. Kelly marched into Walla Walla Valley. Colonel Kelly's orders were to free the valley of hostiles. At the time a large number of Cayuse and Walla Walla were living in the valley. In an attempt to convince the volunteers they were peaceful, Walla Walla leader, Peu-peu-mox-mox, and four of his men rode into the volunteers' camp flying a white flag. In the parley that followed Colonel Kelly demanded that to demonstrate their peaceful intentions the Walla Wallas had to surrender all their livestock and arms.

Peu-peu-mox-mox protested and for good reason. In the month of June the tribe had agreed to and signed the Walla Walla Council Treaty and abided by its terms. Peu-peu-mox-mox argued the taking of their livestock and weapons therefore was not justified. The volunteers' response was to seize the Walla Walla leader and his men and insist they be bound. One of the seized Walla Wallas resisted. In a scuffle that followed Peu-peu-mox-mox and his four men were killed and scalped. Peu-peu-mox-mox's body was partially skinned and ears and hands cut off and preserved in alcohol, later taken to Portland where they were put on display. To make the grisly business even more unpalatable, claims were made that the preserving alcohol was drained away and drank to toast the success of the campaign.

Officials, including Governor Stevens of Washington Territory, attempted to whitewash the affair by insisting Peu-peu-mox-mox was fairly killed. In a follow-up investigation Indian Superintendent Joel Palmer reported that no prisoner attempted to escape until the volunteers began forcibly to bind them. Colonel James K. Kelly, who was in command of the volunteers, went on to serve as US senator from Oregon and Chief Justice of the

Oregon Supreme Court.

As for the Cayuse Nation, its numbers continued to decline. In 1858 Indian Agent A. J. Cain, in his Annual Report, wrote, "They (Cayuse) have been much reduced in numbers from war and disease and with the exception of few . . . are very much impoverished. . . ."

Today the Cayuse, Walla Walla and Umatilla have melded together in an alliance called the Confederated Tribes of the Umatilla Indian Reservation. As of 2002 the population of all three tribes was listed as 2,260.

Even though few in numbers, their spirit remains undaunted. At the foot of the Blue Mountains just east of Pendleton, Oregon, these few survivors have constructed Tamastslikt Cultural Institute with the purpose of keeping alive the traditions and histories of the three tribes.

"We are a small group of people who lived and died close to the land for more than 10,000 years.

We are a small group of people bound together by blood, by culture, by history.

We are a small group of people who have maintained our traditional song, dance, art, language, clothing, religion, and food, despite significant events and changes in our lives.

We are a small group of people with a big story to tell."

"Welcome to Tamastslikt", grand opening August 1, 1998.

Oregon City on the Willamette River, a painting by John Mix Stanley *circa* 1848

ABOUT THE AUTHORS

Bonnie Jo Hunt (*Wicahpi Win* - Star Woman) is Lakota (Standing Rock Sioux) and the great-great granddaughter of both Chief Francis Mad Bear, prominent Teton Lakota leader, and Major James McLaughlin, Indian agent and Chief Inspector for the Bureau of Indian Affairs. Early in life Bonnie Jo set her heart on helping others. In 1980 she founded Artists of Indian America, Inc. (AIA), a nonprofit organization established to stimulate cultural and social improvement among American Indian youth. To record and preserve her native heritage, in 1997 Bonnie Jo launched Mad Bear Press that publishes American history dealing with life on the western frontier. These publications include the Lone Wolf Clan series: *THE LONE WOLF CLAN, RAVEN WING, THE LAST RENDEZVOUS, CAYUSE COUNTRY, LAND WITHOUT A COUNTRY, DEATH ON THE UMATILLA, A DIFFICULT PASSAGE* and *THE CRY OF THE COYOTE*.

\#

Lawrence J. Hunt, a former university professor, works actively with Artists of Indian America, Inc. In addition to coauthoring the Lone Wolf Clan historical series, he has coauthored an international textbook (Harrap: London) and authored four mystery novels (Funk and Wagnalls), one of which, *SECRET OF THE HAUNTED CRAGS*, received a special Edgar Allan Poe Award from Mystery Writers of America.